'You still want to marry me?' Marly asked

'Does your centre still need a donation?' asked Carter.

'You know it does.'

'The offer still stands, Marly. We could help each other. I want a family, and I want you to be the mother of my children.' He stood beside her. Close enough to remember how she'd felt with her lips pressed against his, and the curve of her breast…

Damn it, he never should have kissed her. Now he would never be able to forget it, never be able to look at her without wondering, without wanting to do it again.

'It doesn't *have* to be like this,' he said, more to himself than to her. He would curb himself. He swore it—he wouldn't jeopardise their marriage in any way. He would wait until she was ready, be the perfect gentleman. If only she would agree…

Dear Reader,

You hold in your hand a ticket to a different world—a world full of passion and suspense, a world full of sexy, stubborn and *dangerous* men!

First off the presses is Emilie Richards' *One Moment Past Midnight*, our **Heartbreaker** title, and the hero in this certainly deserves our praise; Quinn McDermott's the kind of man who can find a kidnapped little girl…

Marie Ferrarella's *A Forever Kind of Hero* shows us how a lady private eye and an FBI agent can strike just the right kind of sparks to make fire. This is the second of her **Childfinders, Inc.** books and number three's on the way in July.

In the true tradition of Sensation™ there are two more gorgeous lawmen in *Logan's Bride* and *Cowboy with a Badge* from Elizabeth August and Margaret Watson. And finally, there's a couple on the run with a baby in *The Hijacked Wife*, and a man trying to buy a wife as if he was just going shopping in *Cinderella Bride*. Take a look.

Enjoy them all and come back next month!

The Editors

Cinderella Bride

MONICA McLEAN

SILHOUETTE
SENSATION

*Silhouette, Silhouette Sensation and Colophon are
registered trademarks of Harlequin Books S.A., used under licence.*

*First published in Great Britain 2000
Silhouette Books, Eton House, 18-24 Paradise Road,
Richmond, Surrey TW9 1SR*

© Monica Caltabiano 1998

ISBN 0 373 07852 8

18-0005

*Printed and bound in Spain
by Litografia Rosés S.A., Barcelona*

MONICA McLEAN

gave up a jet-set career as a management consultant to pursue her dream of writing romances full-time. 'What can I say? I'm a sucker for a good love story and a happy ending.' A former stockbroker to boot, she has a BS in business law and an MBA in finance. Though she claims McLean, Virginia, as her hometown, she has also lived in New York, Pennsylvania, Maryland, North Carolina, Ohio…and Texas, if you count living in a hotel (ah, the life of a consultant). She is married—no kids, no pets, no plants—and lists good food, good company and good clothes among life's pleasures. She loves to hear from readers. You can write to her at P.O. Box 127, Fulton, NY 13069, USA.

For Jim, the love of my life, my best friend, my husband. Thanks for supporting my numerous careers and for your unwavering belief in my intellect.

With special thanks to the following individuals, without whom I could not have written this book:

Inglath Cooper, a brilliant and talented author, for being nice to me when I was so ignorant.

Trish Jensen, an author whose writing never ceases to amaze and inspire me, for breaking the news to poor Tyler.

Wendy Corsi Staub, a multi-talented editor and author, for sharing your expertise and saving me ten years of revisions.

Cristine Grace, my new editor, for taking a chance and pushing me to do better.

Every one of my critique partners (past and present), especially: Kacey Allen, Joanne Barnes, Ali Cunliffe, CeAnn Damon, Anne Ha, Debbie Joseph, Danielle Kraus, Connie Marquise, Suzanne McMinn, Carol Opalinski, Hannah Rowan, Sally Steward and Joe Thoron.

Prologue

Cinderella Candidates, the private investigator had labeled the reports—half in jest, half in truth. Carter King extracted the thickest of the folders from the mahogany file cabinet and carried it back to his office.

Gazing down from the top floor of Carolina Banking and Trust, the tallest building in Raleigh, he saw treetops dotting the landscape as far as the eye could see, making the landscape look like a huge plate of broccoli. Somewhere, amid all that vegetation, lay the last missing piece of the perfect life he'd fought, struggled and slaved to achieve with every ounce of his strength.

A woman—the woman who would give him a child.

Marly Alcott, the label read. He opened the folder and took out a photograph the private investigator had entitled "Miss Marly's Kids." Something about this particular shot appealed to Carter over the others in the small cache the P.I. had provided him. For a long time, he stared at the plain, fair-skinned woman with her round glasses and wistful smile. Hordes of small children surrounded her.

Not just any children. Low-income, underprivileged, economically disadvantaged—politically correct terms that said the same old thing: poor. Miss Marly's Kids were poor. Poor, the way he'd once been. A white-trash boy from the projects, as his ex-wife had reminded him on more than one occasion.

He closed the folder without relinquishing the photo and wished he could close out bitter memories of Eva Ann as easily. Carter prided himself on learning from his mistakes, and marriage to Eva Ann had certainly proved the biggest mistake of his life.

This time would be different. Carter had seen to it. No longer was he fool enough to marry for looks, and he sure as hell would never risk marrying "above himself" again. No, sir, this time Carter King had chosen his future wife using the same careful, logical precision with which he executed everything else in his well-planned, risk-averse life—with the sole exception of having married Eva Ann. He'd laid it all out on a spreadsheet, listing his criteria and hired a P.I. to scout out potential candidates. Then he'd selected the only woman with an X in every box: Marly Alcott.

This time around, his marriage would be a union no different from any other joint business venture. Both entities would give to each other, creating a synergy, for one purpose and one purpose only: offspring.

He was thirty-eight years old, and while certainly not on his deathbed, a fender bender the previous week had served as a reminder of how unpredictable life could be. What if he died tomorrow? His lawyer had advised him time and time again to make a will. But who would inherit the small empire he'd built from scratch? Some charitable organization that would hang his framed portrait in a dusty corridor?

No, what Carter needed was an heir, and he wouldn't rest until he got one.

He needed the help of a woman, both in bearing and raising his child. Aside from that, there would be no emotion stronger than friendship, mutual understanding and a shared love for their children—nothing that would upset his regained and highly prized equilibrium.

Only once had Carter strayed from the critical path, bought into the myth of being in love. Being loved. He knew better now. He understood his limits. He could tempt fate only so far.

This time he would get not only what he wanted, but exactly what a white-trash boy from the projects needed.

A Cinderella bride.

Chapter 1

Marly Alcott's stomach growled despite the candy bar and two glasses of water she'd gulped down for lunch. Most days, she packed two lunches to take with her to Little Learners. Although her day care center provided the noonday meal, the tight budget didn't allow for extras, and it was almost guaranteed someone would need a little more from having gone without. Today it was two someones, and Marly who had gone without.

Animated laughter tinkled through the air, the happiness almost a physical presence on the playground. Most days she could sit and watch her children play for hours on end. *Her children*—that was how she thought of them, the only little boys and girls she would ever have. But today, not even their laughter could lift Marly's spirits. Unlike the children, blissful in their innocence, she knew their days on this playground were numbered.

"Hey, Miss Marly!" Five-year-old Tyler Cameron stopped chasing his best friend, Aaron, long enough to point to the sleek black vehicle pulling into the parking lot. "Look!" Tyler shouted. "That funny car's back."

That funny car was a limousine, and it took Marly a moment to make the connection. Then, in a wave of panic, she shoved her wire-rimmed glasses farther up on the bridge of her nose, clapped her hands and shouted, "Children! Inside!"

Limousines didn't frequent this neighborhood, one of the poorest parts of town. Tyler's father, Billy Ray Cameron, a drug lord who had built his business by preying on the poor, had recently taken to driving a similar vehicle. Tyler's mother, Linda, had finally left her abusive husband. Though she planned to testify against him in an upcoming drug trial, she feared Billy Ray's retaliation. Last week, she'd alerted Marly to a possible kidnap attempt.

Marly glanced over her shoulder, relieved to see that one of her teachers, Miss Nancy, had also sighted the limo and was rounding up the children. But when Marly looked back, neither Tyler nor Aaron had moved. The boys stood there, thoroughly fascinated with the vehicle. Horrified, Marly watched the car door open.

"Tyler, Aaron! Get away from the fence." She darted toward them, gravel shifting underneath her sneakers.

From inside the car, one foot appeared. Then another.

"Tyler!" she yelled. "Aaron!"

"But why?" Aaron whined.

"Move it!" She caught them by their elbows and reeled their small bodies around. "Now. Go. Run!"

The urgency in her voice finally outweighed the five-year-olds' natural curiosity, and the boys responded in kind. Without another word, they took off. Their teacher met them halfway, ushering them inside through the open school door. She turned as if to wave to Marly, then faltered midway.

Following her gaze, Marly looked back toward the limo and froze.

She didn't know how she'd expected Billy Ray Cameron to look in person—she'd seen him only in a grainy newspaper photo soon after one of his arrests. But she had pictured someone out of *The Godfather* movies—a giant with slicked-back hair, an ugly scar and a gold tooth.

Certainly she hadn't expected him to look like the man who stood at the edge of the fence, motioning for her to come over. The only thing she'd gotten right had been the giant part. This man was blond, and his face, although more angular than most, didn't appear scarred—she adjusted her glasses—at least not from this distance. His nose might have been a little crooked, probably broken several times in bar brawls or worse, but it wasn't so bad.

In fact, Marly thought, wiping her suddenly clammy hands against her straight cotton skirt, he looked rather…appealing. Nothing like a drug lord at all, which only confirmed that she had lived in a plastic bubble all her life.

"Marly Alcott?"

His voice held a touch of southern drawl, but she wasn't well enough acquainted with the different southern regions to place it. At her nod, he extended his hand over the four-foot fence. "How're you?"

She should have ignored his hand, told him he was on private property and asked him to kindly remove himself and his monstrosity of a car from the parking lot. Instead, she found herself stepping forward and noticing that he had brownish green eyes. Rich, brownish green eyes, like a pair of alligator boots, her mother would have said.

No matter how deceiving his appearance, she couldn't romanticize a dangerous drug dealer responsible for making his son a crack baby. God, the boy was lucky to be alive. Raising her chin, Marly pushed up the rim of her glasses and inspected his outstretched hand as if it were contaminated. She wanted to smack it—she wanted to smack *him*—but couldn't. Years of *proper* upbringing were difficult to forget, no matter how hard she tried. But that was okay. She'd learned to convey what she really felt, while observing the conventional social graces.

Marly held her breath and offered him a limp hand. As soon as he took it, she squeezed. Hard.

Only, he squeezed back. Harder.

She looked up, matching his startled expression, and yanked her hand free.

Suddenly, she felt paralyzed, like a rabbit frozen in the middle of a barren field. There she stood on the playground all alone, acting as if this encounter were some power game, governed by the rules of a society of which she was no longer a part. The man in front of her was a criminal—one who could easily pull out a gun and shoot her right where she stood.

"I'm sorry," he said, his eyebrows knitting. "Natural reflex."

"Wh-what?"

"I hope I didn't hurt you. Your hand," he indicated with a nod.

She stopped rubbing her palm and met his gaze. It wasn't warm, but it wasn't cold. That was enough to surprise her. "What can I do for you?" she asked, backing up a step.

He cocked his head and peered at her. "I'm Carter King. You spoke with my secretary about a donation."

Marly blinked. "You're Carter King? The president of CB&T?" She looked back at the limo. "And that's your—"

"Actually, the bank's. I'm just getting in from the airport. I wanted to see if you might be interested in going to the Children's Hospital fund-raiser tomorrow night. That is, if you don't already have plans. Kind of short notice, but it might be a good opportunity for you…"

Marly barely heard the rest. One of the wealthiest men in town had come in person to invite her to a charity event. He could have had his secretary phone, the woman whose "How are you?" sounded like "Hair yew?" But no. Instead, Carter King, Big Bank President, had to drive up in his fancy car to one of the worst parts of town, scare her half to death and practically break her hand.

"If you only knew," she whispered, closing her eyes briefly, "what it did to me—to us—when you pulled up in that…" She shook her head. "I thought you were a drug lord."

Carter stood motionless. He didn't need to look over his shoulder to see what she saw. If anyone should have known what a flashy car in the projects signaled, it was him. But he hadn't thought about it because it was too convenient to forget. Gone were the constant reminders of his youth—the migraine-inducing beat of music with the bass turned too high, the smell of hard liquor and marijuana lacing the air on a balmy night. Could he actually have forgotten how the flash of chrome, careering through the neighborhood, could inspire sheer terror?

Carter swore under his breath and saw Marly's startled expression. "I'm sorry. I wasn't thinking."

"I-it's okay. You…you couldn't have known."

A long moment passed during which he remained silent, wanting to give Marly the time she needed to regroup. He would tell her soon enough exactly what kind of man he was, what he knew and where he came from. There would be no mistakes this time, no secrets and no reasons to feel ashamed.

Marly finally stopped rubbing her bare arms, drew in a breath and said, "It's nice to meet you, Mr. King. And awfully nice of you to invite me to the fund-raiser."

"Just 'Carter,'" he said. "So is that a lead-in to 'Yes, I'll go' or 'No, I have plans'?"

If she said no, he was prepared to propose right then and there, make his offer and let her chew on that for a while. Lousy timing, but time was running out for both of them. Each was desperate for different things the other could offer. He could help her; she could help him. A barter, plain and simple.

He watched her carefully as she wrapped her arms around her small waist. She was thin. Awfully thin. Narrow hips and a beanpole shape. That worried him when he thought about potential childbearing difficulties, but he'd seen smaller women who were mothers. Somehow, they'd managed.

She shook her head slowly, gazing somewhere around his knees, and Carter summoned the gumption to lay his proposal on the table. But then she said softly, "Yes, I'd like to go with you. Thank you. Did your secretary tell you the level of funding I'm trying to raise?''

"She did.'' He waited until Marly looked up. "She also told me your grant fell through.''

"Yes.'' Her voice wavered around the word. "It's my own fault. If I'd done more research, I would have realized early on that this grant's typically awarded as seed money to start up new projects, not to continue existing programs.''

"But there must be other sources.''

"There are.'' She took a determined breath. "There's a lot of grant money out there. I just have to tap the right sources. I know that now. For all the good it does me.''

"How far in the red are you?''

"Far enough.''

"You sound like you've given up.'' He watched her wrap her slender fingers around the chain-link fence without responding. He noticed the scars on her hands and winced inside. As requested, his private investigator had spared no details about Marly's past. Her medical records enumerated extensive injuries resulting from a village fire while she had served in the Peace Corps.

He turned his gaze to her face. Her complexion was as innocent of makeup as an apple he might have polished on his sleeve—plain but not unappealing.

She'd wrapped her strawberry-blond hair on top of her head in the shape of a donut, reminding him of the classic schoolteacher look from decades gone by. Still, her eyes caught his attention. Even through her glasses, they held the clear blue of the autumn sky. They drew him in, made him believe he could trust her not to manipulate or play games with him. Honest eyes.

"Marly Alcott, don't go shattering my image of you.''

"What image?''

"Champion of the Underprivileged—''

"Economically Disadvantaged.''

"Champion of the Economically Disadvantaged. Good Samaritan Extraordinaire.''

"You seem to know an awful lot about me."

"I've been following your work for some time now. The chamber's been very impressed with your fund-raising skills."

She laughed softly, a laugh that held no humor, just a touch of helplessness. "I think I must have hit every single one of them up for corporate gifts in the past two years. Every one except…you."

"I know. I was starting to feel left out." He grinned for the first time in too long, watching the way her eyes went from sad to hopeful, a slight smile tugging up the corners of her mouth. She did have a nice mouth, pretty pink lips and perfect straight teeth. He wondered if she'd worn braces, if her parents had stashed away a portion of their paychecks month after month, as his own mother had done, if Marly Alcott had grown up thinking even the barest necessities of middle-class life were luxuries.

"Carter King, have I got a proposal for you."

Marly leaned toward the fence as she smiled, and something turned over in his stomach.

Now that was the portrait of Marly Alcott his files had painted, the bride he'd sought for over a year. "I figured you would," he said. "Because I've got one for you, too."

She frowned.

He almost reached over the fence to wipe the crease from her brow, but caught himself up short. Habit. He'd been staring at her photograph for the past month, even traced his finger along the contours of her face, trying to decide if this was a face he could wake to for the rest of his life.

"Six o'clock," he said on a resolute note, starting toward the limo. "I'll pick you up."

"Don't you want directions?" she called out.

He shook his head. "My secretary looked up the address in the phone book. I found it on the map."

Carter had found out everything he needed to know about Marly Alcott. That was how he'd come to decide she was far and away the best of all his candidates, the woman who possessed all the qualities he needed.

The woman he intended to make his bride.

* * *

Linda Cameron dropped off a photo of her ex-husband that evening per Marly's request. Marly shivered just looking at Billy Ray's craggy face. His cheekbones were too pronounced, too angular, and his eyes were deeply sunken into his skull, so that he looked like a skeleton. He had light-brown hair, which he wore in a long, thin ponytail.

There was no way anyone could mistake this man for another. Too bad they hadn't seen the photo earlier—before Carter King's visit.

"Bye, Miss Marly!" chirped a high-pitched voice that sounded like a cricket's.

Marly looked up from the papers littering her desk and waved. "Bye, Betsy Jean. Tell Robbie I hope he's feeling better." She heard the slight southern drawl in her own voice. She'd picked it up from the kids, and it always seemed more pronounced at the end of the day. Wouldn't her mother's so-called friends just love that? Yes, she could just hear them sniffing their disdain at the Shorewood Country Club in South Hampton. But then, they sniffed at everyone. Even at their own, when they fell from grace.

Marly removed her glasses and rubbed the sore bridge of her nose. She squinted at the ledger in front of her. A little more work and she could pack it up for the weekend. If only she'd had the money to hire one more person; she wouldn't have to do the jobs of five people. She stopped herself mid-thought.

New hires were the least of her problems. Right now, the center could hardly afford to pay the existing staff, and from the ledger in front of her, Marly knew she would have to lay off two of her teachers by the end of the month. With the laws concerning teacher-child ratios, it would only be a matter of time before…

A tapping at the door drew her attention. She put her glasses back on, and the hazy figure came into focus. "Oh, hello, Mrs. Edwards."

"Sorry to bother you, Miss Marly."

"No bother. I'm just wrapping things up. Come on in."

Mrs. Edwards came into the room. Her frizzy, platinum hair sprouted from perpetually dark-brown roots. In her hand, she held an envelope, which she placed on Marly's desk.

"What's this?" Marly asked.

"Just cashed my first paycheck from the new job. I got the last two weeks of the boys' tuition here."

"Mrs. Edwards, you don't have to give it all at once out of your first pay. Here." She reached into the envelope and pulled out a few of the sparse bills. "I'm sure there're things you're needing."

Mrs. Edwards stared at Marly's hands for a long moment before raising her gaze. She made no move for the money.

Marly felt a prickle of awkwardness, sitting there with her hand outstretched. Then she realized what she had done.

She let her hand fall to her desk, gazing down at her papers in defeat. One step forward, three steps back. How would she ever foster parents' self-esteem if she kept inadvertently slipping like this? How would she ever fit in? It was worse here than it had ever been in the poverty-stricken villages in which she'd served with the Peace Corps. Every day, she felt as if she were walking on the children's jacks, watching what she said, how she said it.

She remembered the setback that had occurred when she'd told the kids a story about her travels in Europe and they promptly took home that information. The way some mothers looked at her the following week, others averting their gazes. Even if they didn't know her horrible secret, they knew she was different—an outsider at the very least, if not the downright imposter she was.

But despite what they thought, she didn't regard the children in the same way as the women in her mother's circle viewed their "little causes." The children were Marly's life, the only truth to the charade. She wasn't giving out charity at the center. Didn't the parents realize that?

No, they didn't, because their pride had been battered

enough by hard times and bad luck and lotteries that never paid off.

"I-I'm sorry, Mrs. Edwards. I didn't mean to—"

"The boys talk about you at home all the time."

"They do?" she asked, her voice little more than a whisper. She was almost afraid to hear what they said.

Mrs. Edwards cocked her head. "Took me a while before I got used to them jabbering on so much about Miss Marly this and Miss Marly that." She didn't smile. "But then, they started doing things they ain't never done before. Good things. Cleaning up their messes. Picking up their clothes." Her gaze skittered toward the window as she added, "Saying how you told them they should be minding their manners, respecting their mama."

When she looked back, Marly saw the proud eyes of the single parent who worked three part-time jobs, with barely a secondary school education, to provide for her four boys. She could have stayed home. She could have scraped by on welfare. But she didn't. She worked, and she worked hard. And damn if Marly couldn't work just as hard. She wasn't going to lose her center, abandon her commitment to the children of the working poor.

This was her life. Not perfect, not even close to any fairy tale, but her life nonetheless. And she didn't want to lose it. Not now. Certainly not now. She would find a way. She would do whatever she had to do. Anything, if it meant keeping her children's dreams alive.

Anything, if it meant keeping her children.

"You been real nice to let me slide by on paying up for the boys, but I got the money now." Mrs. Edwards indicated with her pencil-drawn eyebrows the envelope on Marly's desk.

Marly agreed with a nod, placing the bills back into the envelope and depositing the whole amount into the safe behind her desk. Only about fifty thousand more of those, and the center would be set, she thought.

God, it wasn't funny. A wave of nausea rolled over her each time she calculated the exact amount the center needed. Never mind the security system, improved meal plans and parenting workshops Marly wanted. She would have to find a fortune just to break even.

"Mrs. Edwards?" she called as the woman was nearly out the door, waiting until she turned back around. "Thank you."

Mrs. Edwards's lips twitched in an unfamiliar manner that might have been a smile. "Thank you, Miss Marly. Bye, now."

Marly gazed down at her hands. At the scars. It had been eight years since the village fire that changed her life forever. Eight years since she'd escaped the terror she'd once feared would never end. Eight years of living in someone else's skin. How ironic it seemed that one person's death could give another a second chance at life.

"Goodbye," she whispered into the empty room.

"Goodbye." Carter hung up the phone and loosened the knot on his tie, then pulled the tie off as he unbuttoned his shirt on the way to the private bathroom in his office. All his toiletries had found a new home in this bathroom. A week's worth of suits hung in the closet. These days, weekend meetings seemed commonplace, and most nights he didn't even bother going home, what with wrestling with the mechanics of the proposed acquisition of a regional bank in South Carolina. When he wasn't doing that, he spent his time wrestling with the mechanics of his own personal acquisition.

Carter pulled the straight pins out of the stiff new tuxedo shirt he'd just purchased at the department store around the corner. Good thing he'd discovered the wonders of using steam to get wrinkles out, since he'd forgotten to drop off his shirts at the dry cleaners' earlier in the week.

"Still buying your clothes off the rack, Carter?" Eva Ann had always had a way with one-liners. A quip here, a gibe there, she never seemed able to resist an opportunity for putting Carter in his place. Not since the day she'd discovered what his place had been.

He could still see the smug look on her daddy's face when

they'd served Carter with the divorce papers. *"Did you really think my little girl would knowingly muddy our family lineage with your peasant ancestry?"*

The memory made bile rise in his throat. He tilted his head back and swallowed, staring up at the ceiling.

This time it would be different.

"Ah, Marly." He sighed, leaning his hip against the marble vanity as he threw the pins into the wastepaper basket. "Here's hoping you need this acquisition as badly as I do." He gave the shirt a brisk snap and hung it from the hook on the back of the door.

Within twenty minutes, Carter had shaved, showered, and changed into a passably wrinkle-free shirt. I-40 provided a straight shot from Raleigh to Durham, and soon he was driving down the quiet, tree-lined streets of Marly's neighborhood.

He found the one-story brick house easily. He'd driven by it a couple of times in the past, hoping for a peek at her in real life, not just in the photographs the P.I. had provided him. Since Marly only rented a room in the house, Carter had been rather surprised to spot her outside one day, planting pansies around the mailbox. Not exactly the kind of thing tenants did—at least none of the ones who rented from him.

Carter hadn't even recognized her at first, seeing her in person, albeit from a distance. She was so small. Not short. Just small. Tiny, delicate. Nothing like the women in his past. He'd always leaned toward tall, well-built, leggy brunettes. Knowing that predisposition, he'd methodically gone through the P.I.'s list and crossed off every single tall, shapely brunette—regardless of whether she met his other criteria.

Plain truth was, despite being long over Eva Ann, he couldn't afford to let another woman pick up where she'd left off. Eva Ann had discovered his weakness, exploited it and then walked out of his life. A man who didn't learn from his mistakes was a damned fool, and Carter had learned to accept full responsibility for avoiding situations with the potential for repeat performances.

He'd fallen for a pretty face once and nearly lost everything.

Good looks weren't among his criteria this time around. He knew too well that physical attraction often led to deeper emotions, and those emotions inevitably led to pain. He'd witnessed it enough times as a boy. His own mama had gone through four failed marriages all in the name of love. Maybe he was fortunate it had only taken him one try, one failure, to realize marrying for love was a modern myth.

But Marly Alcott met *all* his criteria, most especially the absolute conviction that there was no possible way he would ever feel anything even remotely akin to passion for this woman. Yes, sir. Marly Alcott was as risk-free as a Treasury bill, and just as safe an investment.

With that thought entrenched in his mind, Carter parked his car by the curb behind a foreign compact and got out. He waved to the white-haired woman standing in the living-room window, surmising she was Marly's landlady. The curtains fell back as she withdrew, and in another minute, the front door flew open.

Now, *she* was short, Carter thought, watching the woman step out onto the front steps as he walked up the brick path to the door. Even standing on the top step, she only came up to his chin.

"Hey, Mr. King." Her gaze darted over his shoulder, no doubt to his car, and she nervously wiped her hands on an apron bearing the words *#1 Grandma.* "Annie Lou Andrews," she said with an outstretched hand that pulled him forward when he took it. "Come on in. Marly's gonna be right out, said to tell you. I just fixed a nice, cold pitcher of lemonade. Can I get you a glass while you wait? Won't take but a minute," she assured him, ushering him to take a seat in the living room.

"Thanks. That'd be great." He smiled the smile he'd perfected through fifteen years of calming the jitters of old ladies who came into the bank flustered over the status of their deposits. "I think I'm a few minutes early, anyway." He stretched out and slung his arm over the back of the floral-patterned couch. "Beautiful home you have here."

"Oh," she said, raising a hand to her cheek. "Why, thank you. I'll be right back."

Carter watched her scurry off, then looked down at his feet, chuckling.

"You're a real charmer, aren't you?"

He sprang up and whirled at the sound of Marly's voice from the other side of the room. Then he stiffened, his gut clenching in utter shock at what he saw.

No dowdy, shapeless dress with a high lace collar. No schoolteacher's bun. No glasses. *Nothing* he'd expected—and *everything* he hadn't.

Marly wore a dark-blue, strapless evening gown, her straight, shoulder-length, strawberry-blond hair caught up in combs, her ears adorned with simple pearl earrings.

Plain. He'd thought she was plain. Carter squinted and took another look.

She *was* plain. Plain face. Plain hair. Plain figure. It was all there, just arranged differently.

Very differently.

He swallowed—hard. Once. Twice.

"Sorry if I'm late," she said, slipping into a pair of blue shoes by the side of the couch.

"What? Oh, no, you're not. I'm early." He gritted his teeth, hoping Annie Lou would hurry up with his lemonade, regretting not having asked her to put a shot of vodka in it.

He reminded himself that simple appreciation was okay—a perk, albeit an unexpected one. He *appreciated* the change in Marly's appearance. She looked more attractive—for Marly. That didn't mean *he* was attracted to her. Because he wasn't.

Carter cleared his throat and said, "Nice dress."

She looked startled by the compliment, as if she hadn't expected him to notice. "Thank you. Nice tux."

He glanced down at the new white shirt tucked inside his black cummerbund. He looked like any other penguin. But Marly...

He gripped his hands behind his back to avoid rubbing his eyes. Where had she come up with that dress? She looked

every inch like Cinderella going to the ball. The dress seemed
tailored, though he knew she couldn't have afforded it. Tight
down to her small waist, then fluffed out, it fit some shapely
curves, leaving others to the imagination. Her breasts were
fuller than he'd thought, maybe because of the contrast with
her tiny rib cage. He tried not to stare, but as small as she
was, Carter realized she did have curves.

He frowned, veering his mind back to the subject at
hand—the dress. Maybe she knew how to sew and she'd
bought the fabric. That had to be it. His future bride had hidden talents. Naturally, there would be some things the inves-
tigation hadn't turned up, some hobbies and whatnot.

He watched her gaze search the room. "Annie Lou's entertaining me, if you want to finish getting ready. No hurry."

"There it is," she said, reaching for the strap of her purse
that hung from the back of a chair. She put it over her bare
shoulder, turned and smiled. "I'm ready."

"I'll get your coat." He turned, too, looking for a closet.

"Carter." She laughed. "It's eighty-five degrees."

He gazed back. Just because he didn't find her attractive
didn't mean other men wouldn't, and he didn't relish the
thought of other men ogling his wife-to-be, all done up like
that. Why'd she have to go and sew herself an off-the-shoulder
dress? "How about a wrap?" he suggested as a last resort.

She shook her head.

"You're—" he filled his lungs with much-needed air
"—ready, then?"

She nodded.

Annie Lou came out of the kitchen, holding a glass of lemonade.

"Thanks." Carter took the glass and drained it in a few
swallows. "I needed that." Then he escorted Miss Marly Alcott out the door, hoping Annie Lou's parting "Good luck"
had been for him, because he sure as hell was going to need
it before the night ended.

Chapter 2

Marly was going to hyperventilate before the night ended. "Is it warm in here?"

"I can turn on the air."

"Yes, thank you. That would be nice." She raised a clammy palm to catch the breeze, trying to settle into the soft leather interior of Carter's luxury car and will her heart to stop its incessant clamoring.

True, she had found Carter rather appealing on sight, but that was before she'd seen him in a tuxedo, before she'd truly *looked* at him.

Masculine strength was carved into his every feature. His ebony tuxedo fit his broad shoulders and tall frame as if the finest tailor had created it expressly for him. The snowy whiteness of his shirt contrasted with his golden tan, and he'd centered his formal bow tie perfectly. He wore the entire sophisticated ensemble with the easy assurance of a man who was thoroughly accustomed to it.

Marly couldn't take her eyes off him, couldn't stop her pulse from racing or the heat from spiraling through her. The

instant following her first full-length view of him in Annie
Lou's living room, she'd wanted to beeline back to her bedroom and fabricate a story to explain why she couldn't attend
the fund-raiser after all.

This had never happened to her before, this total lack of
composure. But then, it had been a long time since anyone
had asked her out, longer still since she'd accepted an invitation. Maybe that explained why she'd grown quivery and
unsteady at the sight of a man—any man—in her living room.
Or maybe it was this man in particular. This man who gave
new meaning to the term "drop-dead gorgeous."

And now she was alone with him, in his car, on the way to
a charity fund-raiser. Marly lifted both hands to the air vent.
She didn't know if this was her lucky break or the end of the
line, but the stakes were high, too high to risk making any
mistakes.

She couldn't allow her unexpected attraction to Carter to
cause her to lower her guard in public. Not when a man like
Carter was sure to garner his fair share of attention at the
banquet—attention she could ill afford.

Marly rarely attended large gatherings, and never without
good reason. She only hoped her reasoning skills hadn't short-
circuited tonight.

Through her peripheral vision, she saw his hands clench the
steering wheel, the sharp precision with which he used his turn
signal. She stole a sideways glance and noticed tension in his
handsome profile, a slight twitching of muscle as he worked
his jaw.

"You must get pretty tired of going to all these fund-
raisers." She attempted to use small talk to break the silence,
to ease her own tension while pondering the source of his.

"Sometimes. Depends on how much sleep I've had the
night before."

"Did you get enough last night?"

His gaze flickered toward her, then turned back to the road.
"Hardly."

"You've probably been burning the midnight oil with the proposed acquisition."

"You know about that?"

He grinned, and her heart stopped. His eyes crinkled up at the corners when he smiled, and his mouth...oh, God, his mouth...

Panic welled in her. She had to get out of there, away from him. She hadn't bargained on this, hadn't foreseen any of it. Eight years of living alone, and she'd never once wanted for what she couldn't have. She'd never wanted more than to look. She'd never wanted to touch. Ever.

Until now. Damn it.

How was she supposed to keep her wits about her, to stay alert for any signs of danger, with all this shifting and settling inside her?

"Marly?"

"I—I read about the acquisition in the paper the other day." She turned to look out the tinted window, staring at the reflection of her pinkie finger against the glass to avoid looking at him. "They used to be a savings and loan, didn't they? That bank in South Carolina."

"A few acquisitions ago."

"That's what I thought."

"You must follow the news pretty well to remember that."

"Some things, I guess." She fumbled with the purse in her lap, twisting the strap around her thumb.

Silence filled the air. At a stoplight, she felt Carter watching her.

"You seem nervous," he said.

"A little."

"Why?"

She lifted one shoulder, staring straight ahead. "Because," she started, then stopped. She couldn't very well explain that between his effect on her and her apprehension over the impending gathering, she was about ready to jump out of the car. "I guess because I need to talk to several people tonight. I'm trying not to think about it. Besides, I know I've got your ear the whole way back.'' She gave a shaky laugh. ''Maybe you should be the nervous one.''

''Oh, I am. Believe me. I am.''

The light turned green, and Marly glanced at him, bracing herself for his devastating smile. But he wasn't smiling now. In fact, the muscle in his jaw had started twitching again.

They rode in silence the remainder of the way.

Outside the hotel, elegantly dressed men and women milled around. Handshakes, hugs, kisses. So familiar. So distant. Over the years, Marly had learned to fake it, but she'd never learned to like it.

No cameras in sight. *So far, so good.* Her stomach clenched, and she twisted the purse strap tighter, not caring that her thumb was turning blue.

''Hey,'' Carter whispered, turning off the car but leaving the keys in the ignition for the valet. ''We're here. Marly? You okay?''

The attendant had reached her door, opened it, and stood complacently waiting. Marly nodded. ''Fine.''

Carter took the parking stub and stuck it inside his pocket. He watched Marly spin around, looking hesitant…looking too pretty in her dress. He cursed his decision to wait until after the benefit to ask her. Maybe if he'd brought it up in the car, they could have skipped the benefit entirely, gone somewhere quiet to discuss his proposal. Now they were stuck, and he'd have to count the hours, the minutes, until they could leave the fund-raiser and get down to business.

''Second thoughts?'' he asked hopefully.

She shook her head, placed her hand in the crook of his extended arm and tilted her face up at him with a tentative smile. Her lips had a nice shape, he noticed again. He wondered if, when they were married, they would kiss every now and again, just for the sake of kissing. He supposed kissing Marly wouldn't be so awfully terrible.

Her mouth wasn't anything dramatic like Eva Ann's full red pouter, but it had soft curves that didn't lack their own kind of appeal, mainly reflecting moods more genuine than those of his ex-wife. He was so absorbed with his analysis of her lips that it didn't register right away that their moving meant she was saying something.

"I'm sorry. What was that?" He bent his head down to hear her, at the same time realizing he was so close to her bare neck and shoulder he could smell her scent. Sweet, like flowers after a rainfall, making him want to lean closer, to inhale deeply, to savor.

"I said they'd better not be serving rubber chicken."

Her offhand remark made him grin, and he straightened as they approached the entrance, but the memory of her scent remained with him.

Inside, he recognized a few members of the chamber and had started their way, when a familiar female voice with the faintest Indian accent called his name with equal emphasis on the two syllables.

"Reva." He swung around, beaming at the slender brunette carrying a newborn in her arms.

"Hi, Carter. Have you seen my husband? He forgot his reading glasses. I expect he'll figure it out by the time he gets up there to give his speech."

Carter chuckled and touched the baby's tiny fingers. "Sorry, haven't seen him yet. Boy, Sarina's grown since I last saw her."

"Sure." She laughed with a droll roll of her large brown eyes. "What's it been? Two weeks?"

"Yeah, but that's like two years in baby time. Hey, I'd like you to meet someone." He reached over and pulled Marly closer. When she stiffened, he lowered his hand from her shoulder to the small of her back. "Reva, this is Marly Alcott, founder of Little Learners, a day care center for economically disadvantaged children. Marly, this proud new mama's Reva Singh, who is on maternity leave from the legal department of CB&T's Raleigh branch. Also married to the Triangle regional president."

"Good, you got the order right, Carter." Reva laughed. To

Marly, she said, "He used to always say I was the Triangle regional president's wife and leave me to finish the rest."

Marly looked up at him. "What does that tell me about you?"

He grinned sheepishly, rubbing the back of his neck. "That I met Anil first?"

"Nice try."

"Reva, I see Anil over there." Carter waved to a tall man in a light-gray suit, who waved back, then pointed to his wife and imitated a pair of glasses with his hands. Carter nodded.

"Aha. I think he's figured it out," Reva said with a wink. "Nice meeting you, Marly. Don't be a stranger, Carter," she called over her shoulder as she left.

"I won't. You take care." He was about to ask Marly if she wanted to go get a drink, and possibly coerce her into leaving, when he heard someone call his name. His gaze shifted with reluctance from Marly to that of a burly surgeon he'd met while working on the Red Cross blood drive.

"Great speech last week at the Jaycees," the doctor said. "Caught a clip on the eleven o'clock news. Got your good side." He laughed.

Carter turned to introduce Marly, but she'd slipped away from him. He gazed around the room and then over his shoulder, trying to locate her. Finally, he spotted her in a crowd of people by the bar.

"Hey, Carter. Long time no see."

"Why, Carter King. Fancy meeting you here."

In times like this, it really was irritating to know so many people. For a split second, Carter wanted to tell them all to just leave him alone tonight, that he wasn't in the mood to socialize, that he had important business matters needing his attention. But that wasn't the Carter King who'd made it to the top by virtue of his people skills. That wasn't the Carter King who stayed at the top because people liked and trusted him, because despite his cutthroat reputation for negotiation, he was still an all-around nice guy.

"Hey, Ellen. Nice to see you again," he said, trying to

sound as though he meant it, knowing that at any other time he would have.

Carter King was a born charmer, Marly determined, listening to snatches of conversation drifting her way. Balancing two glasses of white wine, she stared at the circle that had formed around him. She didn't need to hear every word he was saying. His tone alone told her he was performing in the center ring.

She slowed her steps, taking in his tall, athletic build, his blond hair styled more like a male model's than a businessman's. She couldn't believe she'd pictured him a squat, balding man with zero personality. But then, that was exactly the kind of man she'd expected to be the president of a large regional bank, the kind of man who would need a date for this benefit.

It wasn't a date, she reminded herself. In philanthropy circles, total strangers phoned each other all the time to attend functions together. Not unlike high society, people wanted to see and be seen. It didn't hurt for a well-known businessman to be seen with a humanitarian.

Carter had no personal interest in her. And she couldn't afford to have a personal interest in him or any other man, even if she wanted to, even if the mere sight of him made her stomach flutter, even if his touch awakened yearnings in her she'd long ago forgotten—no, *especially* because of that.

Obviously, they both had their agendas for this function, and hers didn't include cowering in the shadows, giving in to the awkward and painfully shy little girl who still lived inside her.

She'd already scouted the site for any sign of video cameras or press photographers. Either they hadn't arrived, or they'd come and gone. Regardless, she couldn't afford to be careless. If the wrong people ever recognized her… She shuddered at the thought. She would keep an eye out, taking care to avoid the media at all costs.

Noting that Carter was still chatting away where she'd left

him, cocktail glass now in hand, Marly squared her shoulders and started threading through the crowd in the opposite direction. She needed to get away from him so she could concentrate on the reason she'd agreed to come in the first place. Her center.

She dumped the contents of one wineglass into a potted plant and ditched the glass on the hors d'oeuvre table beside it. One hand free, she stopped to fill a plate with assorted canapés, then continued on her way.

From across the room, Carter saw Marly's sapphire form grow smaller, until it was nothing but a blur, and then disappear. Seconds passed, minutes that felt like hours. Every time he tried to find her, someone stopped him. He moved in five-step intervals, never able to cross more ground than that in one shot. It was ridiculous. At last, he spotted her strawberry-blond hair several feet in front of him and decided to expedite the formalities.

"Carter!"

"Hey, Alan. Nice to see you. Catch up with you later." He brushed past the mayor, waved to his wife.

"Mr. King!"

"Mrs. Reynolds." He kissed the woman's cheek. "Lovely dress. Be sure and send your husband my regards." He was close enough to hear Marly's voice up ahead, talking about her center and their mission.

"Carter!"

He wanted to scream. He smiled, instead, trying not to clench his teeth. "Why, Linda Sue, don't you look like the blushing bride. Best wishes."

By the time he reached the spot where he'd last seen Marly, she had disappeared again. Groaning, he shook his head. He scanned the crowd, but she was nowhere in sight.

"Damn it, Marly," he said with a sigh, bracing one hand on his hip, the other against the wall.

"Looking for me?" asked a soft voice behind him.

Over the rim of her wineglass, Marly watched Carter reel around and blink as if relieved.

"You're still here," he said, exhaling a deep breath.

"Of course I'm still here. Where would I go?" No sooner had she taken a sip than he reached for her elbow, plucking the glass from her hand.

"Would you mind terribly if we left?"

"Right now?" Marly frowned. They hadn't even served dinner yet—not that she was hungry anymore after those canapés—but still...

"Please," he beseeched.

"O-okay."

"Thank you." Carter deposited her glass on the tray of a passing waiter. "If I have to smile one more time, I swear my face is going to crack," he muttered.

She looked up at the angular planes of his face as they navigated a straight path toward the hotel's entrance. "You looked like you were having a good time."

Carter grimaced. "Wait here. I'll get the car from the valet."

She shrugged and watched him dash across the parking lot, a natural rhythm to his stride that displayed his physical fitness. Of course, with a body like his...

Sighing, Marly reached for her purse and unzipped it to extract the three business cards she'd managed to weasel. They were long shots, but if even one of the leads paid off and landed some fast cash for the center, she might have a chance of getting a good night's rest in the near future. What a luxury that would be, for the first time in months. She looked over the names, then put the cards back in her purse as Carter pulled up to the curb.

Although relieved they were cutting out early, she couldn't help but wonder about him. She probably could have managed to make it through dinner. So what had provoked him to call it quits before the end of cocktail hour? Come to think of it, he hadn't seemed overly enthusiastic to start with. Maybe he'd only intended to put in a quick appearance and then take off. Or was it something else?

Why did she keep getting the undeniable feeling something was troubling Carter this evening? She barely knew the man, yet somehow she could sense his tension.

Carter stepped out and circled around the front of the car to open Marly's door. She slid onto the comfortable seat and dropped her head back on the rest. "Thank you."

He rounded to the driver's side. "Are you hungry?" he asked, buckling his seat belt before popping in a compact disc. "We could grab something to eat."

Marly shook her head, brushing her hair against the leather upholstery. "I'm okay. You can just take me home," she offered, figuring the sooner he unloaded her, the sooner he could resolve whatever was on his mind. The sooner she could reel in her senses, stop the unrelenting shivers that kept dancing up her spine every time she looked at him. The sooner she could shove all this wasted attraction into a box and burn it as she'd burned the bulk of her worldly possessions eight years ago.

Carter didn't appear too relieved by her suggestion, judging from the way his jaw set.

"I—I meant, it's okay if you want to—"

"This wasn't a very good idea. Maybe we should have just skipped—"

"Oh, no," she interjected. "It wasn't entirely a wash. I got three business cards, and I still get to bend your ear the whole way home."

He turned to glance at her.

She smiled, a little uncertain.

Then he shook his head and chuckled, and her smile widened. She thought of the Shorewood crowd as well as the crowd they'd just left, and wondered if there wasn't a glint of something more genuine in Carter. Wishful thinking, she was sure, if not downright dreaming. But then, a woman could have dreamed a lot of things about a man like Carter.

She closed her eyes as they pulled out onto the street, thankful when the soft beat of New Age music filled the car and dimmed the sound of her beating heart.

The benefit made her remember how, as a young girl forced to socialize at her parents' parties, she had often relied on her imagination for confidence. And what a vivid imagination she'd had. She would pretend to be a princess—not just any princess, but the most beautiful of them all. All the guests had come from miles around just to talk to her...only, they didn't want to be rude and monopolize her time, so it was up to her to try to speak with each person at least once. That way no one would feel neglected.

The game hadn't changed much. Only, tonight she'd added a handsome prince. She still had a vivid imagination.

"Can't bend my ear if you fall asleep," Carter said.

One eye popped open. "Who's asleep?"

He turned to her briefly, raising an eyebrow. She thought again of the Shorewood set, the snotty way they could make the same gesture. Carter didn't strike her as snotty, despite his wealth. He seemed nice enough. That was his charm—he was nice to everyone. And most of the healthy females at tonight's benefit had probably lusted after him. Not just her.

"I'm ready to listen if you're ready to talk," he said.

She could have happily melted into his soft, southern drawl, but she straightened, instead, determined to set her overactive hormones aside and get down to business. Then she looked at him, and her pulse began thudding again.

Why couldn't he have been a squat, balding man with zero personality?

She took a deep breath. "Well, you already know we didn't get the government funding for the next fiscal year."

"You've tapped all the government resources?"

"No. It was just the main one that fell through, the one that gave us the seed money. I thought...I thought...I didn't think." She pulled a loose comb from her hair before it fell and stuffed it into her purse.

"You're learning."

"I'm trying."

"How bad is it?" His voice was cool, impassive, distracted.

Marly wondered if he had left some unfinished work at the bank and it was bothering him. Maybe that's what had compelled him to leave early. Workaholics were like that. Her father—

"We have a considerable cash crunch," she whispered, rubbing her temple, trying to veer her thoughts back to the subject at hand. "No two ways about it."

Carter's gaze flickered her way. "So what's the game plan?"

"I got a tip last week. There's going to be a notice of fund availability in the *Federal Register* in another month. A grant that's perfect for us. I'm going after it, of course, but I don't know how long it would take to actually see any money even if we're awarded. And that's still an if. I was so counting on getting funded with that last one." She shifted in her seat, adjusting her purse on her lap. "I seem to be an expert at counting my chickens before they hatch."

"Everyone makes mistakes, Marly."

"Even you?"

"Especially me."

His jaw had taken on that hard edge again. She wanted to reach over and touch him, the way she did with the kids at school, to soothe away the unknown source of tension. Instead, she clasped her hands in her lap. Carter was hardly a five-year-old boy; he was a virile man who no doubt had more than enough sources of comfort available to him.

"Let me tell you about Little Learners," Marly said, shifting in her seat.

"Ah, now we're getting to the good part." Carter smiled. "Why don't you start by telling me what makes Little Learners different?"

"Well, in a lot of ways, it isn't any different from other, more costly centers. We have the same activities, events, field trips. We're open from six to seven to accommodate working parents. We serve breakfast, lunch, dinner for the kids who stay late and two snacks. All the teachers have degrees in early childhood development. The atmosphere is nurturing, bright and cheery. For all appearances, it isn't any different.''

"But it is, isn't it? It must take a lot more work to keep your center on par with the others.''

She nodded. "There's the funding, of course, but there's so much more. The children...they come from families that couldn't otherwise afford such quality care, and so often, they're disadvantaged not only economically but psychologically.''

"What do you mean?'' Carter asked, not looking at her.

"I can't even begin to tell you how many former crack babies, physically abused and emotionally neglected children we've had. Not all, but enough. My center gives these children a head start in a society where the odds are stacked against them.''

Marly shook her head. If she lost the center, she didn't know how she would face herself in the mirror every morning for the rest of her life. How would she live with the knowledge she'd failed not only the children but the woman who'd given her freedom, her second chance at life? How would she ever repay such a debt?

She didn't realize they'd come to a stoplight at a busy intersection until Carter's quiet words made her look up from her lap.

"I understand.''

"You do?'' she whispered, wondering what he understood and if he would please explain it to her. In the shadowy interior of the car, she thought she saw Carter smile, a sardonic, self-deprecating smile. It was so odd and out of place that she turned in her seat until she faced him, searching his expression for some hint of explanation. He opened his mouth as if to speak, just as the car in back of them honked.

The light had turned green. Marly's gaze slipped as Carter stepped on the gas. When she looked back, that uncharacteristic smile was gone, as if it had never been there at all. Maybe the shadows had played a trick on her.

"So, do the parents pay anything or is the center completely funded through donations?'' Carter asked, picking up the conversation as though it had never broken.

''They pay tuition on a sliding scale, a percentage of their income up to a fixed ceiling.''

''What if they don't have an income?''

''In order for their children to be accepted at Little Learners, the parents have to be employed or attending school.''

''Well, there's a difference. Why should it matter whether they're employed or not, if their money comes from a job or from public assistance?''

''Because.'' She straightened, flattening her back against the seat. ''I am not handing out charity.''

Carter looked her way. ''Hit a nerve?''

''Yes. I mean, no. I mean, not you. The subject. Yes, it's a sore spot with me.''

He turned back to the road. ''Why is that?''

''Our mission is to provide care for the children of the working poor. Emphasis on the working. It's that in-between group we serve. They make too much for welfare but not enough to escape poverty.''

''So what you're doing, in effect, is helping those who help themselves.''

''Yes. Exactly.''

''So what happens if someone gets laid off or fired?''

''Of course I make exceptions, but believe it or not, these parents are rarely out of work. See, they all have some things in common. They want out, they want a better life for themselves and their children and they work hard.''

''Well, I applaud your efforts,'' he said, pausing as if for emphasis.

Marly held her breath, intuition telling her Carter was leading up to an answer, whether or not the bank would pledge a donation.

''You're making a lot of dreams come true for a lot of folks…''

''But?''

"But," he continued, turning onto her street, "the bank's already overextended their budgeted contributions."

For a moment, Marly couldn't even speak she was so stunned by the timing of Carter's admission. "Well, then." Her voice rose a notch. She smoothed the fabric of her dress against her thighs. "I guess there was no reason to go through the whole song and dance, was there?"

She tried to control her frustration. She didn't care that the only reason he'd asked her to the benefit was for show, that he'd made his motivation obvious by leaving after putting in an appearance. But if the bank didn't have any money to donate, why hadn't he told her that up front, instead of letting her go on so? Instead of getting her hopes up?

Of course she knew the answer to that question. Hadn't she witnessed Carter King in action tonight, always acting as though he was interested in everything anyone had to say? And she'd thought it was part of his charm, how he was so nice to everyone. Ha. Some charm. He was a phony. A big phony for leading her on.

She'd risked a public appearance for nothing!

Carter remained silent as he pulled his car behind hers. Not that she'd expected a response to her rhetorical question. It didn't matter. Their paths would probably never cross again, and if they did, well…she'd deal with that then.

The second the car came to a stop, she unbuckled her seat belt and reached for the door handle. "Thank you for asking me to the benefit. I enjoyed it, and I—it was nice meeting you."

"Wait." Carter touched her arm.

Marly looked down at where his large hand rested on her wrist. She felt hot, flustered. Her cheeks burned with anger. With mortification that after everything, her flesh still tingled at Carter's touch.

She didn't want to admit she'd liked it when he'd touched her this evening, the few times he'd innocently taken her arm, placed his hand against her shoulder or in the curve of her spine. She didn't want to admit she'd entertained thoughts of what it would be like if those gestures weren't quite so innocent, if the chills she'd felt were from a lover's touch, if she were the woman in Carter's life. Not just a humanitarian he'd asked to a benefit for the sole purpose of enhancing his public image.

But that was just her active imagination again. Handsome, charming men like Carter King hadn't graced her doorstep in years, and back in the days when they had, back in the days when she'd worn another face, they'd only been after one thing. Now that she no longer had that one thing, she didn't have to worry about them.

In eight years, she'd never missed the attention. Never.

Until now.

"I really should go," she whispered around a thickness in her throat.

"Please…wait," he said, even as he took his hand from her wrist.

She crossed her arms and stared straight ahead but didn't move to leave.

"You're not going to make this any easier for me, are you?" Carter reached for a button that opened the sunroof, then turned the key in the ignition, cutting off the engine. He rubbed his palms against his trousers. "Marly—"

"The bank's contributions are overbudget. Your hands are tied. I understand that."

"Then why won't you look at me?"

"I've looked at you all night," she said, picking at the silver beads on her purse. "I know what you look like."

He grinned at that. It was just the shred of hope he was eager for. "Marly, I asked about your center for a reason, not just as a conversation piece. The bank's not in a position to make a contribution…but I am."

Her gaze snapped to his, eyes widening. In them, he saw wariness battling excitement. "You?"

"Yes."

She blinked. "A *personal* contribution?"

He nodded. "A quarter million. Cash."

Her hand flew to her chest, as if trying to calm a raging heartbeat. For a minute, he almost thought he could hear it, but then realized the sound was his own.

"To my center?" she asked slowly, her voice hesitant, as if she was afraid she'd misinterpreted words spoken in some foreign language.

He nodded again.

Tell her the stipulation. He heard the voice of his conscience, but his vocal chords refused to respond to the message.

Qualify your offer. Why did it suddenly feel as if his bow tie was cutting off his circulation?

Lay it on the line, buddy. He opened his mouth, but no sound came out. He clamped it shut, feeling suddenly parched, unable to tear his gaze from the woman beside him. Her eyes were filling with tears, her expression transforming from disbelief to astonishment to—

Before he could finish the thought, she was in his arms. His face froze, his eyes widened and his arms started to twitch. He wanted to hold her but was afraid to move.

"Thank you, thank you, thank you," she said squeezing him in a hug of obvious gratitude.

Still, a jolt of awareness surged through his body, so strong for a minute that he forgot to breathe. When he did, he nearly sprang from the car in a panic—until he found the scent of rain-drenched flowers surrounded him. Pleasant and strangely comforting. Settling, grounding—not like the musky scents the others had worn, that Eva Ann had worn; powerful fragrances that threw him off balance and threatened his control.

Comfortable. Marly Alcott had the side of one soft breast pressed against his ribs, one hand on his shoulder, her cheek resting on his arm and her silky hair tickling the underside of his chin. And he felt comfortable with her. Comfortable! This had to be an omen.

She started to pull away. His body cried out. Suddenly, he wanted her to stay put. He wanted a trial run before he proposed, a final test to see if he could go through with it. The shoulder strap of his seat belt held him back, but his free arm shot out to encircle her shoulders, holding her still. She tilted her head up. Their gazes locked and held.

"Carter?" Her voice was barely a whisper.

"Marly." His voice was a sigh. He closed his eyes and lowered his face until his mouth settled on hers.

Her lips were soft, pliant, and when they moved under his, he decided he could definitely get used to kissing her. He slanted his head, brushing his lips back and forth across hers, wondering if he didn't actually *like* the feeling. She felt much better than he'd imagined.

Before he could consider whether or not that was necessarily a good thing, he heard a sound he'd never heard before—not from a kiss. A whimper. Soft. Sweet. Hers. His body's instant response startled him; being in such confines, in such proximity, was almost painful.

"Yes," she whispered, her faint breath like a caress.

His hand brushed across her shoulder to her nape, tangling in the fine strands of her hair. When his tongue touched the seam of her mouth, her lips parted immediately, allowing him entrance.

Carter groaned, deep in his throat, savoring the first taste of her mouth. Sweet. She was so sweet. He wanted to draw this moment out for as long as he could, which amounted to about all of two seconds. Unable to hold out any longer, he angled her head and deepened the kiss, drinking greedily with the thirst of a man who had known what he'd wanted for some time but had been forced to wait too long.

Marly reached up and wound her fingers around his arm, clenching in rhythm with the movement of their swirling tongues, pulling him closer until he thought he would explode. Through sheer willpower, he tore his mouth away from hers.

"Kisses like that are dangerous in a car," he managed to say, trying to regain his breath.

"Kisses like that are dangerous anywhere," she murmured against his sleeve.

But they weren't—not really. It wasn't passion he'd felt just now, but rather...excitement. Yeah, that was it. Excitement over the idea that his acquisition just might work. And the rush he'd felt...well, that accompanied any other successful business transaction, didn't it?

He gazed down at where Marly's forehead had fallen against his shoulder. Her hair spilled across her face, blocking it from view. He reached down and drew the soft strands away, back behind her ear. He could see her smiling, feel the rapid rise and fall of her breasts against his ribs. It made a man feel good to know he could have that effect on a woman, especially if he was about to ask said woman to become his bride.

Carter suddenly felt lower than slime. If he planned on giving as good as he got, he had some explaining to do. "Marly, I'm thinking I should've told you this up front—"

She laid three fingers over his mouth. "You have no idea what this means to me, what it means for the children. Your contribution...it's more than generous. Because of *you,* I'm going to be able to keep their dreams alive. How can I ever thank you?"

It was the opening he was waiting for, but the words he wanted to say lodged in his throat. *Now or never, buddy.* He swallowed. "Marry me, Marly."

Chapter 3

Marly smiled, shaking her head. "Very funny."

Carefully, he lifted her chin, rubbing the pad of his thumb over her kiss-swollen lower lip. He continued to look at her, his eyes dark and searching, his mouth unsmiling.

She wanted to apologize for thinking mean, nasty thoughts about him. She wanted to tell him she was sorry for ever doubting his intentions. She wanted to kiss him again. She wanted even more.

"I'm not kidding," he said, his voice quiet and sensible.

She didn't want quiet and sensible. She wanted him to laugh, to tell her it was a joke, to brush his mouth over hers one last time and remind her she was still a woman.

But even if he did, what would it matter? Because after tonight, she could never see him again. If she'd ever doubted that before, her physical response to him just now convinced her otherwise.

"You're not serious." She shook her head.

He nodded. "I'm very serious."

This wasn't happening. It wasn't possible. The most reasonable explanation was that she'd been zapped off the face of the planet and catapulted into a comic strip.

"You're drunk," she said, opting for the second most reasonable explanation.

"Haven't had a drink in weeks."

She drew back and squinted at him. "I saw you holding a cocktail glass tonight."

Carter lowered his hand to his thigh. "Is that why you ran away?"

"I—I didn't run away. I…saw that you already had a drink. That's all. So what was in it?"

"Ginger ale. I'm not drunk, Marly."

"Okay." She nodded slowly, smoothing her dress across her lap. "Then *I* must be drunk."

He gave her a sidelong look that was as wary as any she'd ever given him. "You dumped your drink in the plant."

"No, that was your drink. I drank mine."

"You don't have to answer right away. I'll give you some time to think it over."

"Think what over?"

"Marrying me."

"Are we back to that again?"

Carter placed his hand on her arm. "I mean it, Marly."

She almost shuddered at his touch. Her response to the warmth of his fingers was so strong, like coming in from the freezing rain to stand before a blazing fire. She'd been numb for so long she could remember little else. She'd had to forget so much. She didn't want to remember now.

"You don't even know me," Marly whispered.

"I know everything I need to know."

"Oh, this is ridiculous. I can't believe they let you run a bank." She gathered up the folds of her dress and opened the car door. Then, because it wasn't nice to insult the man who'd just pledged a magnanimous donation to your center, she hastened to add, "Thank you again for the contribution. I really, really appreciate it. I…I'll be in touch."

In a flash, she was out of the car and practically running across the front lawn. She heard Carter's door open and close.

"Marly, wait."

He was out of the car—the sound of his footsteps followed her, swishing through the long blades of grass.

She ducked under a tree branch. "Don't think I'm not grateful for all you're doing for my center," she said over her shoulder, taking brisk steps to increase the distance between them. "But if you're going to start talking marriage again, I'm really not up for it."

She heard him swat at the leaves of the tree.

"You're going to make this darn near next to impossible, aren't you? If you'll stop running away and just hear me out, I can explain. Five minutes, Marly. Just give me five minutes."

"What—" She spun around and nearly bumped into him, but caught herself up short. "What explanation could you possibly have to convince me you aren't completely out of your mind?"

"Okay." He held up his hand, palm out. The yellowish glow of the porchlight illuminated the solemn expression on his face. "Just listen," he said slowly, "and try to keep an open mind. You remember Reva Singh? You met her tonight?"

Marly nodded and took a step back.

"She and her husband are good friends of mine. They're Indian. As in, from India."

"Yes, Carter. I figured that out."

"They've been married five years, and they're very happy together." He waited as if letting that tidbit sink in before continuing with, "They had an arranged marriage."

"Really? I didn't know that was still a custom."

"Well, not the old-fashioned kind where the parents make all the decisions. Anil and Reva both decided they were ready to get married, then picked each other based on similar interests and compatibility."

Compatibility. Was that what she'd felt in the car when they had kissed? Marly wrapped her arms around her midsection. She didn't want to feel anymore.

Never mind that her entire body was still tingling, her knees wobbly, her breasts heavy. Aching. Alive. It didn't matter. None of that mattered.

She wanted to go back to that cold, numbing place where she belonged. She wanted to embrace the loneliness and the solitude, her steadfast companions in a life she didn't deserve. She wanted to believe tonight was just a dream, that the heavens couldn't possibly be so cruel as to tempt her with all the things she could never have.

Marly shook her head in denial. "You can't possibly be saying what I think you're saying...."

"I need an heir, Marly. I want you to marry me and be the mother of my child. Actually, I'd like two children, if it's at all possible."

"This is crazy," she whispered.

"Oh, come on. It isn't crazy at all. It's logical. It's planned. It's sensible."

"Look, I honestly don't mean to act rude or ungrateful," she said, summoning all the diplomacy she could. "But I'm having a little trouble understanding how two people who know nothing about each other but decide on their first pseudo date to get married and have children can be construed as logical, planned or sensible. I mean, maybe we can go out to lunch sometime—"

"This isn't about going out to lunch sometime. I'm talking about a future. I need a mother for my future children."

"So adopt. Get a nanny. You don't have to get married to have children these days. And even if you do want marriage, Carter, there's a natural progression to these things, an order of events. This is...this is..." She rubbed her temple, struggling for the right words. "Out of whack."

With a muttered curse, he expelled a breath, half-turning to stare at the old maple tree beside him. "This isn't coming out right at all." He shook his head. "Did you ever have this big presentation to make and once you got to the podium nothing went as planned and you had to ad-lib the whole rest of the speech?''

Marly frowned at his profile, noticing the muscle in his jaw was going haywire now and wondering, ridiculously, if he ground his teeth at night. ''I don't make many speeches. I guess it's not my area of expertise.''

''Proposing marriage isn't exactly my area of expertise, either.'' He leaned one hand against the tree trunk, bracing his long frame, as the porchlight cast an even longer shadow across the front lawn. ''Let me try this again,'' he said, turning toward her. ''For as long as I can remember, I've had this vision of how I wanted my life to be, this ultimate goal. I knew if I was going to get where I wanted to go, I had to follow a critical path, do things a certain way in a certain order. So I did. Everything I've achieved can be attributed to having a plan. A well-calculated, logical plan. And every failure's been the direct result of either not having a plan or else not following the plan—losing control.''

Marly felt herself reluctantly drawn to something in the tone of his voice. Pride. Not the luck-of-the-draw kind you got with ancestral bloodlines, but the kind achieved through sweat and tears. The kind she heard every day at her center in the voices of struggling, hard-working parents. She watched his firm, sensual lips as he spoke, listening to the timbre of his voice as well as the words that came out.

''When I was a boy, it meant studying when I'd have rather been goofing off, working summers instead of playing in the sun. Then in college, I had to pass on fraternity parties, keep relationships to a minimum and work harder on academics.'' He stared down at his hands, as if lost in the memories. ''I was twenty-one when I started in banking as a financial analyst. Worked full-time, went to grad school nights and weekends full-time. The bank paid for it.''

''It crossed my mind that you look rather young to be the president of CB&T. I mean, maybe one of the regional presidents, but *the* president? I'd pictured you…older.''

He glanced up. ''Do you know how old I am, Marly?''

She shook her head.

"Thirty-eight, and I'm not getting any younger."

Thirty-eight. Eight years older than she was. Ten years younger than her father, the last time she'd seen him, right after the grand jury had announced their verdict. "I can imagine what you had to do to get...where you are." She swallowed, remembering the last time she'd seen her father, right after the grand jury had announced their verdict, noting similarities between the two men. Had her father been like Carter once upon a time, a hardworking businessman with a drive to succeed? When had he crossed over the line between honorable ambition and self-serving greed? "You must have wanted something very badly to sacrifice so much," she whispered.

"I did, and I don't regret it. But now I want a family." His hazel eyes bored right into hers. "When I'm gone, I want to know that there's a part of me left in the world. Maybe it's a male thing, but I want my lineage to continue."

"No, that's certainly not just a male thing, but—"

"I'm a wealthy man, Marly," he interjected before she could list the available alternatives again. "I'll be a good provider. I swear it."

"I don't doubt that. It's not that at all."

"Then just say you'll think about it."

"Carter." Marly drew in a sharp breath, then exhaled on a sigh. "What can I say to make you understand? I don't believe people should get married just for the sake of getting married."

"Have I said that even once? I told you I want a family."

"But don't you see? It's the same thing." His vacant stare told her he still didn't understand. "I believe that two people should get married because...well, because they love each other." There, she'd said it.

"Did your parents love each other?"

Marly went still, blinking back images she didn't want to see, trying not to give in to the icy tentacles of lonely childhood memories that wrapped around her heart whenever she gave them thought. Choking. Suffocating. "I don't see what that has to do with—"

"Marrying for love is a modern myth."

She drew in a shaky breath. "Excuse me?"

"It's a myth. I tried it. It doesn't work."

"You were married before?"

"Yeah." Carter ran his hand through hair. "A long time ago."

"And you were in love?"

"I thought I was. Anyway, it doesn't matter. What matters is that I was wrong, that I strayed from the plan and got married for all the wrong reasons, and I'm not going to do it again."

"You don't think love is a good enough reason."

"No, and people marry all the time for reasons other than love."

She looked away, her mind wandering to images of the women at the Shorewood Country Club, some young and pretty, others older, their beauty artificially enhanced or fabricated. A good number of them had married for reasons other than love. Mainly money, there was no second-guessing it, and her own mother was no exception.

There must have been any number of women who would marry Carter for his bank account alone. Add in his good looks and charming personality, and she could just imagine the ensuing catfights over him. He would be perfect for someone, someone other than her, even if things were different, even if she didn't have to play the hand fate had dealt her, Marly never could have married anyone like Carter, anyone with the potential to end up like her father.

"Surely there are other women you've dated, women you've known for some time who are—" She wanted to say *more attractive, more charming, more sophisticated.* She settled on, "More compatible."

"No." He shook his head. "*You* are the most compatible woman for me, Marly Alcott."

"But you don't even know me," she cried. No one knew

her—not anymore. That's how it had to be. That was the only way she'd survived. A fresh, new start in a place where no one could connect her with the ugly past. If anyone ever found out, if the wrong people discovered she was still alive, her next breath would be her last. They would hunt her down again, just as they had the last time. Only this time, they'd make certain they killed the right person.

"I know you better than you think," Carter said.

"How?"

"I've been following your work for the past year. I did a background check on you—"

"You what?" Marly felt the blood draining from her face.

"I'll admit it may sound a bit extreme, but under the circumstances—"

"Circumstances? There are no circumstances. How could you, Carter? Why would you snoop into my past?" She pivoted on her heel and marched toward the porch steps, anger overriding fear when a little voice told her that if Carter had known the truth—the real truth—he surely wouldn't have been standing on her front lawn, trying to convince her to marry him. "Did you check my OB-Gyn records to make sure I'm fertile?"

"That doesn't matter."

"Of course it matters. Surely you know where babies come from, Carter."

"There are options…if it doesn't work. If we have trouble—"

"The answer is no," she bit out, trying in vain to dispel the images he'd conjured, visions of them together, trying to make a baby. "I'm sorry, but that's final. I'm not going to change my mind no matter what you say."

"How about the contribution being contingent on your marrying me?" he asked, his voice suddenly cool, calculated. A skilled businessman playing his trump card in costly negotiations.

With one foot on the first step and another dangling precariously in the air, Marly froze, her hand in a death grip on the railing. Her foot landed on the next step with a thud that sounded about as hollow as she felt inside. She closed her eyes, wishing she hadn't heard Carter's words, knowing she had.

"Oh, God," she whispered, dropping her forehead onto the knuckles of a tightly drawn fist. When she glanced up, the expression in Carter's eyes confirmed her fears. "You aren't going to give me the money unless I agree to marry you."

"Think of it as a barter."

His gaze held hers, and she stared back, dumbfounded. How could she have been so dense? Even if she hadn't known up front, she should have guessed it by now. How could she have thought his six-figure contribution was being donated out of the generosity of his heart, no strings attached? Of course there was a catch. When hadn't there been a catch when something appeared too good to be true? God, her entire life had been one big catch.

Was this her punishment for lusting after him?

On knees that suddenly felt like dough, Marly sank onto the bottom step, clutching her purse to her now-queasy stomach as she swayed, then steadied herself. She tried to keep her voice controlled. She didn't want to give away her fear, didn't want to appear weak or vulnerable when she said, "Don't give me an ultimatum."

Carter approached slowly, a deep crease between his brows. "It's not an ultimatum. I don't want you to think of it like that."

Her anger deepened as she forced herself to meet his dark gaze. "Then tell me how else I'm supposed to think of it."

"Like a contract. I want an heir. You want money for the center. I can give you what you want."

"How do you know what I want?"

"You want to keep your day care center. You want to make a difference in lives of the children and their parents. You want—"

She cut him off with an emphatic wave of her hand. "I don't even know you."

"That's not true. You know my name. You know what I look like. You can pick me out in a crowd, just as easily as you can avoid me. You know where I work. You know—"

"I know you're nuts. That's what I know." Marly shook her head, trying and failing to block out what he was saying. She stifled a cry, lifting her hand in a gesture of pleading. "Carter…"

The muscle in his jaw worked for several seconds before he spoke, his voice sounding hoarse when it came out. "I promise you I'll be a good, honest husband."

She shook her head. "No. I'm sorry, I just can't…"

"I'll never cheat on you or be physically or mentally abusive."

"But I—"

"I'll try to support you in every way I can, and I'll see that you're provided for to the best of my ability. Here." He reached inside his breast pocket and withdrew a crisp white business card and a pen. He flipped it over and scribbled something on the back, then held it out to her.

"What is it?"

"My phone number."

"I don't want it."

"It's my private line. You can reach me there day or night. Leave a message if no one answers. Take it, Marly." He stuffed it into the outside pocket of her purse. "You might want it after you've had some time to consider my offer…and your center's finances."

"Carter." She gasped. "Can't we work something out? Something else? I know," she offered, grasping onto the first wild idea that popped into her head. "I can help you find a wife. A suitable wife. I know a lot of people, and—"

"No."

"But, why?"

"Because I want you. I think you'll be a good mother, the perfect mother for a child of mine."

"Nobody's perfect. You can't really expect—"

"You'll be as good as it gets."

"How do you know?"

"I told you before I've been following your work for some time now. You have quite a talent with *economically disadvantaged* children. I...can appreciate that. Just think about my offer. That's all I ask. I can help you, if you'll help me."

Dropping her hand into her lap, Marly bit her lip. An ultimatum. She didn't care what Carter chose to call it; that's what it was. Unless she married the man standing before her, she wouldn't get the money she needed to save the center.

How could he do it to her? How could he? Didn't he know why she could never marry, not just him, but anyone?

No, he didn't. And she couldn't tell him. Nor could she risk his finding out.

Her anger blazed, took on a life of its own. "Damn you, Carter King," she cried, shooting up from the step and running blindly into the darkness of the night.

Marly hunkered down on her knees in the weed-overgrown garden, swiping angry tears with the back of a dirt-caked hand. Even though she'd heard Carter's car pull away long ago, she still wasn't up to going inside. Annie Lou would hear her crying again and come ask if she wanted to talk about it. She didn't.

So she'd made her way to the garden and was taking out her fury on the weeds, yanking at them with a vengeance, pretending they were the little hairs on Carter's big toe.

The autumn night air felt moist as a damp cloth, but she didn't care. She worked fast and furiously once her eyes had adjusted to the darkness, making her way along the garden's edge. All the while, she racked her brain to come up with possible reasons why handsome, charming Carter King would want to marry mousy, penniless Marly Alcott.

In the past, men like Carter had never beaten on her door without a reason, and their reasons seldom had anything to do with *what* she was and everything to do with *who* she was.

She remembered when Preston Britner III, one of the most popular boys in high school, had asked her out. The class wallflower, she'd marked the date on her calendar with a firecracker motif, using every colored marker in her possession. Only later had she discovered Preston hadn't really wanted to date her. He'd wanted to secure a summer internship with her father.

He was the first, but definitely not the last, in a long line of men who'd never looked beyond the surface, never even wondered what lay beneath. And Carter King was no different.

So she was no longer the daughter of one of the richest men in New England, no longer the kind of woman who turned men's heads. But what she now had, Marly realized, was not only a new name and a new face, but a new label, as well. Good Samaritan Extraordinaire—just what a prominent businessman could use to enhance his image.

"Quite an intelligent, well-calculated and *logical* plan," she said through clenched teeth, tugging at the base of a thick, stubborn weed that wouldn't give. "Linking a lending institution with a nonprofit organization." She shook her head, rising onto knees now bare since her panty hose had torn, and brushed the dirt from her hands against her dress. "Blackmailing me into cooperating." Her voice rose to a hysterical note before she groped for the throat of the weed, gripped it with two hands and gave it a vicious wrench.

The ground broke, and Marly crashed onto her bottom with a hard thud. Crumbles of dirt flew in every direction, a few chunks landing in her hair. She didn't care. Instead, she brandished the roots of the humongous weed in the humid night air. "You're even lower on the food chain than this weed, Carter King. Pond scum. That's what you are. Just like the rest of them."

Yes, just like all the rest of the men who'd tried in the past to use her for their own gain. Only, this time she couldn't just run away, go hide in the corner, licking the wounds of her battered pride. This time she wasn't the one with the coveted bounty, the one with the leverage.

"Damn you, Carter." Marly hurled the giant weed with all her might. "Damn you." She raised her face to the inky dark-

ness above her. "So I found him attractive. So I'm just as bad
as the rest of them. It was just a *thought*. I wouldn't have done
anything about it. I swear I wouldn't have...."

She drew up her knees, wrapping her arms protectively
around herself as she buried her face in the folds of her dress.
After a while, she picked herself up, brushed herself off and
made her way back to the house.

She remembered the words Annie Lou had spoken to her
earlier that evening, before Carter had arrived. *"Don't you
give up yet, honey. You're too close. You're going to find an
answer soon. Something will present itself. You'll see."*

Something had presented itself, all right. A breathtaking
man had appeared out of the blue and offered to save her
center. In return for her bearing his children.

No, not just bearing. Raising, too. Creating a family.

A real family, a distant voice whispered, but Marly
squashed the thought.

A real family wasn't possible. Not for her. She'd resigned
herself to that fact long ago. She could never allow any man
to get that close to her. Not anymore.

Another of life's ironies—where once she'd longed for
someone to notice the person inside, now she couldn't risk
permitting anyone even a glimpse. No, Annie Lou and the
children at the center were the closest thing to family she
would ever have.

Her feet were silent on the carpet as she padded downstairs
to her bedroom in Annie Lou's converted garage. Her throat
felt raw, and her eyes burned. She could still taste Carter on
her lips and smell him in her clothes.

Two hours. How could one person change another's life so
drastically after a mere two hours?

In the adjoining bathroom, she stripped out of her soiled
dress and torn panty hose. Two tears trickled down her cheeks,
and she hastily brushed the moisture away with a corner of
the dress.

A Chanel original, it was an eighteenth-birthday gift from
her mother—two sizes too big, as usual. She'd shipped it from

the south of France, along with a generic card and a photo of herself sunbathing aboard her dead husband's yacht, a well-bronzed man's reflection in her sunglasses.

Marly had been foolish to retrieve some of her clothes from storage when she returned from the hospital, but without a nickel to her new name, she'd felt a twinge of desperation. Her mother had died the year before—a car accident supposedly, but she knew otherwise. Thank God she wasn't that desperate anymore.

Not yet, a nagging voice whispered in her mind, followed by an echo of Carter's proposal.

''No,'' Marly muttered. ''I'm not going to let you do this to me, Carter King. Enough is enough.''

She wasn't going to think about him anymore. She would go on with her life as if he'd never existed. How difficult could it be to forget two hours of a person's life? She'd already had to forget twenty-two years.

Chapter 4

How could he forget her when he'd only just found her?

Alone in the darkness of his office, Carter gazed out the window, down on the twinkling lights of the capital city, and wondered if maybe some people were destined to be loners all their lives, and if he was one of them. Sure, he had a lot of friends, a few close buddies like Anil and hordes of acquaintances. Hell, he was constantly surrounded by people, rarely alone except late at night.

But late at night wasn't the only time he felt alone. It happened at different times, catching him unaware. At a party or in the middle of a business meeting. During a sporting event, at lunch in a crowded restaurant or even at a candlelight dinner for two—not that he'd had many of the latter. The last occasion, with a pretty brunette, had sent all his sensors on red alert, reminding him of the dangers involved with a highly attractive woman.

Truth was, he'd never been the dating type, considered it a waste of time for a man who already had umpteen-million social commitments and a bank to run. But that emptiness had continued to grow, even though he refused to acknowledge it. Somewhere deep inside he knew a family would fill that void.

When he allowed himself to envision a family, he realized he wanted the kind he'd never had, the kind he'd only learned about when his mother had read him the story of *The Three Little Bears.* He remembered asking where the papa bear was in their family.

In retrospect, he would have just as soon never claimed any one of Mama's four good-for-nothing husbands as his papa.

So his desire to have a traditional family was grounded in a children's fairy tale. Not that it mattered, because if securing that end mandated participating in a string of shallow, endless head games again—his experience with the dating ritual—he'd concede defeat right now. And he did, shoving away from the window with a grunt of self-derision.

Carter strode across the room and flicked on the table lamp, casting a pool of light around the sitting area of his office. There sat two armchairs and a couch that had doubled as his bed for the past few months while he'd worked on the proposed acquisition of Southeastern Trust. Picking up a thick packet of notes, he folded his long frame onto the couch and reached for his reading glasses, pausing at the file just under the stack of yellow legal pads.

Marly Alcott.

He didn't need his glasses to see her name. Pinching the bridge of his nose, Carter drew a deep breath and shook his head. It wasn't until he'd sat down a year ago and formulated a plan, devised a spreadsheet listing his criteria, that he'd started to hope again, hope that he *could* have it all.

Per his instructions, the P.I. had looked for possible candidates from three different career fields: nursing, social work and teaching. After that, Carter had assigned weights to each criterion and tabulated the results.

Marly Alcott. The only woman with an X in every box:

X Enjoys children
X Understands poverty and what it takes to rise above it
X Can be counted on, trusted not to manipulate
X Needs what I have to offer
X Plain-Jane looks

He stopped reminiscing there and tossed the packet of notes over her file, but the image of her running away into the night wouldn't disappear as easily. He'd hoped that after some time—

Carter shook his head. Who was he kidding? She wasn't going to call. Not this week and not the one after. Tonight, he would take his entire *Cinderella Candidates* file home and shred it. There would be no Cinderella bride. No bride at all. And no family.

Not now.

Not ever.

Not for him.

He'd thought long and hard in the car on the drive back from her house that night, entertaining the possibility that perhaps he'd attained all he was meant to attain, achieved all he was meant to achieve.

Maybe he'd been greedy to want more when he'd already come so far. Maybe he was never meant to have the picture-perfect life he'd dreamed about all those years when he'd watched his classmates' parents pick them up every afternoon from their exclusive private school in the suburbs.

He remembered how he would sit in the classroom window with his face pressed against the glass, watching and wishing. For long hours after all the kids had left, he would remain in the empty classroom and finish his homework, before helping Mama finish scrubbing the school toilets so they could catch the downtown bus home.

How he'd envied those kids and their parents, the way they smelled good all the time and wore fancy clothes and drove expensive cars. Their perfect families. How he'd worked to be just like them. How many years had he driven himself to the point of exhaustion, trying to prove he could be as good if not better than them?

"It doesn't matter, Carter. You can pretend to be something you're not, but you can't change who you are. No matter what, you're always going to be a white-trash boy from the projects who tempted fate and reaped rewards you weren't predetermined to sow."

"Ah, Eva Ann. You always did have such a way with words." Carter's hand clenched into a tight fist as he pounded a rhythm on his thigh. Then he shook his head and smiled sardonically.

He hated it when Eva Ann was right.

Nothing was going right.

After three sleepless nights in a row, Marly forced herself to go to bed early, only to toss and turn yet again. She'd start to doze off, only to awaken again, her mind reeling with numbers.

She'd stared at the ledgers too long and to no avail. No matter how she shuffled expenses or tried to cut costs, she still came up with deficits.

Finally, she pulled on a pair of jeans and a sweatshirt and went outside to the garden. Crouching in the dirt, she admitted there was simply no way her center was going to survive at this rate.

One more month, maybe two at most. By then, the reserves would be dry. She would have nothing left. No money to pay the teachers' salaries. No money for food to feed the kids.

For the umpteenth time that week, she thought of Carter's proposal. Not the children he wanted her to bear, or how they would conceive those children, but the donation that would save her center, the money that could finance their operations for the next two years.

Marly could use that time to apply for every federal grant out there, guarantee the solvency of her center and work on plans for expansion. It would work. She could do it. All she had to do was marry Carter King. And risk his finding out her deepest, darkest secret.

She stopped pulling weeds for a minute and leaned back on her heels to weigh the consequences.

She might have resigned herself long ago to the fact she would never have a family, never marry or have children, never be a wife or a mother. But it still hurt. Even now, years later. She could never let anyone get close enough to her, never risk someone discovering the terrible truth, the secret of her past.

And yet, a small voice whispered that Carter was offering emotional detachment in their marriage—the emotional detachment she would need in a spouse—not to mention the chance to have children. Children of her own.

She didn't know how long she'd been sitting in the garden, when a shuffling noise made her start. She peered over her shoulder, squinting at the back porch from where it came.

The yellowish orange lamplight cast long shadows across the lawn, but nothing moved.

Probably the wind.

She drew a shaky breath, went to wipe her face with her hands, then thought better of it and used her shoulders.

"Miss Marly?"

She spun around at the sound of her name, instantly alert. Her gaze combed the porch, the lawn, the shrubbery.

No one.

She was hearing things—a definite sign that it was time to go in, crawl into bed and let exhaustion grant her reprieve from disparaging thoughts of the fate awaiting her.

Straightening, Marly winced at her sore muscles and slowly climbed to her feet, then took off her dirty sneakers to walk sock-footed through the soft grass.

"Miss Marly?" a tiny voice whispered.

She froze, eyes widening. That was *not* the wind. She stared in the direction of the porch, took a cautious step forward, then paused to listen.

Nothing.

She took another step and stopped, straining to hear the slightest disturbance. She continued until she was within ten feet of the porch.

"Miss Marly?" the voice came again, a stage whisper. "Are you there?"

"Who said that?"

"It's me. Tyler."

Marly halted midstep. "Tyler?"

"Yeah?"

She glanced around. "Where are you?"

"Under the porch."

"Under the porch?" She ran to the small door on the side of the porch and unlatched it, then crouched to peer inside. "I can't see you."

"I can't see you, either." His voice sounded dangerously near tears.

She poked her head around, trying to figure out where his voice was coming from. "Tyler, sweetheart? Can you come out?"

"No," he wailed. "I'm stuck."

"Stuck?" Marly looked around nervously. "Uh, that's okay. Don't you worry. I'll, um, come in and get you." She slipped her sneakers back on. "What are you doing here anyway?"

"Sleeping. I heard a noise, and it woke me up. I was hoping it was you."

Marly took a deep breath. She'd learned that getting the desired answers out of her kids often required several attempts at rephrasing the question. First, she'd get him out. Then she'd figure out exactly how a five-year-old boy had managed to end up a mile from home—let alone in the crawl space underneath the porch—at ten o'clock at night.

"Tyler, sweetie? Can you keep talking to me so I can follow your voice?"

"Yeah." Silence. "What do you want me to say?"

"Anything. Just keep talking so I can hear you." Marly squinted into the dark storage space. Then she pulled back and stood up, wondering if she shouldn't run and get a flashlight. Not that she'd ever seen one at Annie Lou's before. She might have to wake her. What if she didn't have one? Everyone had them, no?

"I gotta go pee real bad."

Okay. She wiped her palms against her thighs. Forget the flashlight. "Hang on. I'm coming." She fell to her knees, ducked her head and started crawling on the ground in the direction of his voice. "Can you hold it?"

"Yeah, but not very long."

She turned right, and bumped into what felt like a garden hose. "Ouch."

"Careful. There's lots of stuff in here."

"Thanks for the warning, kiddo." Marly groped in the dark with one hand to avoid colliding with anything else. She hoped that once she found Tyler she could then finesse her way back out again. She looked over her shoulder. Yes, it would be okay. The light from the door would guide her back. "Tyler? Why don't you sing your ABCs for me."

"'Kay. Which way? Funny or regular?" His voice was getting closer.

"How about funny?"

"'Kay." Tyler plugged his nose and started a nasal rendition of the alphabet.

Marly inched her way forward, winding around barriers and shoving things out of her path.

"Miss Marly—" He broke off, still holding his nose.

"Yes, Tyler?"

"I don't think you talk like this." The kids often teased about her northern accent, trying to mimic her by plugging their noses.

"Thanks, Tyler. I appreciate that."

"You're welcome. Want me to keep singing?"

"Yes, please."

"The funny way?"

"Anyway you want."

"'Kay. I'm gonna do regular now."

He wasn't more than a few feet in front of her now. She reached out and found the fabric of his shirt. "Gotcha!"

Getting out proved easier than getting in, with the light outside the door as a beacon. Once inside the house, Marly let Tyler tend to his call of nature before she started questioning him.

"All done?" she asked as he came out of the powder room off the kitchen.

Tyler nodded, rubbing his eyes before he held his arms out to her.

She leaned down and scooped the boy up in her arms, grimacing at his weight. "Whoa. You're getting to be awfully big. Pretty soon I'm not going to be able to do this."

And pretty soon she would mourn the loss of a three-year ritual. She had carried him for a few minutes almost every day during that time, ever since he'd first come to her center. His separation anxiety from his mother had decreased considerably since the beginning, but he still continued to be love-starved whenever he grew tired, usually first thing in the morning and later in the evening.

So she would hold him for a while as they stood in the window and waved to the other children arriving in the mornings, and she'd cuddle with him a bit in the evenings before his mother came to pick him up. Sometimes, if it got too late, Marly brought him home with her. If the weather was nice, they would walk down to the Circle K and get ice cream cones to eat on the front porch while they waited.

Tyler's mother wasn't usually late, but when she was, Marly always worried that the woman had had a relapse. She'd been struggling alone with her drug problem, refusing to check into a detox clinic, but as far as Marly could tell, she'd been clean for several months now. She'd held down her job as a dancer in a men's nightclub for almost a year, and that was a step in the right direction. Getting out of her marriage to Billy Ray had proved the best thing she'd ever done. For herself and for Tyler.

If only the center could get funding for the workshops

Marly wanted. Workshops that would address the special needs of these parents. Dealing with stress. Staying clean from drugs. Keeping a job. Parenting skills.

"So how about you tell me how you got here tonight?" she asked, trying to concentrate on the here and now.

"Mrs. Barton," Tyler said, his voice already thick with impending sleep.

"Mrs. Barton?"

"Umm-hmm."

"Who is Mrs. Barton?"

"A lady. She's got two dogs, and one of them—the one with the black spots—just had puppies. Do you like puppies?"

Marly nodded, gnawing her lower lip. She could see getting answers out of Tyler tonight was going to be darn near next to impossible.

She closed her eyes, feeling suddenly overwhelmed. *Darn near next to impossible.* Carter had used that phrase the other night.

"All right, Tyler. We'll figure it out later. But for now, I think we'd better get you home before you fall asleep on me."

"'Kay," Tyler answered in a voice that indicated he was halfway there.

She shifted his weight on her hip and reached for the phone to call Linda Cameron. The phone rang once, twice, three times.

Marly looked at the clock above the stove. Ten-thirty. Could Linda have gone out, possibly looking for Tyler?

Four, five, six. The phone continued to ring. Then, on the ninth ring, someone picked up the receiver.

"Hello? Linda?" Marly twisted the phone cord in frustration at the dead air on the other end. "Is anyone there? Linda, can you hear me? It's Marly Alcott from Little Learners."

There was no answer. But Marly heard a resounding click as the line disconnected. Strange. She hung up and dialed again, only to get a busy signal. Was Linda frantic, calling all the neighbors to find her son? Marly hung up and tried one more time. Busy again. Tyler had already fallen asleep.

She gave a deep sigh. Maybe she'd just keep him overnight. She could run by his apartment and let Linda know, leave a note if she wasn't there.

She took him downstairs to her room. His blond hair felt soft on her shoulder, and she smiled wistfully, holding him a bit closer before she tucked him in bed. Then she padded back upstairs, woke Annie Lou and asked her to keep an ear out.

"I have to run over to the Bricks," she explained, giving the nickname for the low-income community where Tyler and his mother lived.

"Be careful," Annie Lou admonished.

"I will." Marly knew the neighborhood well. She'd distributed flyers there in the past. Even though it wasn't reputed to be the most dangerous of the area projects—that honor went to Morrene Gardens, right down the street—she still didn't cherish the idea of venturing out there after dark. Alone.

But Tyler's mother would undoubtedly be worried, and Marly had to let her know that her son was safe.

It took her all of five minutes to drive over and another five to locate Linda's apartment. Because the all-brick buildings looked identical, she ended up parking in front of the wrong one.

Even before she left her car, she heard the noises. People fighting, babies crying, children shrieking. She recalled one of the mothers who lived in Bricks said she'd occasionally wished she were deaf so the ruckus wouldn't drive her insane. Now, with the bass from someone's music pummeling an aggravating rhythm into her head, Marly could certainly relate.

She ran to the adjacent building, keeping her head down all the way. The pounding seemed to increase once she was inside. She braced herself and climbed three flights of stairs, two steps at a time. The sound grew with every flight, until she stood in front of their apartment door. Finding it slightly ajar, she pushed open the door.

The dingy apartment smelled like a fraternity house after a party, the stench of stale beer and urine hanging in the air. A two-inch cockroach accepted the invitation to go outside, scrambling past Marly's feet and into the hallway. She grimaced and held her breath, taking a hesitant step inside as she searched for some evidence of Linda Cameron.

Tyler's security blanket lay on a worn director's chair beside the stereo. It had been nicknamed ''Ratty Blanket'' because it looked as though it had been dragged down every dirty street in the Bricks. No amount of washing would ever turn the tattered, brown rag back into what was once a yellow blanket. Instinctively, Marly reached for Tyler's prized possession and folded it under her arm.

She opened her mouth to call out for Linda, then mechanically closed it without uttering a sound. How would anyone hear her above the blast of music? The vibration of the bass even shook the floor. But when she reached for the knob of the stereo to turn it down, she faltered midmotion, her senses ramming into full alert.

It had been years since she'd had the sensation, but she recognized the tingling all at once. Starting at the base of her spine, it slowly worked its way up until the small hairs on the back of her neck stood in rigid attention.

Something was wrong. Very wrong. Deadly wrong.

She looked toward the bedroom, took a hesitant step forward, then whirled toward the kitchen without knowing why. A swift avalanche of cold, black fear seized the air from her lungs as her gaze collided with Linda Cameron.

The woman was lying on the kitchen floor in a pool of blood, a knife sticking out of her body. Above her, the crouched, still form was unmistakable.

Billy Ray Cameron.

Chapter 5

Shock held Marly paralyzed in its asphyxiating grip.

Billy Ray's long, thin ponytail hung down his back. She caught a glimpse of his craggy face in profile. If he so much as raised his gaze, she'd fall within his peripheral vision.

Run! her mind screamed, but her legs wouldn't respond.

With sickening horror, she watched Billy Ray pull the knife out of his ex-wife's body, his lips twisting with the effort.

Get the hell out of here! Still, she couldn't move.

He rose and crossed to a kitchen drawer, the knife dripping in his wake. He extracted a dishcloth and proceeded to wipe off the murder weapon like a prized possession.

He's killed her! a voice cried out in her mind, banishing the vestiges of doubt. *And he'll kill you, too, if he turns around and sees you standing there!*

Suddenly, Billy Ray's shoulders straightened. He lifted his head a fraction of an inch, like a wild animal sniffing its prey.

Panic slapped her then. Marly whirled and bolted for the door.

''Oh, God,'' she sobbed, half running, half stumbling down

three flights of stairs, looking behind her all the way. Had he turned around and seen her? Was he following her?

Tears blurred her vision as she ran from the building. Her car appeared in the distance, parked in front of the wrong building. Too far away. She wouldn't make it. He would see her running, catch up to her. No. She had to get away. Hide.

She circled around the back and raced for the woods. Low tree limbs smacked into her, scratching her face, catching her hair, tearing her clothing. The dense grove swallowed her in its darkness until suddenly, she wasn't fleeing a low-income community in North Carolina, but a burning village in a far-away land.

The echo of an explosion rang in her ears, the crackle of huts ablaze. Children screaming. The heat of the inferno pressed against her back. The smell of sulfur seeped into the air, oppressive and suffocating, filling her lungs. Faster. Faster. She had to run, to escape.

She raised one arm as a shield to cover her face, another to cover her mouth and nose. She ran like ashes on the wind until she tripped and fell, landing hard on her side, where fiery tongues licked her body. The smell of burning flesh filled her nostrils.

"No," she screamed in agony. Rolling over and over, trying to smother the flames. "No," she cried out, banging her head against a tree trunk, releasing shards of pain and the flood of reality.

Side splitting, heart pounding, Marly picked herself up on rubbery legs, only to pitch forward in a sudden wave of nausea. She braced her hands on her knees, retching in violent spasms. When it was over, she stumbled to the tree trunk and sank onto the damp ground, her body convulsing in aftershock and cold apprehension.

No longer in the village, the Bricks nonetheless offered her yet another nightmare.

No footsteps followed hers in the woods; no one called her name. No one knew. Not yet. Soon, though, if he hadn't already, Billy Ray would see the door she'd left wide open. And if he had an eye for detail, he might even notice Tyler's security blanket missing. Then he'd know for sure someone else had been there, another witness, another liability. Just like Linda.

Dear God, what if Billy Ray thought it was Tyler?

She had to get out of there, get back to the little boy asleep in her bed.

Marly rose and took a shallow breath, grimacing at the stitch in her side. With painstaking steps, she found her way out of the woods. Once in the clearing, she crept along the back of the buildings. She passed the one she'd parked in front of and kept going to the next one. There, she paused to straighten her disheveled clothing.

She took a step forward and froze, like a rabbit surrounded by a pack of wild dogs. Keep going, a voice cried in her mind, and Marly forced herself to listen. Taking one brisk step after another, she bridged the distance to her car, and all but leaped inside. But her hands shook so violently she fumbled with the key, stabbing and missing the ignition on several attempts.

"Please, Hilary..." She shook her head. "Marly... You have to get out of here."

Her gaze swept across the parking lot. Nothing moved. No one approached. But he was out there. Was he watching, waiting to make his move?

"Come on," she urged, her voice a plea. Finally, using one hand to steady the other, she slid the key into the ignition. But there was no sigh of relief as she pulled out of the parking lot. No feeling of comfort as she drove back to Annie Lou's, her gaze alternating between the road and the rearview mirror.

Was he following her? Would he be waiting for her at the house? When would it start and where would it end?

At Annie Lou's, she ditched her car by the curb and ran across the lawn in a frenzied panic. Inside, she closed and locked the door behind her before scrambling to check every window in every room, making sure they were all secured. When she finished, she stood in the middle of the living room, turning in circles with one hand over her mouth until, finally, she collapsed into a shuddering heap.

It was happening again. History repeating itself. Another murder. Another witness. Another trial.

"Raise your right hand and repeat after me. I, Hilary Steele...do solemnly swear...to tell the truth...the whole truth and nothing but the truth...so help me God."

"So help me God," she whispered, closing her eyes.

She drew her legs toward her body and huddled in a ball. She knew firsthand what happened to people who testified against murderers. They became marked targets, and they were hunted down, silenced. Just like Linda.

She looked down at her scarred hands, a lump of fear stuck like tar in the back of her throat. "Just like me."

Not many people got second chances at life. Though she would never have chosen it herself, fate had intervened, taking any decision out of her hands. Yes, she'd been given a second chance, but there had been a price to pay. A very dear price.

An innocent woman had died because of her, and eight years later, the grief of that loss still weighed on her soul day and night. Eight years later, she still felt as though she were living on borrowed time in someone else's life.

Marly raised her trembling hands to her face. She wouldn't do it. Not again. She wouldn't get involved.

This time, there would be no second chances. This time, it would be for real. What would happen to her children? To her center?

No, she wouldn't do it. She couldn't, damn it. She didn't *want* to die.

Not again.

For the fourth time, Carter flipped between radio stations, only to hear the same message broadcast across the air waves: "Local businessman Billy Ray Cameron was brought in for questioning today in connection with the stabbing death of his ex-wife, Linda Cameron. Police officials discovered Mrs. Cameron's body late last night when they responded to a neighbor's complaint of loud music coming from her apartment. No arrests have been made at this time. Authorities declined further comment. In other news…''

Carter snapped off the radio and rubbed the tense muscles in his neck. He'd called himself a fool at least a dozen times on his way over to Marly's center, but he hadn't turned the car around. Though he'd sworn he would shred his *Cinderella Candidates* file and forget all about her, he hadn't seemed able to do it. Not yet.

He had to try again. Just one more time. He had to try to convince her that his proposal wasn't as farfetched as it sounded, that they could make it work and that it would be mutually beneficial for both of them. If she still said no, he would admit defeat and get on with his life.

To his surprise, the playground was empty when he pulled his car into the lot, and when he went to the double doors, he found them locked. Luckily, a teacher in the hallway caught sight of him through the glass and approached. Still, she wore a wary expression on her face and didn't open the door when she asked his business.

"I'm here to see Marly Alcott."

"Is she expecting you?"

He was about to lie and say yes, just to gain entrance into the fortress, when the teacher crooked her head and asked, "Aren't you Carter King?" At his nod, she opened one of the doors a crack. "You're the one who drove up here in the limousine and scared the living daylights out of us."

Carter tried to look duly sorry. "That was me, but I'm a fast learner. See." He gestured to the parking lot and his hunter-green Caravan, the vehicle he'd intended for his "family," should he ever have one.

Just then a pigtailed girl came running out screaming, "Miss Nancy! Aaron cut in front of me at the water station."

"Did not!" said the red-haired boy behind her.

"Did so!"

"Come on in." Miss Nancy opened the door, amid the children's bickering. "Turn right at the end of the hallway. First door on your left.'' She locked the door behind him, then herded the children back inside the classroom.

Carter started down the hallway, taking in the hand-painted Sesame Street murals on the walls. Bulletin boards displayed the children's own creations, from fingerpaint swirls to construction paper cutouts in geometric shapes. There were some crayon drawings, too. One in particular caught his eye. Two stick figures, one big and one small, stood holding hands on a line of green grass. Above their heads was a big red heart. A caption below read: ''Daddy and me, by Nicholas.''

Something twisted deep inside Carter, and he pressed a tight fist to his gut. Only, it didn't help. Nothing would. Not with reality staring him in the face, the reality of a lonely, dismal future. A childless future.

With a stab of pain, Carter realized he couldn't keep up the facade much longer, pretend he wanted a child only for inheritance purposes. Not with the unbearable emptiness that ripped at his soul day and night.

In the years since Eva Ann had left him, he'd immersed himself in his work. He'd driven himself so hard for so long, working late into the night every night, until figures and columns blurred before his weary eyes. He'd fallen asleep at his desk so many nights he finally started keeping a change of clothing at work. Then it became a week's worth of clothing.

Carter had needed the breakneck pace, the mind-numbing facts and figures. They helped him stay focused on one goal and one goal only: reaching the top. And he'd reached it, all right, in record time, only to discover what a bleak place it was when he had no one to share it with.

All this time, he'd told himself it didn't matter. God, how he'd tried to believe it. But it did matter. He was alone, and it hurt like hell. Like it or not, the need for love and acceptance was still inside him, like an open wound that would never heal.

He wasn't fool enough to think Marly would ever love him, but she was more likely than any other woman to accept him for the man he was. And if he could just convince her to help him raise his child, he would settle for that much.

Bracing himself, Carter strode down the hallway toward her office. He found it easily enough—her name was stenciled in an arch above the doorway. He peered inside. The room itself was small, furnished with only a desk, some filing cabinets and a round table in the corner where Marly stood.

She wore a pale-peach sweater and a matching pleated skirt, with her hair pinned up in that same donut shape he remembered from the other day on the playground. Her glasses completed the schoolteacher ensemble. Forehead creased in concentration, she gripped a folded section of the newspaper in one hand, a coffee mug in the other.

He hesitated, his fist hovering in the air, until finally he cleared his throat and knocked twice on the open door. "Got a minute?"

Marly gasped and jumped back, spilling her coffee all over the newspaper. "Oh, God. It's just you."

He would have taken offense if she didn't look so relieved. "You were expecting the bogeyman?"

"Very funny," she said, reaching for a stack of paper towels.

"I'm sorry. Here, let me help you with that." He took the drenched newspaper and started to throw it into the wastepaper basket by the door.

"Wait." She grabbed his arm. "Don't throw that away. I—I'm still reading it."

"But it's ruined."

"It'll dry." She took the soggy remains from his hands, cleared off a space on her desk and lined it with paper towels, before laying out the newspaper as if it were the Holy Grail.

"So what are you reading about?"

Her gaze flickered toward him. "Billy Ray Cameron. The police brought him in for questioning today."

"Yeah, I heard on the radio. It's on all the stations. Murder this time, huh?"

Marly nodded, smoothing the pleats of her long cotton skirt. "His ex-wife, Linda." Her gaze alternated between him and door. "How did you get into the building?"

"One of your teachers recognized me from the other day."

"Oh. Okay."

She seemed to relax a little. But not much. Carter peered at her, one eyebrow raised in speculation. She was awfully jittery for some reason.

"Please stop looking at me like that," she said, rubbing her arms.

"Like what?"

"Like I'm some kind of feasibility analysis."

Carter frowned at her choice of words, at her accuracy.

"Look, was there something I could help you with?" Marly asked. "I don't mean to be rude, but I—"

"You know why I'm here."

She stared at him across the barrier of her desk. "No, I'm afraid I don't."

He turned his palms upward in supplication. "I think it's a feasible plan."

"You still want to marry me?" Her voice sounded shaky, almost uncertain.

"Does your center still need a donation?"

"You know it does."

"The offer still stands, Marly. We could help each other."

Their gazes locked and held for several long seconds, and Carter thought he detected some inner battle waging behind those pale-blue eyes. She was tempted. He could tell from the way she stood, biting her lip and wringing her hands. He could also tell that something had changed since he'd seen her last, if the dark smudges underneath her eyes served as any indication. Had her center's financial picture grown worse?

He took a step toward her. She took a step back. He didn't press. "Tell me your reservations, Marly."

"I—I wouldn't know where to begin." She stared at a spot just over his shoulder.

"I'm a perfect stranger. You've already told me that much, and I've told you about my friends Reva and Anil, and their arranged marriage. Their very successful arranged marriage."

"Carter—"

"Just admit the idea isn't as crazy as it sounds. We would make a good team—"

"Linking a lending institution with a nonprofit organization. A businessman and a Good Samaritan."

"If that's how you want to look at it."

"Isn't that how you're looking at it?" she asked in a small voice.

Carter straightened and met her gaze dead on. "Make no mistake about my motive here. I want a family, and I want you to be the mother of my children. That's it. Don't go looking for ulterior motives where there aren't any."

"Then tell me why you want *me*. I don't understand. Of all the women—"

"Look around." He gestured to the artwork on her bulletin board, the long rectangular framed print of more than a dozen babies that hung on her wall. "It's not too difficult to figure out. If there's a prime candidate for motherhood in this town, it's you."

Marly smiled, but it was a smile that didn't quite reach her eyes. Carter couldn't put his finger on it, but he somehow sensed this wasn't the same woman he'd taken to the charity ball. She'd changed subtly. Or not so subtly. She was less spirited, more withdrawn. And nervous. Very nervous for some reason.

"Is something wrong?" he suddenly asked.

"Wrong?" She turned her back and began straightening the artwork on the bulletin board. "What do you mean? Besides my center's increasingly dismal finances—"

"I'm not talking about the center. I'm talking about you."

In two steps, he traversed the length of the office and stood beside her. Close enough to smell the flowers, close enough to remember how she'd felt with her lips pressed against his, to remember the curve of her breast—

Carter reached out and stilled one of her hands, turning her around to face him as he grasped the other. Both were stone cold and shaking. His gaze flew to hers. Were his wayward thoughts that obvious?

She hastily took back her hands, rubbing them on her arms. "I—I'm just a little cold."

She wasn't cold—she was afraid! Of him, Carter belatedly realized. Damn it, he never should have kissed her. Now he would never be able to forget it, never be able to look at her without wondering, without wanting to do it again. Without scaring her. Damn. Carter raked his fingers through his hair. It wasn't supposed to be like this.

"It doesn't *have* to be like this," he said, more to himself than to her. He would curb himself. He swore it—he wouldn't jeopardize their marriage in any way. He wouldn't force himself on her. He would wait until she was ready, be the perfect gentleman. He would give her whatever she wanted, but take only what she offered, never pushing her further than she wanted to go. If only she would agree...

"Carter..."

He swallowed. "I can get you a cashier's check today."

"I—I don't think so." She stepped back. "You'd better go now. I have a lot of catching up to do. My work. I've fallen behind this week. I...I can walk you out."

Carter frowned. He didn't want to believe negotiations had come to a close, that it was over and he had lost. But one look at Marly's determined expression, and he knew it was true. She'd obviously made up her mind, and no amount of sweet talking was going to sway her.

"That's all right. I know the way," he said, turning to leave. He paused at the door and turned back. "I made it this far by never giving up, Marly. I'm not a man who takes defeat well. But at this point, you've made your position pretty clear, and it doesn't look like you're going be swayed by anything I say or do. So I guess I have no choice but to wave the white flag. Don't worry...I won't be back."

He strode down the hallway, deliberately averting his gaze from the bulletin boards, the red crayon heart clearly etched in his mind, the caption stamped on his soul forever.

Carter King had never been afraid of anything in his life, but he was afraid now. The idea of spending the rest of his days alone scared the hell out of him, but he knew only a miracle would change Marly's mind. It was time to accept his fate.

Past time.

The second time the black limousine snaked by Annie Lou's house, Marly broke into a cold sweat. Letting the curtain fall away, she took a step back and stifled a cry as she bumped into Annie Lou.

"What is it?" the older woman asked, grasping her arm to steady her.

"Billy Ray. His limo's circling the block."

"Are you sure it's him? Maybe it's Carter King again. Didn't he—"

"No." Marly shook her head. "Carter knows better. It's Billy Ray."

Annie Lou pursed her lips. "Where's Tyler?"

"Downstairs."

Just then, a knock sounded at the door. Their wide-eyed gazes met and held in stunned silence. Annie Lou leaped to action first. "Quick." She urged Marly toward the stairs. "Remember the plan."

"But—"

"Go. Hurry."

Marly nodded and ran for the stairs to her room. There, she found Tyler on the floor, playing with some toys she'd brought home from the school.

"It's time, sweetheart," she said, tugging his hand. "Just like we practiced, okay?"

Tyler's eyes widened, but he nodded his assent.

They scrambled down to the cellar, and Marly hoisted him up, into the damp crawl space underneath the living room.

"Miss Marly?" he whispered, still clinging to her neck. "Are Daddy's men going to take me away?"

"No." She pried his fingers loose, kissing his little hands. "I won't let them."

"I'm scared."

"I know, sweetheart. I know. But you have to be a brave boy for me, okay? I'll come get you as soon as they leave. I promise."

Tyler nodded.

"Here, take your action figures. And remember—" She placed one finger over her lips. "Not a sound."

Tyler mimicked her action.

"Good boy," she whispered, closing the wooden door and securing the bar.

Upstairs she heard voices. Annie Lou and a man. She straightened her clothing and climbed the stairs.

"I told you before. She's not feeling well. You'll have to come back another time."

"Look, lady. There ain't gonna be another time. Either you let us in this time, or else—"

"What seems to be the problem?" Marly asked, stumbling into the living room, giving every appearance of being woken from a deep sleep, when inside she was anything but groggy.

Even from the other side of the screen door, Billy Ray looked more menacing than she remembered. His cheekbones jutted out, creating deep hollows in the planes of his crude face. "You Marly Alcott?"

"Yes, who's asking?"

"Billy Ray Cameron, Tyler's father." He tapped one wiry finger against the screen. "Mind if I come in?"

Every instinct screamed *yes!* She wanted to slam the door and bolt it, to run and hide with Tyler in the crawl space. But she did none of those things, instead gesturing for Annie Lou to step aside as she approached the door.

"Hello, Mr. Cameron. I didn't recognize you out there. What can I do for you?"

Billy Ray's gaze dropped to her body, then back up to her face. His deep-sunken eyes narrowed into slits.

Easy, she told herself. *You can't show him your fear.*

But looking over his shoulder, she realized Billy Ray wasn't alone, that he'd brought two of his goons with him. Big, burly men who looked even meaner and more dangerous than he did, if that was possible. Their professional attire did nothing to camouflage the fact that if they wanted to, any one of them could bust past her, never mind kill her with their bare hands.

No fear. "Was there something I could help you with?"

"I think so." He was too calm, too smug. "What do you know about my son's whereabouts?"

Marly braced herself. She'd rehearsed this routine a hundred times in her head, preparing herself for the inevitable confrontation. "Tyler?" she asked. "But I thought he was with you."

"Seems he's disappeared."

"Oh, my goodness." She put one hand on her chest, felt her heart hammering there. "When?"

"You tell me. When was the last time you saw him?"

"Why, yesterday at school. Has he been missing this entire time?" At Billy Ray's nod, she continued in a rush, "Oh, no. This is all my fault. I never should have assumed. Mr. Cameron, please forgive me. I should have contacted the police right away when Tyler didn't come in today. I just didn't think it was unusual, under the circumstances...." Her despair was genuine, with her pulse racing ninety miles an hour and the imminent fear that at any moment she would start screaming.

He looked her over, sizing her up through the slits of his cold black eyes. "Ain't no need to involve the police. Just let me know if he turns up."

"Yes, of course. Is there somewhere I can reach you?"

"Yeah." He smiled then, and an eerie feeling stole over Marly. "Johnny, get the lady a calling card."

One of the thugs reached into his breast pocket and held out a white business card.

Bile rose in her throat, and she tried to swallow it. Big mistake, asking for a phone number. Now she had to open the screen door.

What if she didn't? What if she asked him to leave the card outside the door? Would Billy Ray see through her act?

She stared at him, unflinching. Cautiously, she unlocked the door, her gaze never wavering from his, and cracked it open.

With lightning speed, Billy Ray grabbed the handle and flung the door wide open.

Marly gasped and stumbled back, immediately transported back to the time she'd walked in on Linda Cameron's bloody murder site. There was a crazy glint in Billy Ray's eyes, and when his gaze speared into hers, she felt an imaginary blade slice the air from her lungs.

"Take it," he said, his voice deadly calm.

"Wh-what?"

"Take the card."

"The card?"

Billy Ray snatched the business card from the hand of one of the men and shoved it at her. "If you know what's good for you, you won't mess with me, Miz Alcott."

"No, of course not." She reached quickly for the card, trying to conceal her shaking hand.

"Call me if you hear anything."

"I—I will." She watched the backs of three men as they retreated, waiting until they'd driven away before locking the door. She jumped when Annie Lou touched her arm.

"Are you okay?" the older woman asked. "I was about to call the police."

Marly shook her head and placed her hand over Annie Lou's.

Late that night, long after Annie Lou and Tyler had gone to bed, Marly sat in the living-room chair, huddled into a small, tight ball. She stared at the action figure on the side table, the one she'd discovered on the floor of her room, the one she had forgotten to pick up in her haste to hide Tyler.

What if Billy Ray and his men had stormed the house? What if they'd gone into her room and seen a child's toy on her floor? What then?

Marly buried her face against her bent knees. She'd never felt so alone in all her life. So helpless. She knew this wasn't the last she'd see of Billy Ray Cameron, not by a long shot.

Had he noticed Tyler's security blanket was missing, and if

so, did he mistakenly believe Tyler was involved, that he'd possibly witnessed his mother's execution?

Dear God, it was all her fault. Why had she said her name on the phone that night? Why had she gone into the apartment, instead of leaving a note on the door? What kind of mess had she created?

Damn, she couldn't cry over spilled milk. She had to find a way to protect Tyler, a way to protect them all, until the police arrested Billy Ray.

She focused her gaze on the black telephone beside her, on the white business card she clutched in her hand.

Carter.

How many times had she thought about him in the past five hours, wondering if she hadn't made the biggest mistake of her life? All week, she'd rationalized too much time had elapsed, that surely Carter had come to his senses by now, and the entire issue of his proposal was moot. But he'd come to her center today, let her know he was still prepared to make good on his offer. And she had turned him down.

Marly shivered, remembering how it had felt when he'd held her hands in his, the brief moment in which his warmth suffused the chill wrapped around her heart.

She no longer had a choice. The stakes were too high. It wasn't just her center anymore, but Tyler's safety, as well. Only one person had the resources to save both. All she had to do was agree to marry him and risk his digging up the skeletons buried in her past. After this evening, it was a price she was willing to pay.

But what if there was some kind of statute of limitations on how long she had to change her mind? Had she already exceeded it, lost out on her window of opportunity?

Marly squeezed her eyes shut, said a silent prayer and reached for the phone.

Carter sprang from the couch as the phone's insistent ring penetrated the still of the night. It couldn't be. Could it? It seemed almost too much to hope for, but there were only a

few people who would call him at the bank after midnight.
On his private line.

"Hello?" He wrapped his fingers around the receiver and
held his breath.

"Carter, it's Marly."

He closed his eyes and soundlessly exhaled. "Hey, Marly.
How're you?"

"Not so good. Can you come over?"

"Now?"

"If…if you can."

"Are you at home?"

"Yes."

Exhilaration spread through his chest like some pleasurable
form of heartburn. "Sure, I'll be right there." Carter dropped
the receiver into its cradle and frowned. Funny, he'd never
quite recalled excitement feeling like heartburn. On the drive
over, he questioned his body's strange reaction.

The sound of desolation in Marly's voice could only mean
one thing: that she'd changed her mind. On the one hand, he
was ecstatic. It was what he wanted, what he'd pursued with
single-minded determination during every spare moment outside of work for the past six months. After he'd thought he'd
blown it for good, victory was again within reach, the anticipation of closing a deal heightened by the stakes.

For all intents and purposes, Carter should have been dancing a jig. So why did he suddenly feel about as cheerful as a
turkey before Thanksgiving? He shook his head and backed
out of his reserved parking spot in the bank's underground
garage, then maneuvered the car into the stream of downtown
Friday-night traffic.

Just because theirs was a business arrangement didn't mean
Carter *wanted* to stomp all over Marly's feelings in the process
of closing their deal. At the same time, he couldn't afford to
lose her, let his emotions dull his arbitrating skills during what
was probably the most important negotiation of his life.

No, he couldn't afford to let Marly slip through his fingers.
Not now, not when he'd finally found the perfect woman for

him—the only woman he could trust not to hold his past against him.

Marly Alcott had a rare generosity of spirit, one that knew no socioeconomic barriers. She was a born nurturer, a natural with the children at her center, and he knew beyond a shadow of a doubt that she would make a wonderful mother.

He knew her profile, had studied it for months. It only followed that a woman like Marly still believed in marrying for love, believed it to be a vital element in a marriage. She hadn't been through the hell he had, and he'd see that she never would.

He'd just have to work that much harder to make it up to her. And he would. He would make good on his promise to be a good husband. He would support her in every way he could, and he'd provide for her and their children to the best of his ability. And after a while, she would come to see that love was an overrated commodity. He would show her. Hadn't his mama always said there wasn't a thing Carter couldn't do if he put his mind to it?

Of course, his mama would have slapped him silly before letting him make a fool of himself the way he had over Eva Ann. She'd urged him plenty of times to learn from her mistakes, warning him not to allow hormones to dictate his life.

Carter sighed as he pulled the car to the curb in front of Marly's house and cut the engine. Even though he knew for certain he'd never fall in love with Marly, he would have to make sure he didn't go and do something equally stupid while he was making it up to her.

Just then, a shadowy form moved across the front lawn. Before he could open the car door, the dome light turned on and then off, and she was there beside him, as she'd been the night he first proposed.

"Hi," she whispered.

"Hey." He felt suddenly awkward and excited all at once. He could hardly make out her features in the dark, but her familiar scent filled the interior of the car. He ignored the twitch in his belly, hoping that in doing so, he could stop the sensation from spreading any lower. He didn't want to mix business with pleasure, remember how her lips had felt against his, how sweet she'd tasted. No, he couldn't afford to confuse the issue, wonder how the curve of her body would fit next to his—at least, not until they'd gotten the business out of the way, agreed upon the terms. And even then, he swore to hold himself in check.

"I didn't know if you'd come." Her voice seemed to emanate from a long way off instead of the mere inches between them.

"I said I would."

"I thought maybe you'd changed your mind."

"Marly?" He twisted sideways in his seat, trying to refocus his night vision.

"Yes?"

"You did ask me here for a reason, didn't you?"

She nodded. "You're the only one who can help me."

"Then consider it done," he said, tasting bittersweet victory. "I told you before, and I meant it. I can get you a cashier's check tomorrow."

"Wait, there's more…" She sniffed and looked away, out the passenger window.

Carter frowned, trying not to notice the taste of victory turning more bitter than sweet. He had a sneaking suspicion Miss Marly Alcott was about to up the ante. "Marly?"

For a long time, she didn't answer. Then finally she whispered, "You were right. Something was bothering me earlier today. Besides the center. Something happened last night…."

Carter straightened but remained silent, waiting.

"I'm doing this because…because you're the only one who can help me…the only one I know with the resources."

Her voice was a plea, filled with such desperation Carter had to force his mind to the business nature of the matter at hand. He couldn't fold under pressure, fall prey to a sympathy ploy. He wasn't about to be duped into overlooking Marly's end of the barter if that's where this conversation was headed.

"Go on," he prompted.

"Last night I found one of my little boys from the center hiding underneath our back porch. He stowed away in a neighbor's car, and somehow ended up at the Circle K down the block. I called his mother to tell her where he was, in case she was worried." She stopped and gestured helplessly with one hand.

Aw, man. Something inside Carter twisted. A guy could take only so much of the bleeding-heart routine. If he let her, this woman would have him feeling all mushy and wet, like a pile of leaves after they'd been rained on. Then it would only be a matter of time before he'd be writing her a blank check and kissing holy matrimony goodbye forever.

No, no, no. He had to take control of the situation, instead of allowing the situation to control him. Damn it. He did this every day at work. He needed to focus, concentrate on the issues. Aside from his experience with the bank, Carter also served as chairman of a few boards and often drew upon that experience when faced with delicate negotiations such as this.

It was the chairman's responsibility to remain impassive at board meetings, reserving judgment until all opinions were heard, all arguments presented. Emotion had no place where business matters were concerned. Indeed, it was imperative that one remained emotionally detached in order to do any logical problem solving.

"So what happened?" he prompted after what he deemed a reasonable amount of time.

In the dark, he could feel Marly's wide-eyed gaze on his face, feel her retreat when she turned toward the door. He heard it unlatch and without thought reached one hand out to touch her arm. She was shaking. His gut twisted.

"Marly?"

"I...I can't do this in your car," she said, reaching for the door handle.

Chapter 6

"Marly, wait." Carter reached across the seat, but she'd already opened the passenger door and slipped out. He ran one hand through his hair and slammed his fist on the steering wheel with a muttered expletive.

She'd been on the verge of capitulating. What had gone wrong? What did being in his car have to do with anything?

Carter opened his door and climbed out. Marly was already halfway across the front lawn and didn't look as if she had any intention of stopping or even slowing down.

He swore again and rubbed a weary hand over his face. Late-night stubble scraped against his fingers, reminding him that he should have been in bed, not chasing after damsels in distress for the second time in one week.

He gave a sigh of resignation and set out after her—did this woman ever know how to bruise a guy's ego. He followed her around the side of the house and into the backyard, where he came to a clearing. Overhead, a full moon hung in the sky, its white light illuminating his path to Marly.

He caught up with her in the middle of some sort of weed

patch and laid his hand on her shoulder. Her skin felt soft and smooth to the touch.

She dipped her shoulder to break their contact, and he let his hand fall to his side. "I—I don't know how to tell you this...."

A business transaction. This is a business transaction. Carter tried to retain his objectivity. He focused on the image of a boardroom, he and Marly seated at opposite ends of a long table. He visualized his neatly typed agenda, maybe even some impressive color transparencies of his spreadsheets. He replayed his well-rehearsed arguments tit for tat like a game of chess.

It was going pretty well until Marly sniffled.

Carter's stomach muscles clenched of their own accord. He shifted his weight from one foot to the other, then back again. The sniffling continued. Marly was crying.

With a muttered curse, Carter conceded defeat. Despite his resolve to keep things on a professional level until after they'd settled business matters, he couldn't stand to hear Marly cry.

God help him, he wasn't starting to have feelings for her, was he? No, it couldn't be all that bad. Carter frowned.

"Something happened the other night..." Why had her voice sounded strained? Why was she shaking? *What happened?*

"Marly, turn around."

"What? No. Carter, please."

"Just for a minute," he coaxed without touching her.

"Why?"

"I want to see your face."

"You can see it now."

"No, I can't."

"Trust me." Her voice cracked. "You don't want to see me right now."

"Yes, I do. Marly, please." It was his turn to implore. He held out his hand, but she didn't turn around, so he let it fall. "You called me for a reason. I'm here now. Tell me what's wrong. If I can help you, I swear I will."

"You don't know how much I want to believe that."

"Believe it."

"Oh, Carter." He heard a choked sob. "Something terrible has happened, and I just don't know what to do."

Carter tipped back his head and stared straight up into the cloudless sky, where stars gleamed and winked like searching fireflies. In the light of day, would he wake up to find the word *sucker* tattooed across his forehead?

He straightened and took in Marly's small form against the backdrop of an endless stretch of open space. In that moment, a flash of loneliness stabbed at him. Hers. His. Carter took a hesitant step forward, coming within inches of her. He could smell the flowers. Was it shampoo or perfume? He couldn't tell.

In the pale moonlight, her hair looked more blond than strawberry, and it hung straight in the back, just covering her neck. He started to reach up, to run his fingers through the golden strands, but caught himself before he could act on the uncharacteristic impulse. Marly didn't want that kind of comfort, and despite his identification with her real or imagined isolation, he didn't need to further complicate an already complicated situation.

"You found one of your little boys underneath the porch," he whispered behind her.

"Yes. His name is Tyler."

"So you called his mother to let her know the boy was all right?"

She nodded. "No one picked up the phone for a long time. It just rang and rang. Then someone picked up, but didn't say anything. I—I said my name. I identified myself. It was stupid, but there was no way I could have known."

"Known what? I don't understand."

"Whoever that person was, they hung up on me. And when I tried to call back, the line was busy." She didn't speak for a long moment, and when she continued, the cadence was much slower, as if she was choosing her words carefully. "I gave up and went to bed. I didn't find out until today." Her head drooped lower as she said the words, ''Tyler's mother died last night.''

Carter closed his eyes. Damn, but he understood grief. ''I'm sorry, Marly. But you can't blame yourself—''

''No—''

She turned around then, nearly colliding with him, and Carter's hands went instinctively to her waist, holding her in place. Her head lifted a notch, though she didn't look at him but stared straight ahead. It was enough for Carter to see the tears she'd been trying to hide, and the sight brought with it a fresh wave of guilt at his insensitivity.

Plain. He'd thought she was plain. Carter grimaced. She wasn't the least bit plain, not to him—not the night of the fund-raiser and certainly not now. But what he wouldn't have given to have her tear-stained face and puffy eyes look plain now....

With one hand, he lifted her chin so he could see her in the moonlight. With the back of his fingers, he caressed her cheek. ''I'm sorry.''

''Thank you.''

She had one of the loveliest mouths he'd ever seen, and when she started to chew on her lower lip, his fingers automatically went to stop her. Her lips were so soft and inviting. He could feel her breath, warm and moist against his knuckles. He wanted to kiss her again. He didn't care that Eva Ann would have called the urge base, primitive. He cared only about Marly, about offering her comfort in the only way he knew how.

Slowly, he circled his hand to her nape, supporting her head as he lowered his lips to hers. There was an instant of brushing contact, followed by another and yet another, until his mouth was rocking very slowly over hers.

Marly drew in a sharp breath, her lips parting to whisper, ''Please.''

Cautious not to overstep his bounds, Carter pulled back. But when he gazed down into her eyes, he was startled to see unmasked desperation reflected there.

She wasn't asking him to stop, he realized. Still, she wasn't urging him to go on, either.

Her hands shook where they clung to his shirt, and he had the strangest sense that she was engaged in some kind of inner struggle.

Was she holding herself back? Did a part of her want this?

Carter again vowed to give her whatever she wanted, but to take only what she offered. Never would he push her further than she wanted to go.

Hesitantly, he slid his fingers upward, into the silky strands of her hair. Marly tipped her head back, leaning into his touch. He felt his breath quicken as he lowered his head again, his heart pounding like a schoolboy on a first date.

She closed her eyes and eliminated the last inch of space between their mouths. A tremor of response rocked him from head to toe. She felt so good. Too good. He had to hold himself in check. It would be so easy—too easy—to cross the line.

When her lips parted, he tested the waters carefully, probing with his tongue. He intended only to taste. To give and take only a few seconds of comfort. Nothing more. Lowering his hand to her waist, he drew her into the circle of his arms.

He deepened the kiss, felt her lips move in response as she pressed closer into his embrace. But the moment his tongue touched hers and she moved against him, all tenderness vanished, replaced by an intense, aching need that slashed through Carter's defenses with stunning velocity.

Suddenly, he couldn't hold her close enough, couldn't get enough of her. His tongue plunged and tangled with hers, and all the while she kissed him back with the same hunger.

They clung to each other, frantic hands kneading, gripping. And then just as suddenly, the heat of her touch was gone, his arms empty all too soon.

"Marly?" He held out one hand, but her eyes stopped him from moving toward her. They still held the aftereffects of passion, but they were tinged with fear, as well.

Damn it. He'd done it again. Carter dropped his hand. The

last thing he wanted was to scare her off. Not when he was this close.

What was happening to him, anyway? All these strange feelings creeping up on him, clouding his judgment. It wasn't supposed to be like this. Not with Marly.

"I'm sorry," she whispered. "I don't know what came over me."

"It's all right," he muttered, but it wasn't all right. He was the one who should have been apologizing—not her.

"I'm not usually so..." She rubbed her temple. "Easily distracted." She paused for several seconds before asking, "Where was I?"

He shook his head. Every muscle in his body was tight. He had to step back before he could give in to the impulse to step forward, to pull her into his arms again.

"Oh, yes. I was about to tell you before we...before. About Tyler's mother. She didn't just die...."

"But I thought you said—"

"No. She was murdered."

"Murdered?" Carter folded his arms across his chest. "But who'd want to kill her?"

"Her ex-husband. Billy Ray Cameron."

His eyes widened. "Tyler's mother is Linda Cameron? No wonder you were so interested in that newspaper article."

Marly nodded, saving her words until she could regulate her breathing again.

Had Carter King really kissed her like that? And had she actually kissed him back *like that?*

Her lips still tingled from his touch. A lingering warmth spiraled low in her belly.

She never would have expected such aching tenderness from a man as stoic as Carter cast himself to be. While his gentle touch spoke volumes, gave her the reassurances she needed to hear, the hot, soul-searing passion had taken her entirely by surprise. She'd craved it with a deep-seated need long unfamiliar to her, and he'd given it in a way she would have expected him to reserve for women far more attractive than she.

Marly drew a quick breath. This wasn't the time for her foolish romanticism. She had to rein in her thoughts, get her mind off Carter's warm, sensual lips. His hands on her body, touching her, holding her.

Her fingers curled into fists. She had to stop. That was why she'd run from the car. She couldn't keep a clear head when she associated so many sensations with being in that car. Memories of kissing Carter and equal measures of tenderness and heat and wanting.

And now, she would associate the exact same things with Annie Lou's garden.

"About Tyler," she said when she finally trusted her voice.

"He's Billy Ray Cameron's son, the reason you've got your center locked up tighter than Fort Knox."

She looked down at her hands and nodded. She had to be careful about what she revealed. It was enough to have her own life on the line, not to mention jeopardizing Tyler's—she couldn't risk endangering Carter's, as well.

At her sudden shudder, Carter shrugged off his leather jacket and draped it over her shoulders. The garment felt as inviting as a down comforter, as soft and warm as her mother's fine cashmere, but the faint, woodsy scent that enveloped her…it was all Carter's.

She remembered how it had lingered on her dress that night and how she had savored it, convinced she would never again allow herself that close to him.

But now she was, and she wanted to believe he was the answer to her problems, not the source of additional ones. She needed to believe that.

"Thanks." She stuck her arms through the sleeves. "Can we, um, walk for a while?"

"Sure."

She took his proffered arm and guided him toward the far end of the garden as a stall technique. She needed just a few more minutes to mentally prepare. True, it was an enormous request she was about to make, but was it really any greater than what Carter was asking of her? She hoped he would put it in that perspective—she prayed he would. But first she had to convince him of the urgency without revealing the truth. The whole truth.

Carter looked around. "What is this?"

"Just a field. The soil's not the best. Nothing will grow here. But it's good for walking." She let go of his arm and surveyed the barren field. The moonlight bathed it in white, making it appear covered in snow. Marly looked up at Carter, admiring the lines of his face, his thoughtful expression.

On some level, she trusted him—enough to know he would keep Tyler safe—but she wasn't ready to trust anyone with her life, which she would put at stake the minute she revealed the truth about her involvement.

She knew too well that prison bars couldn't thwart a person's vengeance, that if she pointed the finger at Billy Ray, he'd make sure she paid dearly. She'd been there before. She knew his type, the predators, and she knew how it felt to be their hunted, to be the prey.

Marly shivered and realized her hand had drifted down toward Carter's. Without a word, he took it and started walking. She fell into step beside him. She hadn't realized until the moment he'd first kissed her just how much she'd craved the warmth of another human being. And when he'd kissed her the second time, she didn't think she was ever going to get enough.

She relished the next few minutes of silence, the illusion of being a normal woman without secrets, holding hands on a moonlit stroll with a man to whom she was undeniably attracted. Maybe in another place, another time, another life. But certainly not here, not now, not in this lifetime.

"Billy Ray Cameron is as crooked as they come," Marly said in a calm, even tone that belied the pandemonium inside her. "I've heard stories about him that just make me sick inside. He's corrupted an entire community with his drug trafficking, yet he's never done significant jail time."

"They never can get anything to stick, can they?"

Marly shook her head. "Somehow, he always manages to get off. Not enough evidence. Last month he was implicated in the murder of a teenage boy the police believed was a runner for Billy Ray's drug ring. The prosecution subpoenaed Linda, but she was a reluctant witness. She told one of the teachers at the center that she'd perjure herself before she told them anything. God knows Billy Ray threatened to kill her on enough occasions. He nearly succeeded once when Tyler was three. He used to beat them. Both of them."

At Marly's sound of anguish, Carter squeezed her hand.

"It just infuriates me that people like him go unpunished, while the innocents die. Where is the justice in this world? When Linda left him, I thought she had a prayer. I wish I could say I'd never imagined it would end like this. I know he killed her. I mean," she hastened to add, "he had all the motive in the world."

"Marly?" He turned her to face him. "You said there's something more you want. More than the donation. What is it?"

At his words, her last memory of Linda Cameron flashed in her mind's eye. She withdrew her hand and wrapped her arms around her midsection as a swift wave of nausea threatened to overcome her. Beads of sweat broke out over her upper lip, and she forced herself to take deep, even breaths. She couldn't afford to get sick again, here in front of Carter. How would she convincingly explain that?

"I haven't told anyone about Tyler. Annie Lou and I are the only ones who know he's here. And now you."

"I don't understand. Why all the secrecy?"

"Because," Marly said slowly, regulating her breathing, "with Tyler's mother dead, the authorities will turn Tyler over to his father. And I'm afraid it was Billy Ray who answered the phone, who hung up on me when I called. I'm afraid he knows I've got Tyler, or else he suspects I know more than I'm letting on about his whereabouts. That little boy isn't going to be safe until his father's indicted,'' she said, slamming one fist into her palm.

"Easy there, slugger.'' He took her hands in his for a brief moment. "You're assuming Billy Ray even wants him.''

"Oh, he wants him.'' Marly embraced her hostility toward Tyler's father. Anger was an emotion she could justify to Carter—he would never understand the true extent of her fear. "He came here this afternoon looking for him.''

"Here?'' Carter frowned. "You've got to be kidding.''

"No joke. Scared the hell out of me.''

"Why didn't you call the police?''

She shook her head and started to turn. "I don't want to get involved.''

He caught her elbow. "But you are involved.''

"Look, I don't want to argue about this. Not now. Not here. My number-one priority is to hide Tyler from Billy Ray.'' She wrung her hands together, grappling with the words she needed to say. She had to convey the urgency without revealing the whole truth. "I'm afraid Billy Ray thinks Tyler knows more than he does, that he might have...witnessed something he shouldn't have.''

One of Carter's eyebrows shot up. "Did he?''

"No, but I'm not willing to fork Tyler over so he can explain himself to that *murderer,*'' she said with vehemence, but desperation turned her voice into a plea. "Can't you see? I need to hide him somewhere far away, somewhere no one would ever think to look, somewhere his father could never trace. Just until he's convicted. Then Tyler can be placed in foster care. Please, Carter. Please try to understand. I don't know where else to turn. I need to hide him, and you're the only one I know with those kinds of resources. Will you help me?''

"Will I help you?'' Carter echoed. "Marly, you want to kidnap a child. You realize that, don't you?''

"Yes,'' she admitted with a sad smile. "That's the true irony here, isn't it? I can follow one set of rules that says I'm breaking the law if I don't turn Tyler over to his rightful guardian. Or I can follow another set entirely. The rules right here." She thumped her chest. "The ones that tell me I cannot stand by and let an innocent child suffer at the cruel hand of fate. The ones that tell me I will protect this child at all costs, even if it means breaking the law. I can live with that. Maybe I wouldn't have before, but this is who I am now, and some things I just can't change. This is one of them. So I'm sorry if you think less of me, but you have to know at least this much."

Carter tipped his head back and drew a deep breath. When he straightened, he met her gaze directly. "I don't think less of you. I'd be lying if I said I did. Truth is, I can't fault a logic that aims for the greater good, even if it does defy conventional rules. Maybe that's a flaw we have in common." The corner of his mouth curved upward, revealing a long slash of a dimple in his cheek.

"Will you help me, then?"

"Let's just think this through here. What if the police can't get a conviction? What then?"

"They will. They have to. They've already brought Billy Ray in for questioning. He's got to be the prime suspect. Surely his luck can't hold out forever."

Carter scratched his chin, his appearance thoughtful, as if he was mulling over any mundane, run-of-the-mill dilemma. With a sinking numbness, Marly remembered a line from Charles Dickens about secondhand care, like secondhand clothes, coming easily off and on.

"Is there anything else?" he asked. "Anything you're not telling me?"

The shame of her deception rushed in her ears like the sound of sand pouring from a child's bucket onto the concrete. He had a right to know. She'd allow him that. But there were too many lives at stake, and she couldn't take the risk. She couldn't tell another soul what she had witnessed at Linda Cameron's apartment that night.

"I've told you everything," she said, trying to sound more certain than she felt.

"No, I don't think so. Not everything."

At his words, the air froze in Marly's lungs; breathing became an impossible task.

"You still haven't told me if you'll marry me."

Slowly, she exhaled.

"Marly, please don't make me out to be some kind of monster. I want a child. Two children—"

"Yes, I believe you mentioned that preference earlier." She nodded, rubbing her temple to ease her sudden light-headedness.

"I'm not looking for a surrogate. Is it so terrible to want the mother of my children in our lives?"

"I never thought that. It wasn't so much your intentions as your methods—"

"I told you before, I've already gone the traditional route. It didn't work for me, and I don't have time to sit back and wait for opportunity to knock. You're my last chance, Marly." He lowered his voice, "I...I need you."

Something inside Marly's heart churned. Her eyes burned with unshed tears. She didn't know why, of all the women in the world, Carter had chosen her. But she needed him more than he needed her. She'd realized that tonight, in the aftermath of Billy Ray's visit.

How bizarre it seemed that in the mere space of a week, the pros of a loveless marriage to a complete stranger seemed to have undergone mitosis and multiplied to outnumber the cons. The impossible had become not only possible, but essential. Before her stood the one man who could ensure the welfare of Tyler and the children.

"Will you marry me, Marly?"

She took a deep, steadying breath. "In return for Tyler's protection and a donation to the center in the amount you specified. As long as we agree on the terms, yes. I'll marry you."

For a minute, Carter could do no more than hold his breath, afraid that at any second Marly would retract her words. But she didn't, and the longer he waited, the more tense the silence between them grew.

"Are you sure," he finally asked, "this is an agreement you can live with? Think it through carefully, Marly, because I don't have any intentions of giving you a quickie divorce a couple of months up the line."

"I realize that. You've made your intentions more than clear, and believe me, I've thought this through more times than you can imagine. Marrying you like this—our arrangement—it's not what I planned, not what I foresaw for myself, for my future. But under the circumstances..." She shrugged and turned toward the house. "Futures have a funny way of falling down midflight anyway."

Carter looked away, focusing on some spot off in the distance to lessen the sting of her words and their implication. "You won't regret marrying me, Marly," he said, his voice low. "I know all you've got is my word on that, but I'll make good on it. You'll see."

"Okay, let's discuss the terms."

"I don't know if this is such a good time for us to negotiate," he admitted, aware there were other issues they would have to discuss. "You've been through a lot today. Maybe we should wait until—"

Marly spun around. "But there's no time to wait. Please, just agree to the donation and protection for Tyler. I need to have your word on that much now, so I can get Tyler out of here. The sooner the better. Billy Ray's probably out knocking down every door in the Bricks looking for him. There's no telling when he'll decide to pay me another home visit.

"I'm convinced he's the one who answered the phone last night when I called Linda's and gave my name like an idiot. Billy Ray knows someone's got Tyler, and I'm right up there at the top of his suspect list. Tyler can't stay here. He isn't safe. Please, just give me this much now—the donation and your word you'll help me hide Tyler. We can duke out the piddly stuff later."

"Does he know? About his mother?"

"Not yet. I…couldn't bring myself to tell him. He knows his father's after him, but that's about it. In so many ways, he's this street-smart kid, wise beyond his years. But in other ways, he's just a five-year-old boy, one of the sweetest, most affection-starved kids I know. And he loved her…he loved her with the unconditional love a child has for a parent, even when that parent doesn't deserve such love."

Carter ran a weary hand through his hair. In return for what he was asking of her, Marly's demands paled in comparison. It was an easy concession to make. The wheels had already begun spinning in his mind. He knew exactly what phone calls to make, which people to contact. "You'll have everything," he promised. "The donation, protection for Tyler, whatever you want. I know a place where we can hide him. You won't have to worry. He'll be safe."

"Thank you," she whispered, her voice a little breathless, as if she'd run some great distance and taken her first sip of water.

"Come on. Let's get Tyler so I can take you home."

In the pale moonlight, Marly saw Carter hold one arm outstretched as if in invitation. His handsome face looked worn, like that of a weathered seaman. She went to him willingly, drawing strength from the protection he offered. Tomorrow, she would put up her emotional barriers. But tonight, as they plodded through the garden to Annie Lou's house, they were two combat-weary souls trekking through a battlefield.

At the back door, Marly stopped under the yellowish orange lamplight and pressed a finger to her lips. "Annie Lou's gone to sleep. I don't want to wake her, but I need to leave a note. I think she'd be safer if she went to visit her family for a while. She has a son in Texas."

Carter nodded and pulled out his wallet. He counted five one-hundred-dollar bills, grasped her hand and deposited the money onto her palm.

"What's this?"

"Plane fare."

"Carter, you don't have to—"

"I'm not." He eased her fingers into a small fist. "I'm taking it out of your donation."

Marly looked down at his large, rough hand, surprised again by his gentle touch. "Thank you," she said. "This will help."

"It's a barter, Marly. Fair and square. We each have something the other wants."

"Right." She bit her lip and turned to open the door.

Inside, she wrote the note and left the money, then guided them through the kitchen and down the stairs in the dark. In her room, she released his hand and crossed to the bathroom, where she flipped on the light switch. With the door open a crack, enough light fell into the bedroom for her to check on Tyler without waking him.

One knee propped on the mattress, Marly leaned over the boy. "He's fast asleep," she told Carter, starting to hoist his small body into her arms. At a restraining hand on her shoulder, she stopped.

"You pack a bag. I'll carry him."

She straightened, her gaze automatically roving over his broad shoulders. He was so big. Not just tall but broad. Marly spun around, heat flushing her cheeks. She didn't want to be caught staring at him. Methodically, she pulled an olive green duffel bag from the closet and went about stuffing it. But even with her back turned to him, she could still envision the man she'd agreed to marry.

She went into the bathroom and gathered her toiletries, pausing at the sink to inspect the face reflected in the mirror. It had grown familiar over the years, but she would never forget the first time she'd seen it, the day after the doctors had removed the bandages and a stranger had stared back at her from the glass. Marly Alcott's name didn't seem to fit the face, but then, neither did hers, and that was the important thing.

She stood before the mirror now and tilted her head from side to side as she had done on that day so many years ago. Soundlessly, she mouthed, "Mrs. Carter King."

No, the name still didn't match, not the face and certainly not the person inside.

She lifted a trembling hand to her lips. In the best-case scenario—and she reminded herself she had to hope for the best—they would convict Billy Ray without her involvement, Tyler would be safe, her center saved, and she would be left alive and well. Alive and well, married to Carter King, that is.

For a fleeting second, she wondered what it would be like to be Mrs. Carter King. Did he belong to a country club? Would his wife be expected to host teas? She tried to picture what kind of house he would have, whether it had acres of unused space, furniture you weren't supposed to sit on, objets d'art no one could touch.

She imagined a big, white mansion with tall columns, perched on top of some hill in the middle of one of Raleigh's most prestigious neighborhoods. Her heart constricted painfully at the vision of her own childhood neighborhood, of life ironically coming full circle, when she'd sworn never to go back.

On her father's grave, she had sworn.

Marly hastened to swipe a wayward tear, taking a deep breath in an effort to regain control. She squeezed her eyes shut and whispered a silent prayer for forgiveness. She was doing this for Tyler and the children and for no other reasons. If she had to repeat that affirmation to herself a thousand times a day for the rest of her life, she would.

She emerged from the bathroom to find Carter leaning back, one shoulder against the doorjamb. Funny how the room appeared smaller with him filling it.

"How many bedrooms does this house have?" he asked.

"Three. Why?"

"Is there a reason you're living in the basement?"

"It's not a basement. It's a finished garage."

"Whatever. Why are you down here when there are bedrooms upstairs?"

"Because I need my privacy," she replied, hoping he would let it go at that.

He gestured to her overnight bag. "All set?"

She nodded.

He crossed to Tyler and scooped him up into his arms as if he weighed no more than a stack of pillows.

"You got him okay?" Marly asked, smoothing the hair back from Tyler's forehead.

"Umm-hmm."

Tyler mumbled something unintelligible but didn't wake up. Gently, Marly rubbed the back of one finger over the rosy pillow imprints on his cheek. Glancing up, she found Carter's gaze leveled on her. The intensity in his brownish green eyes held her entranced, made her unable to break away from their intimate circle.

"This is what I want one day, Marly."

For one fleeting instant, Marly allowed herself to remember when this had been her dream, too, a family of her own to cherish forever. How long ago it seemed. A lifetime ago.

"And you'll have it," she whispered, wanting to believe it for herself as much as for him.

Chapter 7

It was never going to work, Marly thought as they zigzagged along the country backroads. Never. Not in a million years. Yes, she had struck a bargain, and she swore she would do her best to uphold it. For her, the price was worth the payoff. But what about Carter? Surely he would come to realize, on his own, that the two of them simply did not make a good match for a lifetime.

For one, they lived in different worlds. Not that she'd ever seen exactly how he lived. New money or old money. How much could it differ? At the core of every affluent lifestyle was money, plain and simple. It took first priority over all else. That's how it always was.

Second, their personalities were completely different, and Carter was used to women far more sophisticated than she. Soon, the novelty of the chase would wear thin.

Third, they had incompatible goals. He wanted to succeed in his chosen field, and he wanted a family. She wanted…to succeed in her chosen field…and she wanted a family.

But it was different. Really. Very different.

Marly wondered why Carter wanted a family so badly, if this was all an image thing with him, as she suspected. A grand scheme hatched to mold his public image into that of a family man. Could it be just a means to some career end? She'd already figured out the public relations benefit of their union.

She studied his profile in the shadowy interior of the car. A man like Carter was made for the society pages, but a woman like her could never share his limelight. She slumped against the window.

"You okay?" Carter turned his gaze away from the road for a brief second.

"Umm-hmm. Just tired." She gazed out into the night. "I thought you lived in Raleigh."

"Moved out to Cary about five years ago. Don't worry, it's not too much farther. We're almost there." They were on a straight stretch of road now, and he glanced over his shoulder at the sleeping form in the back seat.

"Fast asleep," Marly whispered. "Poor little guy. He's just drained."

Carter shook his head, rubbing the back of his neck with one hand. "I'm sorry."

"Yeah, me, too."

"I'm sure the police have been questioning the neighbors. Someone must have seen something."

"Maybe, but it'll probably take some time before they get anywhere."

"Why do you say that?"

"You'd have to understand life in the low-income communities." Marly thought she saw him wince as he shifted gears around a bend. "It's just a lot safer to keep your nose clean, so to speak."

"You don't say?"

"People aren't going to get involved any more than they have to. Call it survival instincts. There's just been a murder, and they'll want to protect their own. It won't look good to be seen talking to the police, especially if it could be construed in any way as narking on Billy Ray.'' She shuddered, remembering the unconcealed threat behind Billy Ray's parting words, when he'd warned her not to mess with him. She, too, had to protect her own now. ''He's not a man who takes disloyalty very well.''

Carter slowed the car, and the beam of headlights cut through the fog to reveal black, wrought-iron gates. Reaching for a remote control in the glove compartment, he explained, ''The fence is for the horses.''

She nodded, focusing more on the assurance of security than the presence of horses.

They wound up what seemed a mile-long driveway until they reached a point where the ground leveled. In the distance stood two structures resembling barns, but as they drew closer, Marly noticed one of them wasn't a barn at all, but a large, rambling farmhouse. Spotlights illuminated a stone chimney through the patchy fog.

''That…that's your house?'' She tried to keep her voice a whisper, so as not to wake Tyler.

Carter's jaw set in a hard line. ''You don't like it.''

''No, no. It's not that.''

''Then what?''

''It just sort of surprised me. I guess I hadn't expected anything this…'' She waved her hand, sensing she was digging herself even deeper into a hole with all these qualifications.

''Anything this what?''

''Well, rural for one.''

''Rural as in hick?''

''I didn't say that.'' Marly felt like an insensitive idiot. ''Oh, come on. We're not even married yet, Carter. Don't start putting words in my mouth already.''

''Then say what you mean. Do you like it or don't you?''

She wondered why her inconsequential opinion of his house mattered so much. It wasn't as if she had any choice in the matter. Would he offer to move if she didn't like where he lived? Doubtful. He'd built his life exactly as he wanted it, a wife and children the finishing touches.

Still, in an odd sort of way, his behavior reminded her of
the children at the center, though they were much more forward in what they expected from her: "Isn't this a pretty picture I colored, Miss Marly?"

She turned her gaze toward his profile and reminded herself
not to forget she owed this man, and owed him big, for helping
her. Carefully, Marly reached out and touched his knuckles,
loosening his death grip on the steering wheel. "Your house
is charming."

He shot a glance at her out of the corner of his eye. "I
wasn't fishing for a compliment. If you don't like it—"

"I like it. I just stuck my foot in my mouth, and I'm sorry.
It's just that I was so afraid you were going to live in some
ostentatious place in some stuck-up neighborhood. I didn't
know if I could go through that—" She cut herself off before
she could say *again*. "What I'm trying to say is that if I
sounded surprised, I was. But it was in a good way."

She let her hand drop into her lap, not wanting to prolong
their contact. If she were honest with herself, she would admit
she liked touching Carter more than she should. But there were
so many things she couldn't be honest about—why complicate
matters further by owning up to insignificant feelings toward
a man who wanted to marry her and father her children? Life
was already tumultuous at best.

"This isn't easy for me, Carter. It's as though I'm giving
up my entire life and assimilating into yours."

"That's not true."

"Isn't it? This is your house."

"It will be *our home*." He directed a pointed glance at her.
"And I don't expect you to give up anything. I don't *want*
you to give up anything. I'm only asking you to share a part
of yourself."

A part of herself. Marly glanced down at her abdomen. Dear
God, was it really possible? For as long as she could remember, she had always wanted children, always coveted the
chance to create her own family, a family so different from

the cold, lonely one into which she'd been born through no choice of her own.

She was almost afraid to think about it, after all these years of chastising herself for wanting something she could never have.

Where once she faced nothing but a barren field of dreams, did she have a chance now, a chance to create something wonderful?

She tried to imagine a part of herself and a part of Carter, together in one little body, but found she couldn't accept the possibility as something real. Not yet. Not after wanting it for so long, wishing that somehow there were a way, and knowing it was hopeless.

Years ago, she'd accepted her fate as something she couldn't change. And now this. Out of nowhere, this handsome prince had come into her life, like some kind of fractured fairy tale. But she couldn't risk believing in it, couldn't bear the thought of awakening to find her worst nightmare a reality.

Marly shivered as Carter maneuvered the car around back, then pulled into one slot of a three-car garage. Overhead, a light flickered on. Carter got out and unbuckled Tyler from the back seat, before lifting the boy into his arms.

"Mama?" Tyler mumbled, his eyelids fluttering open to reveal bleary, unfocused eyes.

Marly felt a fresh stab of pain.

With a look of helplessness, Carter turned to her.

"Shh, it's okay," she whispered, brushing her fingertips over Tyler's eyelids. But it wasn't okay—Tyler still had a long road ahead of him, and they would have to take things one day at a time. Their first priority would be to get him out of harm's way. "Close your eyes, honey. Go back to sleep." She gestured for Carter to hold him closer, and when he did, Tyler snuggled into his arms. Within a few seconds, his breathing fell back into a deep, even pattern.

Marly stood on tiptoe to peek at his face. "Is he asleep?" she mouthed. At Carter's nod, she preceded them to the side door. She felt him tap keys at her waist and reached down to take them. "Which one?" She held up each key until Carter gave her the okay, then inserted the proper key into the lock.

"Wait a minute," he whispered, his lips close to her ear, his head next to hers.

She held herself perfectly still, afraid to move, afraid to breathe, for fear of brushing her cheek against his lips.

There was danger in their shared comfort tonight. How easy it would have been to lean back, to lay her head on his shoulder and confess to what she had seen, to the guilt and fear that ate at her soul. But she couldn't, no matter how much she wanted to. Just like the secret buried deep in her past, she couldn't risk confiding this truth to anyone. She couldn't put her life on the line. Not again. Never again.

"You have to disarm the security system," he said, and instructed her how to do it.

Marly nodded and pressed the four-digit code once inside the door.

Carter sidestepped her. "I'll be right back."

"Where are you taking him?"

"Just upstairs to the guest room."

"Oh, okay." Marly took a hesitant step into what appeared to be a breakfast nook. A table and six chairs were assembled in front of a huge bay window with a cushioned bench seat. She noticed only one place setting at the table, and felt another twinge of shared isolation with the man who appeared to eat all his meals alone.

Her gaze swept across the spacious, U-shaped kitchen, where whitewashed wood and beveled-glass cabinets afforded a view of a neat and orderly lifestyle. Burgundy-tiled countertops splashed warmth into the otherwise-neutral decor. The kitchen seemed to have two of everything: an indoor grill on an island in the center, another range on the counter with double ovens just to its side and a double glass-doored refrigerator within arm's reach.

Marly felt as though she'd stepped back into another world, until she glanced up at the ceiling and noticed a simple, hand-stenciled border. It seemed oddly out of place with the ultra-modern appliances. She didn't know why, but she liked that.

Wandering down the hallway, she flipped light switches on and off until she came to a large, airy room with cathedral ceilings that could only be the living room. A large stone hearth in the center. Wall-to-wall bookshelves at the far end. Navy blue leather furniture with burgundy throw pillows. The decor was simple, yet inviting—neither plain nor pretentious.

Lured by two framed photographs, she crossed to the mantel. She lifted one and peered at two people sitting on a silver bench eating hotdogs: a blond-haired woman who looked at least forty and a young boy of ten or so. In the background, a wall displayed colorful graffiti. The boy held a backpack between his feet and flashed a big, crooked grin at the camera. The woman's smile was only slight, the gray shadows under her eyes making her look tired. One of her hands rested on the boy's leg. The protective gesture combined with the glitter of pride in her eyes seemed to convey a deep, maternal bond.

Marly replaced the first photograph and reached for the second. It was a graduation photo from Buckhead Preparatory High School, as indicated by the blue print on the bottom. She could tell it was the same woman and boy. The boy looked as though he'd aged about a decade, although the woman appeared to have aged two. Her gray shadows had turned to circles beneath eyes that now seemed hollow despite their sparkle. Her hair hung limp and lifeless around her sunken face.

Though she sagged against the boy, this time no weariness weighed down her smile, which spread from ear to ear. Instead, it was the boy whose crooked smile now appeared only slight. Wearing a black graduation cap and gown, he towered over the woman by more than a foot, one arm encircling her shoulder. It was almost as though their roles had changed, and he was now her protector.

Marly replaced the photograph and retraced her steps out of the room. Down the hall, she found a room with another stone fireplace and a wet bar. Her gaze swept from light oak floors to soaring ceilings, while her mind grappled to make sense of the images she'd seen in the past few minutes, to connect them with the man she would soon marry.

There was something terribly disquieting about Carter's home. Decorated with simple furnishings, the rooms used colors and textures that seemed to aim at warmth and comfort, as if in invitation to come home and be oneself.

It was too much. Too earthy. Too artless. It was out of character, out of sync with the portrait she'd painted of Carter. She shook her head, trying to make sense of it all and coming up empty. She was too tired, too exhausted, to think anymore. The past week had been filled with sleepless nights and unparalleled fear. Now, for the first time in too long, she felt the first signs of peace.

Carter would keep Tyler safe until this Billy Ray situation passed. She believed that. And she, in return, would do whatever she could to make their marriage work. She owed him that much. She just prayed that in the years to come, she could keep up her guard, lest he slip by her lowered defenses and realize she wasn't the woman he thought he'd married.

Crossing to the wet bar, she scanned the labels until she found a bottle of brandy. After removing the cap, she poured herself a generous amount, watching the thick liquid slosh around in the snifter. As a young girl, she'd often watched her father swish his brandy. The way the brandy clung to the glass always reminded her of the toilet bowl cleaner the maids had used.

Raising the goblet to her lips, she sniffed the aroma concentrated at the small opening before taking a tentative sip. The blackberry-flavored liquid swirled around her mouth. When she swallowed, it burned a hot, pleasantly numbing path down her throat and into her stomach. Marly closed her eyes and wrapped both hands around the glass, taking another sip and then one more, until she'd drained the contents of the glass and the brandy's warmth numbed her frazzled nerves.

She poured another finger of brandy into her snifter before recapping the bottle and returning it to the shelf. Then she carried the goblet to a green-and-white pin-striped armchair and eased her stiff muscles down onto the cushions. Her head felt heavy, her entire body weighed down with fatigue as she raised her sore feet onto the matching ottoman, careful so as not to jostle the brandy.

In her mind's eye, she saw the mother and son and wondered, what kind of man had the boy in the photos become?

What kind of man was Carter King?

He was a jerk.

Carter leaned against the entryway to the great room and shook his head. Curled up in one of the chairs lay his Cinderella, fast asleep with her "glass slippers" on the floor nearby, her fingers laced around a brandy snifter. He stooped to pick up the sneakers, lingering for a minute by her side.

If he had even one shred of decency in his body, he would have grabbed the opportunity to level with her earlier. She'd given him the perfect opening. It would have been so easy to say, "You're wrong, Marly. I do understand. I spent eighteen years of my life in the slums."

Eighteen years of my life.

Sometimes he wondered if he'd been honest with Eva Ann from the start, things might have worked out differently between them, and they both could have been spared the ugliness of their breakup. To think that they'd built their entire relationship on witty, meaningless repartee and equally meaningless sex. Sure, it had been all right in the beginning, until Eva Ann had tired of what she called his insatiable appetite. But one thing was for certain: they never would have married had she known the truth about him—nor he about her.

She'd been a spoiled, pampered princess who had grown up with everything she'd ever wanted, yet she'd expected even more from Carter. More as in more than everything. Kind of a neat concept if he thought about it. Problem was, he really hadn't thought about it during the three years he'd spent foolishly trying to give Eva Ann the world. Her world, that is. Certainly not his. And, as she'd told him on more than one occasion, most memorably when she'd dropped the divorce papers in his lap, Eva Ann was a firm believer in "never the twain shall meet."

That's why this time was so different, so important. Carter had thought this relationship through with his head instead of his hormones. Marly was different, the P.I.'s extensive background check had revealed. Different from any woman he'd ever known, different from any woman he'd ever find again. If anyone would understand and not judge him, she would. If anyone would value what he had to give, she would. And if his calculations proved correct, Marly Alcott wouldn't give a rat's tail about muddying a family lineage with his peasant ancestry.

Carter reached behind the couch and withdrew an afghan. He thought about taking her upstairs, letting her sleep on a mattress instead of in a chair, but despite her obvious exhaustion, she looked so content to be sacked out right where she was. And damn, if he didn't like the sight of her curled up in his favorite chair.

With infinite care, he reached to take the brandy snifter from her hands, noticing the splotchy pigmentation from the scar tissue. He also noticed her fingertips left no prints on the glass, just smudges. But not just chance—Marly had no fingerprints, he learned from the P.I.'s report. The fire had burned them right off.

Carter winced, remembering all the gory details contained in the dossier. It happened when she was abroad, serving in the Peace Corps. There had been some sort of explosion. Her village had turned into an inferno. She'd escaped, just barely, after a futile attempt to rescue her best friend from the blaze.

She was a survivor, his Cinderella. Just like him, she'd been to hell and back. But unlike him, she wore her battle scars on the outside.

Marly Alcott had worked harder and given selflessly to others more than any woman he'd ever known. If anyone deserved riches, she did. And he would see that she got them.

He draped the afghan over her body, folding the corner back

under her chin. He leaned down and tucked a fallen lock of hair behind one ear. Soon, he would show her all that worry had been for naught. Soon, he would tell her about his past.

Soon.

Carter didn't sleep. Though he closed his eyes, he lay awake well into the early hours of morning, trying to chunk all the little details that still needed ironing out. He wondered if Tyler needed a child psychologist to help him with the trauma of his mother's death, and if the place he had in mind could accommodate such requests.

Before even the first rays of morning sunlight filtered in through the windowpane, Carter rose and showered, then went upstairs to check on the boy.

A lamp in the corner cast a glow over the guest room, out-lining a small form in the middle of the queen-sized bed. Re-laxed in sleep, Tyler looked cute and content, but then, what kid wasn't cute when he was asleep? Mama had often said that was when she liked her children best, and with Carter's siblings, that came as no surprise.

Leaning against the doorjamb, he watched the steady rise and fall of the comforter that covered Tyler. Though the guest room itself was rather plain and nondescript, the boy's pres-ence made Carter envision how he'd redecorate if he had a son. Race cars and sports paraphernalia, play tools and musical instruments that made a lot of noise.

Of course, a girl would be fine, too. Growing up the young-est of five boys, he didn't know much about girls—even less about women, he mulled. Still, Anil and Reva sure were crazy about Sarina, and Carter imagined he'd feel much the same if he had a daughter. Either way, he wouldn't be too picky when the time came. Only one thing was for certain: boys or girls, his children would have their own rooms.

Even when he and Mama had been on their own, neither of them had had their own room. At the time, the efficiency apart-ment had seemed like a giant step up, since in their old place,

Carter had shared sleeping quarters with his four brothers, while Mama had slept on the living-room couch.

His brothers, all much older than he, would often leave home for stretches of time, only to return days, weeks, sometimes even months, later. Mama cried when they left and cried when they came back, so Carter never knew which was worse, having them gone or having them around.

His mama always had a hard time saying no to a person in need. As he looked back, it wasn't difficult to see how she'd ended up marrying so many times and giving birth to five babies. She'd never been one to refuse her home to anyone, not in the beginning, anyway. All that changed the day she'd packed their bags and announced to his older siblings that she and Carter were moving out of their subsidized housing project in the inner city of Atlanta and they weren't coming back.

The full impact of her decision hadn't hit Carter until much later in life, when he'd realized not only what a grave disappointment his brothers had proved to be, but how much faith his mama had put in him and his abilities. His mama...

Shifting from the doorjamb, Carter swallowed around a sudden tightening in his throat. Damn, but he missed her.

He'd just turned to leave the room, when a slight movement caught his eye. Turning back, he noticed Tyler's head was no longer on the pillow, but buried underneath the comforter. Not wanting the boy to suffocate in his sleep, Carter approached the bed and peeled back the edge of the comforter, when like a sand crab, Tyler's head burrowed even deeper. Puzzled, Carter again tugged back the comforter, and to his surprise, watched a little ball scamper underneath the covers and across to the other end of the bed.

"Tyler?"

A small thump resounded on the wooden floor.

"Tyler? You all right?"

Silence.

Curious, Carter rounded the foot of the bed just in time to catch two round pools of trepidation peering up at him before darting under the bed.

Frowning, he took a step back and then another, until he retraced his steps to the door. There he crouched, leaning back on his haunches. "Hey, Tyler." He tried to make his voice as nonthreatening as possible. "There's nothing to be afraid of. My name's Carter. I'm a friend of Miss Marly's, and I'd like to be your friend, too. Miss Marly brought you here to visit for a while. She's downstairs right now. Would you like to go see her?"

Nothing.

"I'd leave you alone, but it's a pretty big house, and I wouldn't want you to get lost trying to find her. You sure you don't want to come downstairs with me? It's still pretty early, but we could get something to eat. Are you hungry?" Carter thought he heard something shift underneath the bed. "We could cook up a good, old-fashioned Sunday breakfast. Pancakes, eggs, bacon, sausage, the works. I'm getting hungry just thinking about it." His stomach growled on cue. "Of course, there's always cold cereal if you prefer that."

One little hand poked out from the dust ruffle, lifting the edge up just enough that Carter could see the whites of two eyes.

He tilted his head sideways. "What do you say? You hungry?" He heard a slight shuffling and imagined Tyler nodding underneath the bed. "Well, come on, then."

The boy hesitated for a brief moment, then slithered out on his belly. He looked wary, refusing to make eye contact with a stranger, but Carter didn't press. He started down the corridor, allowing Tyler to maintain a safe distance behind him, pausing every few feet to make sure he hadn't lost him.

In the den, Marly slept where he'd left her. She'd turned onto her side in the night, her legs slightly bent. Tyler went to her like a magnet, all thought of food apparently abandoned. Carter tried again to tempt him, but he shook his head and immersed himself in tracing the pin-striped pattern of the armchair.

Unabashed, Carter went to the kitchen thinking to lure the boy with the tantalizing aroma of breakfast, but by the time he returned, Tyler had ensconced himself in the chair next to Marly and fallen asleep. He shook his head and started to leave.

"Smells great" came a soft voice, still raspy with sleep. "You didn't tell me breakfast in bed was part of the deal."

Carter closed his eyes, and for just a minute imagined how it would feel to awaken to that voice after a night of love-making. His lips twitched at the thought. Not bad. Not bad at all. "Do you want it to be?" he asked.

"I—I was just kidding."

He turned around but saw no evidence of humor reflected in her face. He felt suddenly awkward. Had he stepped out of line again? Was she, too, remembering last night in the weed patch? The feel of their bodies pressed together, his hands in her hair, his lips against hers....

Damn. Carter raked his fingers through his hair. He'd chosen Marly because she was safe, because he didn't envision himself falling in love with her, because he wasn't attracted to her. But the direction of his thoughts told him otherwise about the latter, and that was a bad sign.

A very bad sign.

Chapter 8

Why did he have to be so handsome? He was dressed in faded blue jeans and a Duke Blue Devils sweatshirt, his broad shoulders nearly filling the door frame. His shower-dampened hair only increased his lazy sensuality. And those long legs... Of course she found him attractive. She wasn't dead. Not yet, anyway.

Her attraction to him was perfectly understandable. A perfectly understandable nuisance at best, but at least it made sense. Unlike Carter's attraction to her.

"What time is it?" she asked.

"A little past five. You don't have to get up yet."

"Too late. I'm up." Marly eased herself free from where Tyler had sandwiched her in the chair and self-consciously ran a hand through the knots in her hair. "I'm an early riser."

"I'm an insomniac."

"And a workaholic, I imagine."

"That, too. It's not as if there's been anything to come home to. I mean, until now."

She didn't return his smile, but followed him into the

kitchen, massaging a kink in her neck. Strange how even the most trivial facts held paramount importance now. Little pieces that would somehow fit into the big picture. Sleeping habits. Work styles. Priorities. They had done everything backward, agreeing to marry before they had a chance to get to know each other. Still, it was to her benefit. She had to remember that.

"Have you seen my overnight bag?"

"Yeah, I stuck it in here." He gestured for her to follow him down the corridor.

They came upon a large room she gathered was the master bedroom. She must have missed it in the night. It was decorated in dark greens and burgundies, and a king-sized four-poster stood in the center. Plush cream carpet provided the necessary balance of light with the dark color scheme.

Her overnight bag sat on a chair in the corner, but she hesitated to enter the room, as if by crossing the threshold, she would somehow admit there was no going back. The notion seemed silly after a few seconds, since she knew in her heart she'd already crossed the point of no return sometime last night in the middle of Annie Lou's garden.

She turned her gaze to Carter and noted the room seemed scaled to fit him, high ceilings and a large bed.

He looked so clean-cut this morning, with his fresh shave and golden hair that seemed to fall naturally into place. She could even smell the barest hint of soap on his skin. A wave of self-consciousness washed over her, and she tugged at the hem of her T-shirt. "Would you mind if I got out of these grungy clothes?"

Carter's brow raised almost imperceptibly. "Not at all."

"I mean," she rushed to add, "I'd really like to take a shower. Can you keep an ear out for Tyler? I shouldn't be more than a few minutes."

"No problem. Towels are in the linen closet." He flicked on the bathroom lights and gestured toward a door.

"Thank you."

"You're welcome."

They stared at each other a few pounding heartbeats before Carter turned and left. For some stupid reason, Marly felt a strange sense of loss. She shook it off, closing the door and locking it.

In the bathroom, she washed quickly, trying not to notice the simple elegance of the gold fixtures, the ceramic tile, the double sinks or the oval Jacuzzi that sat under the skylights. Instead, she focused on the impracticality of the glass-encased shower stall and all the scrubbing it must take to keep the doors clean.

Afterward, she brushed her teeth, changed into jeans and a navy blue sweatshirt and towel-dried her hair. She pulled her hair away from her face with a navy blue headband, plucking the wisps of her bangs free. As if on autopilot, she went through all the motions of getting ready, and it wasn't until she'd finished and was leaving the bathroom that her gaze zeroed in on the mahogany four-poster smack dab in the middle of the bedroom.

She'd noticed it before, but hadn't allowed herself to think of the implications. Until now. She slumped against the door frame, one hand fluttering to massage her throat.

The thought of actually sharing a bed with Carter was both electrifying and terrifying, with emphasis on the latter.

Her response the night of the charity banquet, when Carter had told her about the donation, had been purely spontaneous, an overreaction to the tumultuous emotions racing through her. And last night in the moonlit field, the need for his touch had all but overwhelmed her.

She'd given in to her desire without stopping to think about what she was doing, about where they were going. Now she did stop to think, about making love with Carter, about sleeping with him through the night and waking with him.

Marly brushed her fingertips over her lips. She could still feel the warmth of Carter's mouth and, if she closed her eyes, remember how she felt in his embrace. For those few minutes, he had made her feel safer than she had in a long time, safer than she'd ever felt before. And wanted. Wanted for the

woman she was, and not for the things she could give him.
But that wasn't entirely correct.

In a way, Carter was like the other men…only he didn't
want material possessions. He wanted children. And she had
promised them to him. Only, they hadn't discussed time
frames or sleeping arrangements.

And though she wanted Carter with an almost desperate,
primal longing, the reality of intimacy was far more than she
could deal with right now. There was the actual act and then
the aftermath—explanations she wasn't ready to give.

Not yet.

She would simply have to tell him so. Surely he would
understand.

"You're not sleeping in a guest room, and that's that."
Carter plucked Marly's overnight bag right out of her hands
and started walking down the hall with it.

"Don't you think you're being just a tad unreasonable?"

"No," he called over his shoulder.

Marly tossed a glance in Tyler's direction, worried that their
voices might awaken him, but the boy was sound asleep. With
a frustrated sigh, she took off after Carter, catching up with
him in the master bedroom.

"Carter, please," she beseeched, closing the door behind
her. "I've known you all of a week. Surely you can understand that I'm not ready to sleep with you."

"Look, I told you before and I'll tell you again." He
planted her overnight bag on the chair and crossed his arms.
"I'm not going to pressure you into having sex with me. Not
now, not ever."

His vehemence surprised her. "I didn't think you would.
It's just that little technicality about how babies are made.…"

"Exactly why I think it's important we get used to sharing
a bed, even if we sleep fully dressed at opposite ends at first.
We're going to be married, for crying out loud. I don't want
my wife sleeping in another room."

"But I'm not ready to share your bed, damn it!" Out of

nowhere, the tears began. Anger, sorrow, despair, fear and anxiety all poured out in an uncontrollable flood. She turned her back, embarrassed that Carter should witness such flagrant lack of control. She remembered how her mother would get so disgusted with her so-called crocodile tears, the times she'd been sent to her room, told not to come down until she could learn to control her emotions.

Marly bowed her head. How she wished she had her own room to escape to now.

When she felt Carter's hands on her shoulders, she stiffened. She didn't want his pity.

"I'm sorry," he whispered.

"Me, too, but you might as well know you're marrying a wuss."

"Stop." Carter squeezed her shoulders. "You don't believe that for a second and neither do I. You've been through so much in the past two days. You've had to deal with an untimely death, the added responsibility of a five-year-old boy, not to mention being coerced into marriage by a complete stranger."

Marly sniffed. "You're not helping."

"But I will if you let me. Come on, Marly." He turned her around to face him and wiped her tears with the pads of his thumbs. When she wouldn't look up, he bent his knees and peered up at her. "Won't you please stop fighting me? We're on the same side here."

"Easy for you to say. You hardly strike me as the kind of man who has anything to be afraid of. Plus, you're the one holding all the cards from where I stand."

Carter straightened, and the abrupt motion drew Marly's gaze. "Then maybe you need to stand a little closer."

Suddenly, she found herself in the circle of his arms, her hands flush against his chest. Hardened planes of muscle tensed beneath her fingertips. She could feel his heart beating, the warmth beneath the sweatshirt. And she could feel the intensity in his eyes when he said, "We're all scared, Marly. Every one of us. We wouldn't be human if we weren't. So don't think for one second that you've got some kind of monopoly going here.''

Marly blinked, the mere notion of anyone or anything intimidating a powerful man like Carter too ludicrous to contemplate. ''Name one thing. Just one thing that frightens you.''

''I can name several. I'm afraid of failure. I'm afraid of not being able to make a difference in the world. I'm afraid of dying without having children. I'm afraid of leaving this world in the same unremarkable fashion in which I entered it.'' He shrugged. ''What can I say? I'm a selfish bastard.''

''No, I don't believe that,'' she said, because his words touched her somewhere deep inside. They spoke to her soul, and for the first time, she accepted Carter as an ally rather than an opponent. ''It takes a very brave man to admit those things. And Carter, you will have children. I want you to remember that even if…'' She swallowed, trying to fight another onslaught of tears. For so many years, she'd faced the stark reality of an uncertain future alone. She'd long stopped believing in happily-ever-afters.

''Even if I have to wait five years to consummate our marriage?''

''No, I—''

''Good, because you know I'm a man of my word, and five years would make for one hell of a testosterone backup.''

''Very funny.'' She rolled her eyes and stepped away. How could he make jokes at a time like this?

A time like this. She shook her head, then laughed at the ludicrousness of it all. Her life, their situation, the very notion that a man like Carter would wait five years for her.

She'd stopped believing in fairy tales the day Preston Britner III confessed to his ulterior motive for dating her. From that point forward, she'd learned more than she'd ever cared to find out about the games people played, the sacrifices they made, to get what they wanted.

She didn't suffer from any delusions. She wasn't, nor had she been for a very long time, the kind of woman who turned men's heads, the kind of woman a man like Carter could have at the snap of his fingers. Which led her to suspect he had ulterior motives.

If he was playing games with her, she wanted to know the rules up front. She wanted to know exactly what he planned to gain out of their arrangement. Besides the fact that he wanted children and thought she was a prime candidate for motherhood, what made her so special?

"Answer me this," she said, her voice calm and steady. "Why, of all the women you could have, would a man like you choose to marry a woman like me?"

His eyes narrowed. "A man like me?"

"Yes. I think it's a fair question."

Carter tipped back his head and inhaled deeply. When he straightened, the breath he let out sounded as if he'd held it for years instead of mere seconds. "Okay, I'll tell you why a man like me would choose to marry a woman like you." His voice sounded bleak and empty as he parroted her words. "Because once upon a time, I was a boy not unlike Tyler—only my father was the addict, and my brothers were the drug dealers."

"What?"

Marly's eyes widened in bewilderment. She wore faded jeans and little makeup. Her cheeks were pink from scrubbing, and her hair fell in silky waves on her shoulders. With Marly, what you saw was what you got. She was so natural, so unpretentious, so different from all the women he'd ever known.

"It's true," he said in answer to her unspoken question, raking his fingers through his hair.

Her gaze never left his as she took slow, hesitant steps toward the bed, where she felt the mattress behind her with one hand before hoisting herself up. "Go on."

Carter knew he had to level with her. He couldn't chicken out this time. He shrugged, not really knowing where to begin except at the beginning. "I grew up in one of the worst projects in Atlanta. My old man was husband number three for my mother. He left us around the time I was five. She married once more after that, but it was short-lived. No kids out of that one. Of course, I was her fifth. She decided to call it quits after me.''

"Where is she now? Your mother.''

"She died of cancer ten years ago. Didn't quite make it to her fiftieth birthday.''

Marly covered her mouth with both hands. "Oh, Carter. I don't know what to say. I'm so sorry. I had no idea. I saw the photographs on the mantel. The one where you were little, sitting on the bench with the hotdogs.''

"That's us at the bus station.''

"And the other one. At your graduation. Wait a minute. It said Buckhead Prep—''

"I went there free. She was a janitor at the school. We took the bus out to the suburbs every day.'' Three facts he'd tried so hard to conceal all those years ago, but his efforts had proved futile. There simply wasn't any way of hiding the fact that he was different. He'd known it, and it didn't take long before the other kids at school found out, too.

But he'd never expected Eva Ann's daddy to stumble across the truth, not with all the precautions he'd taken to make sure his past stayed dead and buried. He should have suspected the man would go digging. Still, he had no one to blame but himself for not coming clean when he and Eva Ann had decided to marry. He wouldn't repeat that mistake now. He had to make sure Marly understood what she was getting into.

If his calculations proved correct, she wouldn't bail out on him. Still, he braced himself for her reaction, some sign of pity or disgust, after the initial shock wore off. Experience had taught him that every decision model, no matter how good the criteria, still contained a margin of error. He only hoped like hell Marly didn't fall into that margin.

He watched her fingers toy with the edge of her sweatshirt. When she cleared her throat, her voice came out low and shaky.

"Let me make sure I've got all this. You grew up in one of the worst projects in Atlanta. You went to a private school because your mother was a janitor there. And you took the bus?''

She made the last part sound so incredulous that Carter felt compelled to add, "Every day."

"Umm-hmm." The crease between her brows deepened, and she kept her gaze averted. "So now how do I fit into this?"

"Because you work with kids like me, like the kid I was. Because you understand that world, the world I come from. I need someone who understands…so my kids will understand."

Marly nodded, fanning herself with one hand. Slowly, she slid down from the bed and went to stand by the French doors. She rubbed her arms as if to ward off a chill as she stared out the panes of glass, into the inky darkness, a dazed expression on her face.

Carter took her vacated spot on the bed. Even though he'd had plenty of practice in the boardroom, patience didn't rank high on his list of virtues. Propping his elbows on his knees, he rested his chin in one hand and tried not to fidget, but the verdict was slow in coming. Marly didn't move for a long time, and when she did, he watched her forehead drop against the windowpane. She lifted one hand to cover her face.

Carter's gut clenched automatically, but nothing could have prepared him for the devastating blow of four whispered words from the one woman he'd least expected to say them: "I am so ashamed."

As soon as the words were out of her mouth, Marly turned around to see Carter rise from the bed in one swift move, his jaw set in a rigid line. "Where are you going?"

"Out." His tone was terse. "I need to make some phone calls."

"Wait. Before you leave, I owe you an apology—"

"You don't have to apologize for speaking your mind."

"No, not for what I've said, but what I've thought, what I've been thinking."

He paused, one hand on the doorknob, and shook his head. "You lost me."

"I stereotyped you, and that wasn't very fair."

"I'm sure it was a shock for you—"

"Yes, it was. But all that aside, I still didn't have any business jumping to conclusions about your life and your values. So please know that I'm sorry for misjudging you."

Carter peered at her for a moment, his eyebrows knitted. "Marly, this might sound like a dumb question, and feel free to tell me so, but we are talking about the same thing, aren't we?"

"You're going to make me spell it out, aren't you?"

"Please."

"Oh, all right. I suppose I deserve it." She clasped her hands. "I apologize for thinking that just because you're well-off now, you were born with a golden spoon in your mouth, that you're a Class A snob who's so absorbed with money and power you could never appreciate life for its nonmaterial worth. Um, that's the gist of it. Do you forgive me?"

Carter scratched his chin. "You really thought all that?"

She nodded.

"So what changed your mind?"

"What you just told me. About your past and your fears."

"You said you were ashamed."

"I am. Of myself." She saw him stiffen. "What? You didn't think—"

"Apology accepted." He opened the door and gestured for her to precede him. "Ready for breakfast? I really do have to make some phone calls."

"Not so fast." She strode across the room, bridging the distance between them with several quick steps. She closed the door and wedged her body between him and the exit. "Carter King," she said in her best schoolteacher stage whisper. "Don't you dare tell me you thought I was ashamed of you."

He didn't reply.

"You did, didn't you?" She shook her head. His hazel eyes

looked so dark and haunted as they held her gaze that she wanted to crawl inside him and hold him. "You couldn't have been further from the truth. Do you know what I thought when you first told me? When I recovered enough to form a coherent thought? I stood at that window and thought *my God.* All this—" She gestured around the room. "The house, the cars, the horses, the bank. You built all this from nothing. Do you have any idea how that made me feel?"

"Ashamed?" Carter said, one eyebrow raised, the slightest smirk playing on his lips.

But she wasn't going to let him turn this into a joke. Judging from his initial reaction to stomp out of the room, he didn't find it funny, either.

"Besides feeling ashamed *of myself,*" she qualified, "I felt proud. Of you, of your accomplishments. Of the man you've become." She looked down at her hands. "I know, it sounds kind of silly. I mean, we hardly know each—"

Before she knew what was happening, Marly felt the door press against her back and Carter's body move within scant inches of hers. She gasped and looked up. At the same moment, Carter's head came down. His lips covered hers, and she leaned in to him, like a flower turning toward the sun. Once withered, half-dead, all alone in the darkness, her petals unfolded now to bask in the brilliant light he poured down upon her.

He kissed her softly, then not so softly, his hands rubbing up and down her arms. His head lowered to her neck, his mouth feathering the hollow of her throat with hot, moist heat that drew a broken sigh from her.

Greedy lips drew his mouth back to hers. She held his face to hers with one hand, the other clenching the fabric of his shirt. Her mouth opened at the touch of his tongue, and she moaned softly at the remembered taste that was all his.

They clung to each other like two long-lost lovers, reuniting after an unbearable separation. Through two layers of denim, Marly felt him grow hard against her. Though her mind told her to move away, warned her that sunlight would burn if she got too much, her body moved, instead, to cradle him.

The memory of the four-poster flashed in Marly's mind, the image of naked limbs tangling in the night. Sleeping in Carter's arms. Waking to—

Suddenly, she remembered the reason she couldn't do this. The nightmares. Carter's inevitable questions. She pushed against his chest. "No, stop. I can't. Not yet. I'm not ready…for that."

Carter broke away. He took a step backward as if to distance himself, as he wiped his mouth with the back of his hand, like a child wiping off a milk mustache. "I'm sorry," he said, his voice ragged around the edges. "I wasn't trying to push you. I—it won't happen again."

Marly sagged against the door, trying to control her racing heartbeat. She knew she would have to tell him eventually, that he would find out. And when he did, there would be questions, questions she wasn't ready to answer.

When she finally convinced herself she wasn't going to hyperventilate, she reached for the doorknob and opened the door. "So how about that breakfast?" She looked up and saw Carter still trying to catch his breath.

"What breakfast? Oh, that breakfast. Yeah, right. Come on out whenever you're ready." He ran his fingers through his hair and all but raced out the door.

Marly started after him, then turned back, her gaze alternating between the four-poster and her overnight bag. She raised her fingers to her lips, and her face flushed with heat. "God, help me," she whispered, closing the door behind her.

Chapter 9

At the rate he was going, Carter wasn't going to last five minutes, never mind five years.

It wasn't supposed to be like this, he silently protested, tipping his head back against the wall.

Tall, voluptuous brunettes had always stirred his blood. He would have anticipated this stiffening in his groin from them. But why the hell was he lusting after a dainty blonde with bright-blue eyes and the sweetest of smiles? Where had this attraction come from? And why now, when he knew the very success of this relationship depended on him controlling his libido?

As long as he could keep his attraction to her under control, she wouldn't be able to breach his defenses. But if he ever let himself go with her, he'd never be able to get that control back. Eva Ann had taught him a bitter lesson, one he would never forget. Marly might never turn on him, but he couldn't take the chance and let his guard down.

He opened a kitchen drawer and checked the velvet box inside. Then he drained the remainder of his coffee in one large gulp and reached for the phone. He didn't relish the idea of waking Anil so early on a Saturday morning, but the situation with Tyler took precedence over any formalities.

"Anil, it's Carter. I'm sorry to wake you—"

"Wake me? Oh, that's rich. We're in the middle of a feeding over here. You want a turn?"

Carter smiled. "Thanks, but I'll pass this round. Listen, the reason I'm calling…I need a favor."

"Sure, name it."

"The Summit." Carter had counted on Anil's recognizing the significance of the name of the private school where Anil had spent his youth, along with children in danger.

His friend didn't fail him. "This is serious."

"Yeah."

"How soon?"

"Today."

"I don't suppose you can tell me…"

Carter gripped the phone. "No. I'm sorry."

"That's all right. I understand. Give me an hour."

"Thanks, Anil." He hung up and turned around to see Marly watching him curiously.

He remembered her words of pride for a man she barely knew, and felt a surge of warmth deep within him. Beneath the warmth, something else rumbled to life. Wanting. The embers of a too-familiar yearning, banked but still burning. What was it about this woman that was slowly driving him crazy? Carter couldn't explain it.

He looked at her, and he itched to feel the well-worn denim of her jeans, to see for himself if it was as soft as it appeared and to know the shape of her bottom in his hands. He wanted to lift her sweatshirt, touch the skin of her stomach and run his fingers along the gentle curves hidden beneath the baggy material. He wanted to feel her breasts in his hands—

"Carter?" A glimmer of fear reflected in her eyes. "Is something wrong?"

"No." *No.* He forced his thoughts to a careening halt and spun away. He didn't know what sparked this unexpected attraction, only that he couldn't allow it to blaze to life, risk letting it grow out of control. "I was just seeing about arrangements," he said, his back to her as he poured himself another mug of coffee and reached for a notebook. "Hungry?"

She took a piece of bread from the loaf on the counter and popped it into one of four slots in the toaster. "This is fine."

Carter shrugged and carried his mug to the window seat. He stretched his legs out on the cushions and opened a notebook on his lap. But his gaze focused on the sunrise in the meadow beyond, and his thoughts centered around the woman he was about to marry.

He swore he would hold himself rigidly in check, even when he did finally take her to bed. He would be the perfect gentleman. He wouldn't let himself drown in her. He would simply consummate the marriage and satisfy his wife as swiftly as he could, while preserving the distance between them.

"Is this seat taken?" a soft voice asked.

Carter angled his outstretched legs to make room for her. She sat down and drew one leg to her chest, lacing her fingers over a bent knee. He frowned and returned his gaze to the meadow, trying to ignore the delicate scent of dewy flowers that teased his nostrils. He tried to concentrate on something, anything, besides the overwhelming desire to press his face against the curve of her neck and inhale deeply.

"You've changed your mind, haven't you?"

"What?" His gaze snapped back to her. Was he so transparent now that she could tell what he was thinking?

There was a jarring, jagged-edged silence and then she repeated, "You've changed your mind. I can tell." Her voice sounded sad, yet tinged with an edge of fear. "You don't want to go through with this, do you? Our arrangement, the marriage, the—"

"You can't be serious." Carter bolted upright, bringing his legs to the floor. Coffee sloshed around in his mug, the notebook fell and landed with a loud thump and Marly stopped speaking. "I haven't changed my mind," he said in a steady voice. "I'm not *going* to change my mind. I've just been sitting here, paranoid I'm going to do something that'll make you change yours."

"You were?"

"Yes."

"Like what?" she asked.

He could hear the undercurrent of relief. He shrugged. *Like undress you with my eyes.* He had to change the subject. Now. "There's something I wanted to ask you. Your teachers at the center? Are they all female?"

"Yes, why?"

"Earlier when Tyler woke up, I think he was more than just shy with me. I think he might be afraid of me...because I'm a man."

Marly pursed her lips. "I could see that. I don't think he's had many ideal male role models. I know he's afraid of Billy Ray, and he's mentioned Daddy's men more than once, always with a bad connotation." She glanced down at her hands and drew a shaky breath. "The other night, he told me how his mother had promised him she wouldn't call Daddy's men again, but he knew she did. It's amazing. He knows so much about things he shouldn't...and so little about things he should. He was a crack baby. We've had to work extra hard to get him up to pace with the other kids his age." She stopped and shook her head. "I'm sorry. I'm rambling."

"Don't apologize. In fact, stop apologizing. We're both in this together now, all right?"

"For better or worse?"

He smiled down at his coffee. "Yeah, something like that."

Marly took a deep breath. "I feel like I'm walking on eggshells."

Carter glanced up. "Me, too."

"I don't suppose it's going to get any easier with the passage of time."

"I doubt it."

She leaned forward. "Then tell me what you want from me,

Carter, what you want from this marriage. Go ahead and spell it out. It isn't going to get any easier, any less awkward, and I have to know.''

''All right.'' He bent down and placed his mug on the floor. ''It's pretty straightforward, I suppose. You know I want a child, preferably two, but we can wait and see how we do with the first one. I want your promise to help me raise him or her. We can lead separate lives privately if we choose, but we're a team when we're with our children. I want them to know they're loved, to believe they were conceived out of love.''

''But you told me—''

''Marly, this may be a business transaction for you and me, but not for our kids. As far as they know, it's the real thing. So adultery is out. Divorce isn't an option, and if we run into marital problems, we'll seek counseling.''

She nodded and laced her fingers together to keep them from shaking. Carter had obviously spent a great deal of time thinking things through to be able to summarize an entire relationship in such concise, clear-cut terms. Though she appreciated his honesty, in many ways his thoughts of family seemed cold and calculated. Yet in many other ways they didn't.

She couldn't deny that the kind of marriage Carter wanted had a certain appeal for her. He was offering her the space she needed, the emotional detachment she required in a relationship. But even more, a chance to have the children she'd always wanted, the children she'd believed she would never have. It was as close to the real thing as she could get.

''Marly?''

She raised her gaze to his. His eyes were more green than brown this morning. Fringed with thick golden lashes, Marly thought they were the most beautiful pair of eyes she'd ever seen.

''No matter what, I'll see that you're taken care of,'' he said.

''How?''

''Your finances. Your center.''

Her chin lifted a fraction. "You would take care of my center?"

"Yes, ma'am."

"Even if something happened to me? If I died?"

Carter scowled. "What kind of question is that?"

"I have to know. We're discussing all the potential things that could go wrong, aren't we? Well, what if I die next week? Will you see that my center receives funding, that my children are taken care of?"

"You're not going to die next week."

"Can you please just answer the question. Will you or won't you?"

"I said I would."

"What about Tyler?"

"Him, too."

Marly exhaled and slumped in relief. "Thank you. You don't know how much that means to me."

"I'm beginning to." Carter leaned forward. "I think you'll approve of the place I have in mind for Tyler. It's a kind of safe house, a private school for children in trouble. Very secluded, secured like a military base. The only way in is by referral.

"Most of the kids have parents who are prime targets of assassination. Political figures. Diplomats. Others should be in the Witness Protection Program, but aren't for one or more reasons. You get the idea."

She nodded. *Others should be in the Witness Protection Program, but aren't for one or more reasons.* How easy it was to look back several years and pinpoint the exact fork in the road where a person made the wrong turn. If her mother had known of this school, would she have pursued the option for them? It was just one of the questions Marly would never be able to answer.

"Where is this place?" she asked.

"Just outside Asheville, in the Smoky Mountains. We can drive there today."

"Do you think they'll take Tyler?"

"We'll find out soon enough. That's what I was doing just now on the phone. I know someone who used to go there. So do you."

"I do?"

"Anil Singh."

"Really?"

"Yeah, he spent several years there when his father worked for the World Bank."

"It must have been very lonely for him." She worried her lip between her teeth.

"What?"

"I don't know how I'm going to do this when the time comes. The center's been the only stable thing in Tyler's life, and to take that away at the same time as his mother... I mean, he knows about death and dying. Living in the projects, he's seen enough of it. But this is different. This is his mother."

"The school has several child psychologists. I already checked with Anil."

Her eyes suddenly widened, her expression growing disturbed.

"I didn't mean to upset you. It was just an idea. If you'd prefer—"

"No, it's not that." She slumped, propping her chin in one hand. "Do you remember the shooting at Lakewood Elementary last year?"

"Sure."

Marly wouldn't soon forget the crazy woman who had chosen an elementary school in the prestigious suburb of Lakewood as the sight for her morbid shooting spree. Four children had been wounded critically. One died.

"They brought psychologists into the school for the children," she told him. "To help them deal with the tragedy. I thought it was a great idea. And then, just a few short months later, there was a shooting at one of the projects. Gang wars. Two eight-year-old boys were caught in the cross fire, one of them the elder brother of one of my kids. I went to the funeral. I talked with the mothers. I learned no psychologists were brought into their school, no professionals to help their children deal with the horror of their classmates' deaths.

"I was appalled that the administration had viewed such a tragedy as a normal, everyday occurrence in the lives of these children, that they hadn't provided them with any special counseling. And now...now, I'm afraid I've done the same thing with Tyler. I've been so concerned with his physical safety—"

"Stop right there. You prioritized in a time of crisis, Marly. That's all. And once you've seen to his physical well-being, you can turn your attention to other matters. I know you would have raised the question of a psychologist even if I hadn't."

"You seem to have a lot of confidence in me."

"Yeah, I do. I know you, Marly. A lot better than you think. I've done my homework."

Marly looked away. The guilt of her deception suffused her cheeks with heat. Carter didn't know her, not really. How could he? She wasn't anyone—not the person she'd been born, not the person in whose skin she lived. For eight long years, she'd been a nonentity, a woman without a past, living another woman's life.

Mrs. Carter King. The name whispered through her mind, and she wondered if, over time, she could truly make it her own.

His jean-clad leg brushed against hers, but she didn't move away, savoring, instead, the odd sense of connection with the man who would give her an identity that was all hers.

He was hard and strong, and Marly realized for the first time that she had his strength on her side, that she wasn't alone anymore, fighting one never-ending battle after another. She felt suddenly greedy, almost afraid to ask about the donation, but Carter seemed to read her mind.

"We can get a cashier's check this morning," he said. "The bank's open on Saturday."

"No, that's okay. Monday's soon enough. I want to get Tyler situated first. There is one other thing. I don't want any publicity. No media of any sort."

"Any particular reason why not?"

"Yes. I am a very private person, and I don't like the lime-light. Is this going to be a problem?"

Carter scratched his chin. "Not right now. We may have to reevaluate after we have children, though. School plays. Ath-letic events. Those sorts of things."

"Okay," she agreed. She'd cross that bridge when she came to it. "I do have to call Annie Lou before we leave and tell her…about us." After five years of living with the older woman, she could anticipate her reaction. "I suppose I should warn you that Annie Lou's an incurable romantic."

"You don't think she'll approve of a hasty marriage?"

"Oh, she'll approve, but only because she's going to think it was love at first sight."

Carter rose from the window seat. "So let her believe it." Crossing the kitchen, he pulled the small jeweler's box from the drawer where he'd stashed it. "I, um, have something for you."

He hoped it wasn't too simple. Eva Ann had returned the one he'd gotten her, opting, instead, to pick out her own. He'd pretended it hadn't mattered, but for some reason, it had.

He brought forth the box and popped open the top.

Marly's hands slid from her knees.

The small box in his outstretched palm suddenly seemed heavier. "You're probably thinking this was awfully pre-sumptuous on my part. Maybe it was, but I bought it after the first time you turned me down." He shrugged. "I don't know. I thought maybe you'd take the offer more seriously if I had something to back it up."

She didn't utter a sound, simply stared at the half carat diamond solitaire nestled in velvet lining.

"I wanted to get a bigger stone, but I could just see you refusing to wear it to work." When her expression contorted in an expression of pain, he hastened to add, "It's okay if you don't like it. I can take it back if you want to pick your own."

"No." She lifted her gaze to his, and he thought he detected a sheen of moisture gathering in her eyes. "I don't want another one. I want this one. It's…perfect."

Carter swallowed. "You'll wear it, then?"

"Yes, of course I will."

He didn't realize until she said the words how very much he'd needed to hear them. "May I?" he asked, taking her scarred hand in his. She nodded, and he slid the ring over her finger. A perfect fit.

The diamond sparkled, and Marly gripped his fingers with hers. "It's beautiful," she whispered, staring down at the stone.

So are you, he wanted to say but, instead, took a step back and, for some reason, held his tongue.

She looked too good, sitting there in the window seat, nestled among the cushions and plants. She looked as if she belonged there, as if she belonged here, in his house with him. But it wasn't a done deal. Not yet. Not until he got his bride to the altar.

Chapter 10

Marly's heart skidded with warning, and her defenses rose in reaction. She could play a part for Annie Lou and the rest of the world, but she had to remember it was only an act. Her future husband was a charmer, and he could make it exceedingly easy for her to fall into the trap of accepting their make-believe love story as something real if she wasn't careful.

They were silent for a few moments, until Carter said, "There's one other thing we have to talk about."

At those few words, a well of panic superseded her apprehension. Her mind whirled down a mental checklist, and she realized they had covered almost all the basics, which left only one item. "What's that?" she asked, praying it wasn't the one topic she didn't want to tackle again.

His eyes confirmed her fears before he spoke.

"Sleeping arrangements."

She fidgeted in her seat as his gaze continued to hold hers. She tried to find the words to tell him why she needed more time, when, from the other room, a small voice called out her name. Tyler. "In here," she called back, breathing a sigh of relief for the postponement of her confession.

Tyler came barreling out of the den, then froze in his tracks when he saw Carter.

"Hey, Tyler." Carter gave the boy an easy smile. If he'd been the least bit frustrated by the interruption, he recovered quickly.

Tyler's gaze darted between Marly and Carter.

"Hi, honey. Come on over here." She gestured with her hand. "Have you met Carter?"

"We met earlier this morning, didn't we?"

Tyler nodded, taking small, cautious steps toward the window seat.

"Oh, come on. You're not shy this morning, are you?" She clasped Tyler in a quick hug, ruffling his hair.

His arms circled around her waist. "Is he your boyfriend?" he whispered, careful to avoid looking at Carter.

"Well, actually…" Marly glanced at Carter, who pretended he hadn't heard the question, even though she knew he had. She took a hesitant breath and thought she might as well get used to saying it. "Carter's my fiancé. Do you know what that means?"

Tyler shook his head.

Marly cleared her throat delicately. "It means he's the man I'm going to marry."

"When?"

Marly looked at Carter. "When?"

"Monday."

She swallowed. Monday was only two days away. In two days, she would be Mrs. Carter King.

"Are those pancakes?" Tyler's attention turned to a plate on the center island.

"Sure are," Carter said, rising from the window seat. "You hungry?"

Tyler nodded. She fixed him a plate and watched as he shoveled the gooey mess into his mouth. All the while, she noted how he kept stealing glances in Carter's direction. Carter must have noticed, too, because he busied himself straightening the kitchen.

"Hey, Tyler?" Marly asked, when Carter turned on the sink faucet. "What would you think about taking a vacation with Carter and me?"

"Where?"

"Oh, a surprise place."

Tyler eyes lit up for a second, but then the shadows came and chased away his momentary joy. "Mama won't let me."

Marly's hands tightened on her wadded napkin. The longer she waited to tell him, the more she prolonged his grief. "Tyler," she whispered, willing herself to be strong, for his sake. She leaned over and wiped the syrup from his face. "There's something we need to talk about. Why don't we go over here, to the family room." She felt Carter's hand on her shoulder.

"Do you want me to come?" he asked.

"Please."

Marly sat on the couch and pulled Tyler into her lap, dreading this moment more than she'd dreaded anything in her life. Considering several moments in her life, that said plenty.

Carter sat down on the chair flanking the couch and nodded his encouragement. For some reason, his presence was a balm to her. She wasn't sure she would have been able to do this without him. The thought frightened her. She'd already relied on him on several occasions. And, damn him, he'd come through for her each and every time.

Tyler stuck his thumb in his mouth. Marly gently raked his hair back, over and over, in what she hoped was a soothing rhythm.

"Tyler, what I'm about to tell you, you're going to have a tough time understanding. Just remember that I'm here. I'm not going anywhere, all right?"

"We're both here," Carter said. "We're both here for you, Tyler."

Tyler's wide blue eyes turned to Carter.

Carter smiled at him and, leaning forward, asked, "So tell me, who's your best friend at school?"

Tyler's thumb made a popping sound as it left his mouth. "Miss Marly."

Carter's eyes sparkled as he glanced at her. "Besides Miss Marly. Who's your best friend?"

"Aaron Duncan," Tyler said after some thought.

"He's a nice guy, huh?"

"Yeah."

"Who do you not like the most?"

Marly frowned at Carter. She had no idea what he was getting at. He gave her a "trust me" look. Strangely, she realized—at least on some level—that she did.

"Sammy Joe Franklin," Tyler said, wrinkling his nose.

"He's a real creep, huh?"

Marly felt she should protest. She didn't.

"He's a creep," Tyler agreed. "He steals stuff."

"So I guess you could say there are some good guys and some bad guys in class, right?"

Tyler thought about that. "Right."

"Well, that's exactly what it's like for grown-ups, too. There are some good guys and bad guys. Your daddy's men, for example. I think we can safely say they're bad guys, right? They're grown up Sammy Joe Franklins."

"Yeah."

"Now, take me, for example. I much prefer being a good guy. I'm like a grown-up Aaron Duncan. I would never, ever do anything to hurt you. In fact, I hope we end up being the best of friends."

Tyler studied him. "Do you do crack?"

Carter slowly shook his head. "I don't know why anyone would want to do crack."

"Do you smoke reefer?"

"I don't smoke anything. I hate smoke. It makes me cough."

"Do you like to down a cold one?"

Carter chuckled. "Well, now, there you have me. Yeah, every once in a while, I like to have a beer or two. Not more, though. I don't like feeling out of control."

Now, there's an understatement, Marly thought.

"Do you think we might become friends?" Carter asked.

"Do you play basketball?"

"Love to. I even have a hoop out in the driveway."

Tyler's eyes nearly bugged out. "You do?"

"Sure do. And a swimming pool out back. Do you like to swim?"

"I don't know. I ain't never been swimming."

Marly read understanding in Carter's eyes and something unfurled in her chest as she watched him try to win Tyler's trust. Oh, yes, Carter King would approach fatherhood as he approached everything else in life. He'd excel at it.

"I'll teach you to swim if you'd like," Carter said, and Marly could see the muscles in his jaw working.

Tyler looked at Marly. "Can you ask Mama if I'm allowed?"

She swallowed and blinked back tears. "I'm afraid I can't do that, sweetheart."

"Why not?"

She took one more look at Carter for reassurance. He gave it to her in the form of a sad smile. "Honey, your mama's gone to Heaven to be with God."

"When's she coming back?"

Marly pressed a kiss to Tyler's forehead, overcome for the moment with emotion. Then she sat back and looked him in the eyes. "She's not coming back, Tyler. God took her forever."

Something flickered in the little boy's eyes. An age-old wisdom that had no business being there. "You mean she's dead?"

Marly nodded.

His eyes widened, tears already brimming. But if Marly was expecting an outburst, she didn't get one. Instead, Tyler's fingers curled around the bunched fabric of her sweatshirt, and he buried his face against her shirt, sobbing quietly.

"It was them drugs," he said in a small voice, his lower lip quivering.

"What drugs, Tyler?"

"Them drugs Mama took. That's how come I ran away."

"You mean the night in Mrs. Barton's car?"

"Yeah." His voice cracked. "Mama made the powder into a line on the table and put a straw in her nose, and then she sniffed it all up. Then she stuck a needle in her arm, but it didn't work. It never works. Those shots ain't never made Mama better, just sicker."

Marly shuddered at the ease with which this five-year-old boy told of his mother's drug use. He knew so much, too much, about drugs. And yet, some vestiges of innocence remained. But for how long? She wrapped her arms around him, holding him close, trying to fight back her tears.

"I'm sorry, sweetheart. I'm so sorry."

"Tommy Redding's dad got sick and died, too. And Johnny Cooper's mom, too. And Mama. When I seen her lying there on the floor, I knew she was gonna be dead this time and Daddy was gonna take me away," he whispered. "I don't want to go with him. Please, Miss Marly. Don't make me go."

"I won't." She held him closer. "I swear it, Tyler."

Carter, bless him, spoke up. "We're going to do everything in our power to keep you safe."

"Really?" he asked.

"Really. You have my promise on that."

Tyler stuck his thumb back in his mouth, curling his index finger around the bridge of his nose. Though he clung to Marly, his gaze remained on Carter, and newly won trust shone in his eyes.

Marly imagined her own expression was the same.

Carter watched Marly's expression out of the corner of his eye as he tossed some items into their cart—toys, comic books, a deck of cards and some candy. "Just this once," he whispered to her, adding a tube of bubble gum-flavored toothpaste to the assortment. They had stopped at an outlet mall in Burlington so they could buy some clothes for Tyler.

Marly didn't argue, and he knew she wouldn't. Not at a

time like this. Spoiling was one thing, consoling another, and Tyler would need a lot of the latter in the days and weeks to come. He seemed to understand with relative ease why he had to go away, why he had to hide from Daddy's men, but the thought of being alone frightened him.

"Miss Marly?" he asked in a small voice from the back seat. "How come you and Carter can't stay with me?"

"Oh, sweetie." Marly turned in the seat and loosened her seat belt, drawing one leg up and angling it for balance. "I wish we could, but Carter and I have to work. Otherwise, who's going to run the center? And who will run Carter's bank?"

In the rearview mirror, Carter saw Tyler's head droop. "We'll come visit you every weekend," he felt compelled to repeat.

Marly smiled. "And remember, you're only going to be gone for a very short while, and you'll make so many new friends. Remember when you were new to Little Learners?"

Tyler shook his head.

"Well, you were, once upon a time. But you made friends so quickly, and you know why? Because you are always nice to everyone, and that's why they all want to be your friends."

"Like Aaron?"

"Yes, like Aaron."

"And Betsy Jean?"

"Umm-hmm. And even Sammy Joe."

"Miss Marly?"

"Yes?"

"I love you."

"I love you, too, Tyler."

Carter cast a sideways glance and caught Marly blinking back tears before she turned toward the window. Her words echoed in his mind and churned something deep in his gut, but he knew better than to entertain any foolish hopes of hearing her say them for him. He'd already been down that road before, and look what it had cost him. No, Carter King was through tempting fate. By winning Marly, he'd already reaped much more than he ever deserved.

They drove five hours that day, across the North Carolina piedmont and high up into the mountains. Marly had put the middle seat of the Caravan down and thrown a comforter, along with some pillows over it. Tyler finally curled up with his security blanket and fell asleep in the makeshift bed, worn from their journey.

At a little past two in the afternoon, Carter snapped on his directional signal and took the exit ramp off the interstate. An hour later, they pulled into a small town with a motel where they would stay for the night. They could eat and rest up, then take Tyler over to show him the school. Then tomorrow morning, they would say their goodbyes.

Carter pulled the car into the parking lot. When they came to a stop, he could hear Tyler's soft, even breathing in the back seat. "Be right back," he told Marly, leaving the keys in the ignition.

The motel was nestled in a small valley, with the foliage of autumn all around. He walked the short distance to the main entrance, breathing in the fresh mountain air.

Inside, a dark-haired, lanky teenager sat on a stool, with one eye on the front door and the other on a college basketball game.

Carter squinted at the small television. "Is that the Carolina-Duke game?"

"Yeah, Tarheels are ahead by six."

"Won't last. They're playing on Blue Devils' turf."

At the sound of the buzzer, the teen stood and mocked a free throw. "God, would I ever like to go there."

"Nice form. You thinking about playing hoops in college?"

"Nah. I ain't going to college."

"How come?"

The teen rubbed his fingertips together. "No money."

Carter shook his head. "Don't let that hold you back if it's something you want. There's plenty of financial aid out there. You just have to tap the right sources." He took the notepad from the front desk and tore off a sheet. "Here, write your name and address. I'll send you some information."

"Really? Hey, great." He scribbled a few lines and handed the paper back to Carter. "So you need a room?"

"Two beds, if you've got them."

"Sorry, no double doubles left."

"I'll take whatever you have, then."

"Single double?"

"That's fine. Just one night." Carter paid cash for their room and pocketed the receipt along with the teen's address.

"Everything okay?" Marly asked when he climbed back into the car.

He nodded and handed her their room key. "Hungry? The clerk says there's a restaurant next door."

"Yeah, I am. And I'll bet Tyler is, too. Maybe we can wash up first?"

"Good idea." He circled the vehicle around the back of the motel and parked in front of their room. After getting out, he opened the back door and carefully lifted Tyler into his arms. The boy opened his eyes, disoriented for a moment, before he settled his gaze on Carter. Then he looped one arm around Carter's neck and closed his eyes again.

Carter swallowed, a barrage of paternal instincts coming at him hard and fast. He looked up to find Marly smiling at him as if she could read his mind.

"One day," she whispered, then turned to walk ahead of them. She turned the key in the knob and pushed open the door, coming to a standstill once inside. "Carter?"

"I'm sorry. This is all they had. You two can take the bed. I'll sleep on the couch."

She frowned and closed the door behind them.

That afternoon they ate burgers and fries, before venturing over to check out the school. The guard posted at the gates asked for identification, then checked a computer for their names.

"Hope you didn't have any trouble finding the place," he said, returning Carter's driver's license.

"No, the directions were quite sound," Carter replied. Once inside the gates, he murmured, "That's the password."

Marly nodded and stored the information. As they drove around the grounds, she pointed at two youngsters riding ponies. "Look, Tyler."

His face was already pressed against the glass. "Am I gonna get to do that?" he asked, his voice a mixture of skepticism and awe.

"You sure will," Carter answered. He could tell Marly was relieved by the summer-camp atmosphere.

The headmaster of the school was a close friend of Anil's, and he greeted them heartily, before taking them on a tour of the grounds. Tyler held Marly's hand, his eyes wide with curiosity. Everywhere they went, they saw kids laughing and playing.

"What's that?" Tyler asked, pointing to where several kids had gathered around a watering hole with their fishing rods.

"That's a lake where we go fishing. Note the life preservers," he said to Marly, who nodded her approval. "You think that's something you'd like to do, Tyler?"

Tyler shrugged. "I don't know. I ain't never been fishing before."

The headmaster crouched and gestured for Tyler with a just-between-us nod of encouragement. When Tyler went over to him, he confided, "We put extra fish in the lake so they're easier to catch."

Just then, a peal of laughter drew their attention to a group of kids around Tyler's age who were playing freeze tag. Those tagged stood frozen in their spots like petrified trees. One little girl hung back, watching from the fringes. She had dark-brown hair, tied back in a ponytail with a bright-red ribbon. From the expression on her face, she obviously wanted to join in the fun, yet every time she took a step forward, she would hesitate, then step back again.

Tyler pointed toward her. "She looks like Betsy Jean."

"You're right. She does," Marly agreed.

The headmaster smiled. "Do you like playing tag?"

"Yeah." He looked up at Marly.

"It's his favorite game," she explained. "He's a great runner."

The headmaster raised an eyebrow. "Would you like to join in?"

Tyler shrugged and kicked a rock.

"Sweetie?" Marly lifted his chin and gave him an encouraging smile. "Why don't you go see if that little girl wants to play. I think she might need a friend."

Tyler squinted at the figure in the distance. "'Kay." He let go of her hand and started down the hill, gradually gaining speed until he was running.

Marly took a step toward Carter, followed by another, until she was standing beside him. His hand moved automatically to the small of her back. Together they watched Tyler approach the little girl.

Tyler pointed at the other kids. The girl shrugged, noticeably shy. They appeared to converse for a bit, and then he took her hand, once more gesturing toward the others. This time she nodded once, and together they ran into the field.

"That's my boy." Marly smiled, turning to gaze up at Carter.

God, she had the most beautiful lips he'd ever seen.

"It's going to be all right, isn't it?" she whispered.

He returned her smile, glancing down at his stomach, where one of Marly's hands rested. "Yeah, I think so," he said, resisting the urge to scoop her into his arms and swing her around.

They ate dinner in the school's cafeteria, then spent the rest of the night back at the motel playing cards. Each time Tyler started to get melancholy, they tried to distract him. Marly taught them some games, and Carter did a few magic tricks.

"How'd he do that?" Tyler asked Marly. She shrugged. The boy turned to Carter. "How'd you do that?"

"A magician never reveals his secrets."

Tyler tilted his head to the side and grinned. "Aw, come on. I ain't gonna tell no one."

Carter laughed. "Okay, how about this. Each time we come visit you, I'll show you how to do one trick. What do you think?"

"Okay, but can you show me just one trick now?"

"Yeah, I think I can do that. Here's what you do." He taught Tyler how to separate the deck into two piles by color. "See, you have them pick a card from the red deck and put it back in the black deck. Then you can tell which one they picked."

"'Cause it's the only red one!" Tyler laughed.

Carter glanced over at Marly. She sat cross-legged on the floor beside them, a sad smile on her face. He wanted to tell her that it would all work out, that time healed all wounds, but he settled for a gentle squeeze of her hand. She squeezed back.

"Come on, Tyler," she said, getting to her feet and holding out a hand for him. "Let's get you washed up for bed."

"Aw, is it time already?"

"It's past time. You want to thank Carter for teaching you the magic trick?"

"Thanks," he said, stacking the two piles of cards together and handing the deck to Carter.

"You're welcome."

"Good night." He wrapped his arms around Carter's neck in a quick hug.

"Good night," Carter whispered, his throat suddenly tight.

Hilary smoothed the thin blanket over the edge of the bed and cleared a spot for her friend to sit. Outside, cooling winds blew through the village, but their huts trapped oppressive heat inside. They planned to stay only long enough to rest their tired muscles before going back out to help distribute the food rations.

"Do you really think we look alike?" her friend asked with a laugh. "All day long they've been calling me Hilary."

"I don't know. I guess there's a slight resemblance. We could pass for cousins, maybe. But I think it's our hair and

skin color that throw them off. They aren't used to the lighter shades.'' Hilary stood up and stretched. *''God, am I sore.''*

''Me, too.'' Her friend flopped back on the bed and threw one hand over her forehead. *''Wake me up when it's time to go home.''*

''Have a nice nap, Rip Van Winkle.'' Hilary laughed. *''I'll be right back.''* She left the hut and started for the well to fetch a bucket of water they could boil and drink later. She wasn't fifty feet away, when an explosion sounded behind her, pitching her face first into the dirt.

Tiny rocks scraped into her hands and knees. Scrambling around, she gaped in horror at the sight of orange and red flames lighting up the black sky.

Her hut was ablaze in the night.

''No!'' she screamed, stumbling to her feet. But the winds were already sweeping the conflagration through the village. *''No!''* she screamed, running into the inferno. *''Marly!''*

Marly bolted upright in bed, her entire body drenched with perspiration. She was shaking so hard she didn't trust herself to get out of bed without falling. Every breath she drew prickled her lungs like wooden splinters.

She looked beside her and noticed the other side of the bed was empty. Her gaze combed the darkened room for Tyler, and detected his small form on the couch next to Carter. They were speaking in hushed tones. With the pounding of her heartbeat filling her eardrums, she couldn't decipher a word.

She leaned back against the pillows. Thank God she hadn't screamed in her sleep. She didn't need to frighten poor Tyler any more than he already was. And Carter. She'd caught a break this time, but her luck would run out before long. They would marry soon, and naturally, as husband and wife, they would sleep together. That was part of matrimony.

He would find out about her nightmares, and knowing Carter's logical mind, she would have to provide a rational explanation. She wondered how much he knew from the background check. And how much she dared to supply.

She couldn't risk any additional scrutiny, lest Carter discover the horrible truth of that fire.

Oh, God. If the wrong people ever knew…if it ever got out… Marly shriveled down under the covers, securing the blankets all around her. She forced herself to calm down. There was no point getting worked up over nothing. Eight years had passed. If they didn't know by now, chances were they never would. And when the time came, she would tell Carter what he needed to know about the fire. Just enough to appease him, to justify her recurring nightmares, and nothing else.

Slowly, her heart rate slowed until it sounded somewhat normal again. She took a deep, cleansing breath. From the other side of the room, the whispers continued, only now, she could discern the words.

"Carter, do you still miss your mama?"

"I sure do. I miss her all the time. I always will."

"I wish my mama was here."

"She is here, Tyler. She's right here, in your heart."

"What's that mean?"

"It means just what Miss Marly said. That you'll always remember your mama, remember the fun times you had. That she'll live in your memories."

"I remember one time when Mama and me went to Carowinds. You ever been there?"

"No, but maybe you can take me sometime."

"'Kay, but you gotta drive, 'cause I'm just a kid."

"Deal, but in the meantime, I want you to think about all the good times you had with your mama. Don't ever forget them."

"I won't. I wish…I wish she would come back." He sniffed.

"Tyler, your mama's an angel now, and she's gone to a place where there aren't any drugs."

"Heaven?"

"That's right. Your mama's healthy and strong again. And you know what else?"

"What?"

"She's watching over you now."

"She can see me from Heaven?"

"That's right, and it's okay for you to be sad, but she doesn't want you to be sad for too long."

"Can she hear me?"

"Umm-hmm."

"Mama?" he said with wonder.

"She can't talk to you, but you go ahead and tell her whatever you want. She can hear you."

"Mama...I love you." He sniffed. "I wish you didn't take them drugs from Daddy's men. I...miss you." He paused. "Carter, do you talk to your mama?"

"Every night. In my prayers. And I ask God to make sure she's okay and to look after her."

"You think He listens?"

"Yeah, I do."

Marly smiled into the shadows, relief mixing with an equal amount of fear. For all his logic, Carter King had a deep sentimental side. She never would have guessed, and almost wished she didn't know. From the beginning, her feelings for him had thrown her off balance, but the attraction had run only skin deep. These glimpses of the man beneath the veneer warned her of far more dangerous threats.

In time, Marly might allow her future husband into her bed, but never, ever could she allow him into her heart.

Chapter 11

"**I** got the bags. You get the door," Carter said, tossing the keys to Marly.

She caught them with one hand. Once inside, she pressed the buttons that disarmed the security system. She propped the door open with one of Carter's boots and stepped inside, coming up short as a sudden rush of sensations threatened to overcome her.

The first time she'd entered Carter's house, she'd come as a complete stranger. Everything had been new—the sight, the smell, the feel of the house. This time it wasn't so new. Stored impressions hurtled back at her, recent memories giving rise to a strange feeling of familiarity. They wrapped around her, enveloping her in their warmth, as if welcoming her home.

Marly's purse slid from her grasp, dropping to the floor. She wrapped her arms around her middle, embracing the feeling of coming home as something dear to her, yet so elusive in her life.

"You okay?" Carter asked, coming in with their bags.

She nodded.

He stared at her for a long moment, before whispering, "Welcome home."

"Thank you." Her attempt at smiling failed. "Need help with those?"

"No, I'm fine."

As he took their bags down the hall, Marly held up a hand in protest, then let it fall to her side without uttering a word. In the past twenty-four hours, she had softened, like a wax doll left too near a flame.

A false sense of security, a voice warned.

But they were going to be married. Tomorrow, no less. What sense did it make to prolong the inevitable? Carter would find out about her nightmares sooner or later, and when he did, she'd have to provide a satisfactory explanation. There was no getting around it.

That night, she took a long bath, letting the whirlpool jets pound the tension from her muscles. She changed into a cotton nightshirt, pulled on her robe and padded down the hallway to the study. Carter sat at his desk, staring into the flames of the fire in the fireplace.

"I'm going to sleep," she told him.

He nodded. "Good night."

"Aren't you coming?"

"In a while. I have some work to do."

"Oh, okay. Good night, then." She started to leave, then turned back. "Um, Carter?"

He glanced up, and she thought she caught a troubled look in his eyes, but then it was gone, and he was just looking at her expectantly.

"What side of the bed do you sleep on?" she asked.

"The right."

"The right if you're facing the bed, or the right if you're in the bed?"

"Facing."

"Okay, thanks. Good night."

"Good night."
She turned and closed the door.

Carter opened the bedroom door and peered inside. Marly slept on the far left side of the bed, by the windows. Wearily running a hand through his hair, he crossed to the closet and undressed. Last night in the motel room, he'd worn sweats to bed and practically burned up in the night. He wasn't used to wearing anything when he slept in his own bed. Reluctantly, he reached for a pair of boxers. It was the best he could do.

Moonlight filtered through the French doors, revealing Marly's pale arm where she hugged her pillow. Carter pulled back the comforter and maneuvered underneath the covers, careful not to disturb her. He turned on his side, his back to her, and closed his eyes, willing sleep to come quickly, before he could think too much about the woman in his bed.

He'd seen her nondescript robe earlier and had tried, with little success, to keep from wondering what she wore underneath. He imagined dowdy flannel, with buttons up to her neck; only, that didn't help, because he liked buttons, and he liked unbuttoning buttons.

He imagined shapeless sweats; only, that reminded him of how he'd broiled last night, which led to other thoughts, and eventually he was wondering whether she wore panties to bed. Finally, he conceded defeat. In his mind, all paths led back to the same place. He wanted Marly naked. Underneath him. Plain and simple. There was no getting around it.

Carter punched the pillow and turned it over, trying to shut off his mind. He pictured a blackboard, visualized numbers written slowly, one by one, backward from ninety-nine. Ninety-eight. Ninety-seven. Ninety-six…

He continued the methodical countdown as long as he could. The numbers eventually became garbled, disjointed. A dull, gray haze seeped through his consciousness.

Carter didn't know how long he'd been asleep, when he heard a loud thump and bolted upright. Marly's side of the bed was empty, and his bleary gaze combed the bedroom for some sign of her.

He heard her before he saw her, a cry of agony that snapped him up out of sleep before he fully understood what it was. Heart hammering, he leaped from the bed in time to see her rolling across the floor.

Rolling like a person with her body on fire!

"Marly!" he cried as she hit the wall. In three quick strides, he was kneeling beside her.

"No!" She patted at her body frantically. "Go away!"

He realized she wasn't talking to him, but trying to smother imaginary—or in this case, remembered—flames.

"Marly..." He gently caught her shoulder. "Wake up, Marly. It's just a dream. It's over now. The fire's gone. You're safe, sweetheart. Can you hear me?"

"Put it out!" She threw her head back and screamed. And then in the next breath, she was awake, her eyes wide and filled with terror.

Carter pulled her toward him without really thinking about what he was doing until he had gathered her trembling limbs in his arms. "You had a nightmare," he whispered against her temple. "It's over now. You're safe." Carefully, he reached out and touched the back of his hand to her heated forehead. Tears coursed down her face, and he brushed them away with his knuckles.

"The fire," she said in a shaky voice. "It was so hot. It burned...my hands." She lifted her hands up as if to inspect the scars.

Carter reached for one hand to cradle it against his cheek. He turned the palm over and pressed it to his lips. "Shh...I know. But it's over, sweetheart. It's over."

"You know?" she whispered.

He nodded, and she shivered, laying her head against his shoulder, her body dewed with perspiration. After a while, they were encircled in each other's arms. Carter leaned his head back, against the wall, content for the moment just to hold her.

His unease didn't start until it dawned on him she was all but naked, dressed only in panties and a thin cotton nightshirt.

He tried not to think about it—this wasn't the right time—even though he could feel the imprint of her breasts against his bare chest, her bottom against his thigh, her silky legs....

She moved just then, a slight shift of her body that made him grit his teeth. Too late. With a grimace, he realized he was more than a little aroused—his body's swift response to the wanderings of his mind.

"I think," he whispered, "that we'd better get you back in bed." *On your own side, with me far on the other.*

"No!" The circle of her arms tightened. "No, please...not yet."

"Marly..."

Her whispered plea was just a warm breath of sound against his throat, and Carter felt his gut pull tight as she shifted again, this time turning more toward him. "Just a few more minutes."

"Just a few," he managed to whisper, his voice sounding as hoarse as it felt.

Her hair tickled his shoulder, but he tried to block the sensation, tried to force his mind from imagining the erotic way it would look fanned across his pillow. He clamped his eyes shut and tried to ignore the smell of flowers, musky in the aftermath of her nightmare, musky as he'd imagined she would smell after they made love, damp, bare skin against skin.

Damn it! It wasn't supposed to be like this. He wasn't supposed to feel this way, not about Marly. He vowed to be a gentleman, even if it killed him.

But he could feel the slow rhythm of her breathing, her heartbeat. He could feel her take a deep breath, feel her breast brush against his chest. And then he felt the touch of her fingers on his cheek and made the mistake of looking down and into her eyes.

He had seen that look before, and he knew that in her current state, Marly would follow wherever he led. He clenched his teeth so tightly they ached, because he knew he couldn't do it, couldn't take advantage of her, and risk losing himself in the process. Not tonight. Not when she was this vulnerable, when her own defenses were lowered, when it would be so easy to let go and never come back.

"Carter?" she whispered, trailing her petal-soft fingertips over his lips.

God help him. He was going to die.

He swallowed. "Tell me what you want, Marly."

She shook her head. "I don't know."

That's what he was afraid of. He had vowed to give her whatever she wanted, but to take only what she offered, never to push her further than she wanted to go. Tonight he wouldn't need to push. Tonight there would be no boundaries if he gave in to the fierce desire inside him. Tonight there would be no return.

Carter closed his eyes, struggling with indecision, finally opening them and meeting her stormy gaze. He knew what he had to do. He knew what she needed, and he knew he could give it to her, without compromising either of them. There were ways, and he knew them all.

He eased her down, off his thigh and onto the carpet. At her whimper of protest, he closed his mouth over hers, drawing her into a hungry kiss. Her whimper turned into a soft moan as she turned partway in his arms.

His hands circled around her rib cage, under her nightshirt, to cup her breasts. He kneaded them in his palms, teasing the nipples between his thumb and forefinger, while his hungry mouth moved to her neck.

Carter inhaled deeply. He loved the way she smelled, the way she felt in his arms, the small noises she made in the back of her throat.

"Carter..." Her voice sounded sultry in the sudden heat of their bedroom.

"Shh. Just relax." He brushed his lips over hers again and again, until her resistance wore and her hands threaded into his hair. "Yes, like that." He trailed one hand down to her waist, and then lower, slipping underneath the elastic waistband of her panties. "Like this."

She gave a sudden gasp as his fingers found her warm, wet and ready. Oh, so ready. Her bottom pressed against him, the muscles rubbing his swollen flesh. He wanted to turn her around, to pull her over him, to guide her hips until they found a perfect fit. He wanted to bury himself deep inside her, over and over again, until he lost himself in her warmth.

He pressed his lips against the hollow of her throat and whispered her name, but it came out a ragged moan. He sucked in a breath and clamped his eyes shut. He wanted her so badly at that moment that it bordered on pain.

"Carter, are we going to...?"

"No," he reassured her, responding to the glimmer of fear in her eyes. Not tonight. He swore it. "Just you. Just...you."

He brought her to the edge swiftly, held on to her as she gripped his arms, tumbling over the precipice and into oblivion. Again, he sent her soaring and felt her release as she convulsed around him. Again and again, like a puff of milkweed tumbling on the wind, until he was certain he'd eradicated all coherent thoughts from her mind. Until she writhed against him, and he could stand no more. Until she cried out his name and went limp in his arms one final time.

Only then did he gather her up from the floor and into his arms, and carry her to the bed, where he laid her down, then covered her damp body with the sheet.

"Carter?" she whispered, but her eyes were already closing.

"Right here." He bent down to kiss her eyelids, grazing her cheek with his knuckles. Something shuddered through him, a wave of desire mingled with tenderness, so raw and unexpected it made him take a step back, followed by another, until he'd safely rounded the foot of the bed.

He took his place, far on the other side, where he lay perfectly still, afraid to move, afraid to even breathe, every inch of his body hard and aching for her.

It sure was hell being noble.

Carter shaved and showered while Marly slept. Flinging a towel around his waist, he used the bedside telephone to call the office and check his voicemail.

Twelve messages waited. The first eleven came as no surprise, but the twelfth one raised an eyebrow. It was the P.I. he'd hired for Marly's background check. Although the message wasn't anything more than a request for Carter to call back, he strode down the hall to the kitchen phone and dialed the number with wary apprehension.

"Mike. Carter King here. Returning your call."

"Hey, thanks for getting back to me, Mr. King. Something's turned up. I don't know if it's a big deal or not, but I thought you might want to know. Seems someone's poking around town, asking a lot of questions about that woman you had me investigate, Marly Alcott."

Carter frowned and flipped a page in his notepad. "Any idea who?"

"Not at this point. I got a tip from a friend of a friend."

"Hmm. Can you look into this for me?"

"Sure thing. I'll get on it right away."

"Thanks, Mike. Oh, and one other thing. See if you can figure out what they're after."

"Will do, Mr. King."

Carter's jaw tightened as he replaced the receiver. He remembered Marly accusing him of snooping into her past when he told her about the background check he'd run. She sure as hell wasn't going to like knowing someone else was doing the same. Especially if that someone was Billy Ray.

Carter wondered what he wanted and why he was so interested. Billy Ray wasn't going to find anything incriminating, if that was the objective, but the fact that he was looking didn't sit well with Carter.

He leaned his hip against the counter and frowned at the blank page in his notebook. Then he scribbled some notes, tore out the page and tucked it into his briefcase before going back to the bedroom to dress for work.

"Good morning," a soft voice greeted him when he entered the room.

Something tightened in his gut. "'Morning," he replied, checking to make sure the towel around his waist was still secure. "Sleep okay?"

"Umm-hmm." She looked warm and tousled, propped up on one elbow. When she wouldn't look at him, he read the faint pink glow in her cheeks as embarrassment. And for some reason, that bothered him.

It took every ounce of his willpower not to cross the room and crawl into bed with her. He could spend the entire day reacquainting himself with her body—never mind that he had every line and curve already etched in his mind. He would trace every pattern again, some maybe twice, others maybe more. He would match the feel of her to the sight, and he would drink it in. And when he was done, she would know there was nothing even remotely embarrassing about her body.

"I didn't hear the shower." She finally raised her gaze to his and asked, "Have you been up long?"

He almost laughed at the double meaning. If she had glanced down, she would have seen the unconcealable bulge beneath his towel, but she didn't. So he didn't tell her the sight of her waking up was one of the most incredible turn-ons he could remember. "Not too long," he answered, instead. "I need to get to the office. I'll pick you up at your center around noon, if that's all right. We can ride over to the court-house together."

She nodded and drew the covers back, glancing down at her bare legs, then back up at Carter. Slowly.

He knew the instant she recognized the evidence of his arousal. Her gaze flew to his, and for a long moment, they both stared at each other in silent acknowledgment of what had passed between them.

But Carter could look only so long before he wanted to take, and then it wouldn't be long before he'd want to take again and again.

"Bathroom's free if you want it," he said, ducking into his closet. He dressed quickly after grabbing the first navy suit, white shirt and red tie he could find. He took his shoes back to the bed and sat down to pull on a pair of dress socks.

Marly hadn't closed the bathroom door, and he watched through the corner of his eye as she dragged a brush through her hair, the lines of her body feminine and graceful.

Other memories of her body washed over him in a heated rush, and before he could steer his thoughts away, he was remembering the night before in vivid detail. Her soft scent and sweet taste, the sound of her labored breathing, the feel of her slippery warmth and the wide-eyed look of surprise on her face just before she found release.

His loins tightened painfully, and he shot to his feet. He grabbed the car keys from the dresser and shoved them in his pocket. "See you around noon."

He couldn't dash out of the house fast enough. Every second he passed in Marly's presence sapped him of more and more self-control. And soon, if he didn't get a grip, he was going to be fresh out. If he wasn't already.

Carter swore and shook his head. The model he'd set up on his spreadsheet had told him Marly was different, that she was special, that she was his last hope. But the model had been way off base in measuring one critical factor: his attraction to Marly.

Like it or not, he wanted her in ways he'd never wanted another woman, and that gave him reason to be afraid. Very afraid.

She was afraid. Very afraid. Before last night, Marly wouldn't have guessed intimacy had so many facets. She'd never let another soul know about her nightmares. They were too real, too personal. The side of her Carter had seen she'd never shared with anyone. And the side of her that he brought out she'd never known existed. It was, by far, the most mind-blowing experience of her life. He had rescued her from the depths of terror and taken her to unparalleled heights of ecstasy.

Every nerve ending in her body buzzed alive when he'd

walked into the bedroom that morning, wearing nothing but a towel. He was the most virile man she'd ever seen, tall and broad, with ropes of muscle everywhere. And oh, how the sight of his obvious attraction to her had made her hands itch.

She'd wanted to run her fingers along his neck, feel the strength of his arms, touch her lips to his bare chest. She had wanted him with a hunger she didn't know she had. He had awakened something in her, and she didn't know if she would ever be the same again.

That afternoon, in the car on their way to the courthouse where they would soon marry, she felt a sense of connection with him, a sense of belonging with him. It frightened her to trust him on yet another level, to allow him any closer to her inner fortress, but last night, he had made her feel so safe and protected. Oddly, he'd made her feel cherished.

How was she supposed to keep the fortress around her heart intact when he was so adept at scaling walls?

Marly shivered at the memory of coming apart in his arms and rubbed the gooseflesh on her arms.

"You okay?" Carter glanced over at her.

She nodded. "Fine."

"Did you talk to Tyler this morning?"

"Umm-hmm. He's keeping up a brave front, but he misses his mother terribly."

"He has a session with the child psychologist today. I'll call later and see how it went."

"Thanks. I appreciate that." She wiggled the ring on her third finger, already growing attached to it, reassured by its presence. Reassured by the man behind the symbol.

"You don't have to take the flowers inside if you don't want to."

"I want to," she said, lifting the small bouquet of white roses to inhale their perfume. She wore a simple linen suit she'd picked up from Annie Lou's that morning, and the roses added a touch of understated elegance. "They're beautiful." She smiled at his handsome profile, marveling that the strong and powerful Carter King was also a man capable of such gentleness, such selflessness, such giving.

She found herself suddenly curious about his first marriage, what had gone wrong and why it hadn't worked. She built up her nerve and finally broached the subject.

Carter shrugged and flexed his fingers on the steering wheel. "There isn't much to tell," he said, repositioning one hand on the top of the steering wheel. With the other, he rubbed the back of his neck.

"What was her name?"

"Eva Ann."

"Why didn't it work between you?"

"We were very different people. Different backgrounds, different outlooks. She came from a rich and powerful family, and I... Well, you know about me."

"And that's why you divorced her?" Marly asked.

"I didn't divorce her. She divorced me. You see, when her daddy found out his little girl had married a boy from the wrong side of the tracks, well, let's just say they didn't want to muddy the lineage with my kind."

Marly smarted. "That's the most absurd statement I've ever heard."

"What can I say? It was my own fault. I should have told her the truth before we got married. I guess deep inside I always knew how she would react. And the more time that passed...well, it just snowballed in the end. That's why I don't want any secrets between us, Marly, why I had to come clean with you. I wanted you to know exactly what you were getting into."

She couldn't bear to look at him then, to flaunt her deception in his face, so she stared straight ahead. "But if you were in love—"

"We were never in love. Only *I* was fool enough to believe anything else. And don't worry, I'm not about to go repeating that mistake, either."

Marly bit her lip. She knew he meant the words to reassure her, so why did she feel something inside her dying just a little? Had the events of last night somehow given her a glimmer of hope where none should have existed?

She was a fraud, and that would never change. Her lies would forever hang between them, preventing anything more than the arrangement to which they'd mutually consented.

"Carter?" she asked, trying to squash the hurt she had no right to feel. "There's something else I've been meaning to ask you. About last night…"

"Last night was for you."

"No, not that." She felt the stain of a blush creeping up her cheeks and hoped he wouldn't notice. "When I told you about the fire that burned my hands, you said you already knew. Was this part of the background check you had done on me?"

"Marly, I hope you can understand why I would—"

She waved away the rest of his explanation. "It's water under the bridge. I was just wondering how much you know."

He frowned as though he hadn't anticipated that question. "Just the facts, I guess."

"Like what?"

"Well, I know it happened overseas, when you were in the Peace Corps. Your village caught fire."

"Anything else?"

"Yeah. I know about your friend who died. I'm sorry."

She nodded and looked down at her hands. "Do you know anything about her? My friend?"

"No, should I?"

She shrugged. "Her name was Hilary. Her family was a lot like Eva Ann's, but she was different." She stared at her diamond ring as it sparkled in the sunlight. "She would have been honored to be your wife."

A warm hand touched her sleeve, followed by a brief squeeze. "Thank you," Carter whispered. His voice sounded rough, strained.

Marly glanced up, and in the split second when their gazes met and held, she felt something reach out and touch her deep inside. When he turned his attention back to the road, she tried to do the same, but it didn't work.

She rubbed her thumb against the band on the inside of her finger and reminded herself that she'd gone into this arrangement with her eyes wide-open. Carter had been straightforward with her about his past and his intentions for the future. He didn't want or need her love.

But what if she needed his?

Chapter 12

Had he been a true gentleman, Carter might have softened his words when he told Marly he wasn't about to go repeating past mistakes, but he had to make sure she understood that love wasn't part of their agreement. Not now. Not ever. That didn't mean he didn't care about her, that he didn't think the world of her as a generous and giving person...as a warm and sensual woman. More sensual than he'd expected, more than was probably safe, more—

"Carter?" the justice of the peace was asking.

Maybe if she looked at him, if she gave him a sign. Any sign. Distress. Disgust. Anything. But she couldn't—or she wouldn't—look anywhere except straight ahead. She'd even signed the marriage license without blinking, didn't stiffen a bit when he'd asked if she'd take his name. No arguments. Nothing.

So the white-trash boy from the projects decided to continue tempting fate, continue reaping what he'd never been intended to sow. Because, after all, Carter knew that although he could pretend to be a gentleman, deep down he could never change who he was. And finding Marly was the best thing that ever happened to him. Yeah, he was a selfish bastard to the core.

"I do," he whispered, gazing down at the top of Marly's strawberry-blond head.

He would make it up to her. He would. He knew their ceremony was nothing like the kind most women dreamed about, but she wouldn't live to regret their union, regret becoming his wife. No, not at all. Short of actually loving her, he would be the best damn husband in the world. She would see.

"I now pronounce you man and wife. You may kiss the bride."

The bride stared somewhere over his shoulder as she lifted her face for him. Her lips didn't even move as he brushed his mouth over hers.

In that brief moment, he felt a stab of regret for what he knew could never be, for the boundaries that would forever separate them, the white-trash boy and his Cinderella bride.

He stepped back, and Marly's gaze fluttered away.

"Thank you," she said to the justice of the peace and the witnesses. After walking a few feet, she paused without looking back.

Carter gave his own thanks and shook everyone's hand, trying to ignore the judge's raised eyebrow, then went after Marly.

She waited until he fell in step beside her, then walked with him as far as the door, without speaking.

"Carter?" she finally said.

"Yeah?" They stared at each other, and he wondered if she felt any different, or if it was just him. He wanted to ask her a million things. He wanted to drop to his knees and thank her for giving him this chance, to reassure her that he wouldn't blow it.

"I have to deposit the check," she said quietly.

The check. Carter rubbed the bridge of his nose to refocus. *A business transaction. This is a business transaction.*

When he didn't respond right away, she added, "I suppose I should switch my account to your bank."

"That would probably be good." He forced a smile and opened the door. "I'll walk you over."

"Thanks."

"Sure."

She paused in the doorway and worried her lower lip. "I mean, for everything, Carter. I just hope I won't disappoint you."

He smiled then, for real this time, and brushed the pad of his thumb over her lip. "You couldn't disappoint me, Marly." He kissed her quickly, ending it before she had time to react. "Come on. Let's deposit that check."

They stepped outside into the sunshine. Marly took his proffered arm, and they walked the few blocks to the bank together. Carter introduced her to everyone as the new Mrs. King, which raised more than a few eyebrows.

"Your wife?" one of the longtime tellers exclaimed.

Damn, but he liked the sound of it. "That's right." Carter put a hand on Marly's shoulder, squeezing softly.

"Well now, just how long have you been keeping this little lady a secret, Mr. King? Far as I can tell, you've been hoarding her all to yourself!"

"That's right, Jonathan. She's all mine."

The teller laughed, and Marly glanced up to shoot Carter a warning look, but he didn't care. She was his wife, and he wanted all the world to know.

"Hey, there's someone I'd like you to meet," he said, after they'd opened two new accounts, one joint and one for Little Learners.

"Carter, I don't have much time. Maybe we can do introductions another day." She indicated the face of her watch. "I have to be back at the center in half an hour."

"It'll only take a minute."

"Carter?" She turned around, placed her hand on his sleeve, the first physical contact she'd initiated that day. "Do we have to do it just now? I'm feeling a little overwhelmed."

He touched her fingers, held them under his own hand,

wanting to tell her not to worry, that she wouldn't regret her decision. "Marly—"

She squeezed his arm. "Please?"

"Okay." He scowled and hung his head. "I just wanted to show you off."

"Oh, for Pete's sake." She grimaced. "You have got to be the world's biggest ham. You know that?"

He looked up. "Is that good or bad?"

"I'm not sure yet, but you can quit with the boo-boo face. I work with kids, remember? I know a pout when I see one."

"Is it working?"

She smiled and rolled her eyes. "One more introduction and then we're going."

"Great." He grinned and steered her toward the mayor's wife and made introductions. All the while, he kept hearing the same two words echoing in his mind: my wife.

Marly Alcott was his wife now.

Marly King.

His breath quickened, as an unexpected wave of possessiveness shuddered through him.

Carter gritted his teeth. Damn, if he wasn't doomed already.

Alone in her office at Little Learners that evening, Marly twisted her wedding band around so the channel-set diamonds faced upward. Her eyes grew misty, and she clamped them shut, warning herself not to succumb to melodrama.

But behind her closed lids, she saw her new husband—her beautiful, handsome new husband—slide the wedding band over her finger. It was a moment she wouldn't soon forget.

She'd been so overcome with emotion she could barely speak. She'd been afraid that if she even looked at him, she would burst into tears.

God help her, she'd never realized it was possible to ache for another person the way she ached for Carter. She couldn't get him out of her mind; couldn't stop thinking about him, remembering him.

What had he started? What had he awakened in her?

All these nerve endings she hadn't even realized she had were now buzzing alive. First her heart and now her body, and somehow the two had intertwined in their longings.

Did that explain the heaviness in her heart, the dull throbbing low in her belly when Carter had put his arm around her and introduced her to everyone at the bank?

It scared her to admit the depth of her need for him, even to herself. She wanted him. It was that simple and that complicated. She wanted Carter as she'd wanted no other man. She wanted to be his wife, in every sense of the word. But what scared her most was the unmistakable yearning for the one thing she couldn't have.

She didn't suffer from any grandiose illusions. He'd seen to that. He treated her like a princess, in all but one regard.

So why did she have to keep reminding herself that love wasn't on her agenda, either? Why couldn't she be happy for what she had? Why did the knowledge that her otherwise-perfect husband would never love her have to hurt so badly?

Marly sighed and kicked off her shoes. She'd overcome greater obstacles in her lifetime. Surely she could survive a loveless marriage. Couldn't she?

Well, for starters, she could stop overanalyzing every little thing. Every word, every gesture, every feeling. She touched her fingers to her lips, remembering the times Carter had kissed her, wondering how long she would have to wait before he kissed her again.

"It's hopeless," she whispered into the empty room. Shaking her head, she retrieved her To Do list from the top desk drawer and scanned the remaining items.

Her first order of business had included ordering a new security system for the school. That done, she'd crossed various other tasks off the list throughout the day, leaving only a few.

Intending to pare the list down even further before she left for the day, Marly reached for the phone and called the local food distributor to increase their rations.

"Is this a one-time order, Miss Alcott?"

"No, it's permanent, so if you wouldn't mind updating our standing information, I'd really appreciate it."

"Will do. Anything else?"

"Oh, I almost forgot. I have a new name. I'm Marly King now."

"A newlywed?"

"That's right."

"Well, congratulations."

"Thank you." Despite herself, she smiled as she hung up the phone, skimming her To Do list for the next item.

"Looks like you got yourself a little windfall there, Miz King." Billy Ray Cameron's voice washed over her like an icy waterfall.

Marly's smile faltered. How the hell had he gotten inside the building? Had she forgotten to secure the door after the last child had left? Her heart clamored an erratic rhythm. God help her, she couldn't remember.

An overwhelming sense of panic suffused her. Each time she saw him, Billy Ray appeared more menacing, the wild, unbalanced glint in his eyes more evident. All survival instincts told her to run. But she couldn't. Not this time. She had to play out her role. It was the only way.

"Hello, Mr. Cameron." She forced a congenial tone. "Are you here with Tyler?"

Billy Ray's eyes narrowed with suspicion as he approached. Planting his palms facedown on her desk, he leaned forward so their gazes were level.

Her blood ran cold. She almost stopped breathing altogether.

"If I remember right, I done already warned you once about messing with me." He tilted his head to the side and pursed his lips in a patronizing gesture. "Do you need a Yankee translation?"

Marly shoved back in her chair and jackknifed to her feet. *No fear. No fear. No fear.* "I—I understood you perfectly. I take it you haven't found Tyler."

"You take it right."

"Oh, I'm so sorry, Mr. Cameron. This is just awful. Have you called the police yet?"

"No, and I'll give you three guesses why not."

"Guesses? Why, I don't know."

"Well, maybe if you think real hard—" he tapped his temple "—it'll come to you."

She frowned. "I don't know what you're implying, Mr. Cameron, but if there's something I can do to help—"

"As a matter of fact there is." With measured steps, he rounded her desk, coming dangerously near her, before stopping. "The police seem to think I'm hiding Tyler, but you and I both know he ain't with me, don't we?"

Marly didn't respond.

"Yeah, that's right. We do," he said, answering his own question. "So now why don't you start by telling me exactly what you know, Miz King."

"I'm sorry?" God, she was shaking something awful.

"What you're holding back."

Her hand fluttered to her throat. "I'm afraid I don't quite understand—"

"Cut the crap, woman." Billy Ray slammed his knuckles down on her desk. "I'm on to you."

Marly lifted her chin. "I've told you before, Mr. Cameron, and I'll tell you again—"

"I ain't buying it."

She didn't like the way he was staring her down, the cold glint of his eyes piercing out from the sunken pits in his skull. Try as she might, she couldn't eradicate the image of him pulling the knife from his ex-wife's body, the way his lips had twitched from the effort.

A sudden wave of nausea rolled over her. She wanted to scream but knew she couldn't. She wanted to run, but there was nowhere to go. It was just her and Billy Ray and—

"Excuse me, is this a private conversation?"

Marly's heart thudded with relief at the sight of Carter standing in the doorway. She'd never been happier to see another person in all her life.

"Yeah, it is, so butt out," Billy Ray said.

"I believe we're finished," she corrected.

"I don't think so."

"You heard the lady, Cameron."

Billy Ray swung his gaze to Carter. "I'm sorry," he said with exaggerated patience. "Have we met before?"

"Carter King." He tipped his head back. His voice was deep and quiet, like wrapped thunder. "Pleased to make your acquaintance."

Billy Ray's eyes narrowed on Marly. "This ain't over," he said, his voice low but not low enough.

Carter unfolded himself from the door and came to stand at his full height. "If you've got business with my wife, I suggest you go through me from now on." He was much larger than Billy Ray, taller and broader. But even more than his obvious strength, Carter King radiated power. It oozed from every pore of his body, and even Billy Ray appeared to take note.

The shifty drug lord retreated slowly, then pivoted on his heel and strode from the room. Carter kicked the door shut behind him. Marly breathed a sigh of relief and all but ran into Carter's arms.

"Thank you," she whispered against his chest. "I don't know what I would have done if you hadn't shown up." She was shaking so hard, like a quivering mass of jelly. He held her close, and she closed her eyes, wanting to crawl inside his skin, to absorb some of his strength.

How much more could she take without giving?

Marly pressed a glass to the refrigerator's water dispenser. "Can I get you some?" she asked Carter without turning around.

"No. Thanks."

They'd barely spoken after Billy Ray had left, aside from Carter's suggestion that they go out to dinner and Marly's request that they go home and change first. Some wedding day. She frowned into her water and took a tentative sip.

"I talked to the psychologist this afternoon. She says Tyler's behaving normally for a child who has just lost a parent. He's coping better than most.''

''He's seen more death than most.''

''That's true. Marly?''

''Hmm?'' She took a bigger swallow.

''I want you to consider calling the police.''

She sputtered and nearly dropped the glass.

''I know what you said before....''

''No, Carter.'' She put the glass down on the counter and spun around, nearly colliding with her new husband.

Carter's hazel eyes were dark and intense, reflecting the determination of a powerful businessman unaccustomed to hearing no for an answer. ''Marly, this is the second time he's come around, and I have to tell you I don't take too kindly to *any* man harassing my wife, let alone two-bit scum like Billy Ray Cameron.''

''I understand, but I don't want to involve myself any more than I already have.''

''Don't you think Billy Ray's going to want to involve the police? Even if it's just to get the heat off himself?''

She shook her head. ''He isn't going to draw attention to Tyler's disappearance. He…thinks Tyler knows something incriminating. He can't afford to let the police find him first.''

''How do you know this?''

Marly shrugged. ''I just do.''

His jaw set with the hard edge of frustration. ''And you're sure Tyler doesn't know anything?''

''I'm sure.''

Carter leaned against the island in the center of the kitchen and crossed his arms. ''Okay, look. I still think you should consider telling the police Cameron's hounding you.''

''But I don't want—''

''Marly, you don't have much choice, with Cameron so damn intent on involving you.''

''No, don't say that. I have a choice. No one can make me…'' She swallowed down a knot of fear. No one could make her testify again. No one could force her involvement.

She wasn't a fifteen-year-old girl this time, required to obey her mother's decisions, but a grown woman in charge of her own life and her own life's choices.

So why did it seem that the more things changed, the more they stayed the same? She could run, but she could never hide. And in the end, she was still the same little mouse, backed into a corner.

Carter reached out and tugged her toward him. She went to him willingly and stood in the vee of his long legs, her hands resting on his shoulders, his hands on her waist, as if it was the most natural position in the world.

He gave a heavy sigh and said, "You're right. No one can make you."

Marly worried her lip as she studied the chiseled planes of his face. He was extraordinarily handsome, this man who was now her husband. She dropped her hands to his chest, staring at the splotchy pigment of her scars.

"There's something I have to tell you," she said, choosing her words carefully. "About the fire and my friend...Hilary."

"You don't have to talk about it if you don't want to."

"I do, because I want you to understand. It's just a little hard, even after all these years. You see, it was a bomb that started that fire."

Carter frowned. "What are you saying?"

"They killed her."

"Who killed her?"

She drew a shaky breath. "I don't know where to begin, except at the beginning. Hilary...witnessed a murder. Her testimony sent three men to prison. All three were major underworld players. One of them was her father. They blamed him for the foul-up and later killed him in prison, making it look like a suicide.

"Next was her mother. A Boston blueblood. She was a conceited, self-absorbed socialite who never really understood how the other half lived." She frowned, a mixture of anger and pity welling inside her. "She died when Hilary was in college. Car bomb. Of course the investigators said it was a faulty starter.

"Hilary joined the Peace Corps and fled the country, but in the end, even she underestimated the long arm of the underworld. They planted a bomb in her hut. We were both in there. If I hadn't left to go get water…"

"Shh, don't say it." Carter felt strangely uneasy as he held his wife. His hands traced over the gentle curve of her waist to grip her hips.

Just thinking about her near brush with death troubled him. She'd become an integral part of his life in such a short time. The thought of losing her, past or present, didn't sit well with him.

"I'm sorry," he said.

"Me, too." She fingered his tie. Her lower lip started to tremble, and she bit down on it. "Carter, I'm sorry I didn't tell you this earlier. I should have…"

"Hey, it's okay." Her lips were red from gnawing, and he lightly traced the contours with his index finger.

"No," she whispered. "It's not okay. You still don't know what I'm trying to get to, and I'm still afraid to tell you. But you have a right to know.…"

He frowned. "Know what?"

Marly's eyes filled with tears she quickly blinked back.

"Marly, what is it?"

"I saw him," she whispered. "It was me, not Tyler. I saw Billy Ray at Linda's that night. I saw him pull his knife from her body."

Carter felt the air being sucked out of his lungs. "You were there?"

Marly nodded, covering her mouth with both hands.

He shoved a rough hand through his hair and swore, pulling his wife to him. "Tell me everything."

He listened intently as Marly filled in the missing pieces of the puzzle, and suddenly everything made sense.

"You didn't go to the police because of what happened to Hilary."

"I couldn't."

"Marly, look at me." He took her hands in his. "Billy Ray is no underworld figure. He's a small-town hood, and the local authorities could squash him like a bug."

"Then why haven't they squashed him yet?" She pulled her hands away. "I'm not getting involved, Carter, so don't even try to make me—"

"I would never make you do anything."

"You made me marry you."

He could tell from her pain-stricken expression that she regretted the words as soon as she'd spoken them.

"I—I'm sorry. That didn't come out right."

He shrugged. "It's true."

"It's also true that you've done nothing but help me, and I don't want you to think I'm not grateful...for everything. That's why I had to tell you. I just hope you can understand—"

"I do, but I want you to understand something, too. There's a killer running around loose. He's managed to evade the law for years, and you, sweetheart, have the evidence to fry him. No, I'm not going to force you to go to the authorities, but I want you to think about it. I want you to think long and hard, and whatever you decide I want you know that I'm behind you. You're my wife now, and I would never let anyone hurt you. I swear it."

"I believe you. And Carter, about what I said just now... I don't want you to think I'm going to throw that in your face for the next ten years."

"Ten?" He raised an eyebrow. "Lady, you're going to be married to me for a lot longer than ten years."

"You forgive me, then?"

"Yeah."

She trailed her fingertips across his jawbone, her gaze traveling over his lips. "Sometimes I'm not sure you're quite real."

Carter swallowed. "Oh, I'm real, all right."

"Can you believe we're really married?" she whispered.

"No. Can you?"

She shook her head. "Carter?"

"Hmm?"

"There's something I've been wanting to do...." She raised herself up on her tiptoes and brushed her mouth over his.

A fine tremor coursed through his body.

"Is this okay?" she asked, as if unsure about some kind of etiquette.

"Yeah," he murmured, bracing himself as she stepped a little closer into the juncture of his thighs. Surely he could withstand a few minutes of her sweet torture.

"Good." She threaded her hands into his hair. "I couldn't wait much longer."

Whoosh. Her words ignited him like a match dropped in kerosene. He was hard in an instant and wanting her badly.

Marly might have been waiting for kisses, but he was waiting for more. Much more.

How honored would his new bride feel if she knew he wanted to make love with her on the kitchen counter?

Just one more second, then he would end this, before things could get out of hand. Just one more second.

Her breasts brushed his chest, and he slid one finger inside her suit jacket, grazing her nipple. It pebbled at his touch, and Marly shivered, pressing closer against him.

Just one more second, and then he would pull away.

Her hands moved down his shoulders, rubbing his upper arms. Each puff of breath sounded increasingly labored. Just one more second... She moved her hips against him.

Ah, hell. Who was he kidding? One more second and he'd have her on the kitchen counter.

Carter gripped her hips, savoring the way her body molded to his. It felt like ripping off the top layer of his skin when he set her away.

"On second thought," he managed to say, "it is getting late. We should probably get going. You must be hungry."

She looked a little disoriented as she shook her head. "Not really."

"No? I'm starving."

"All right," she agreed with a smile, but as she moved away, he saw it falter.

It still didn't register that anything was wrong until she was halfway down the hall to their bedroom. A sniffle. That was all it took. "Marly?"

No response.

"Marly, what's wrong?" He started after her.

"Nothing. I'm just going to change. I'll be right out." She ducked into the bedroom.

He followed, before she could close the door.

The room was bathed in semidarkness, with only one bed-side lamp burning. He didn't bother turning on any others. Marly stood by the windows, her back turned.

He knew she wanted to be alone. He also knew he couldn't leave her.

Carter crossed the room and stood behind her, listening to the sniffles. "Married less than eight hours, and already I can tell when you're crying from the very first sniffle."

"Great."

"Not so great when I don't know why." He tucked a lock of her hair behind her ear. "Talk to me."

She shrugged. "It's so hard to believe we're really married, that this is our wedding night."

"It does feel pretty strange, doesn't it?"

"Yeah." Her voice cracked.

"You want to talk about it?"

She shrugged again. "I guess all young girls have this idea of how it's going to be, you know, their wedding...their wedding night. They dream about these things...."

Marly felt Carter's hand on her shoulder, nudging her around to face him. "Tell me your dreams," he said, his eyes searching hers.

She shook her head. "I can't."

"Why not?"

"Because they're just girlhood dreams. I'm a grown woman and a realist now."

He shrugged. "Tell me anyway."

"No, you'll laugh."

"I won't. I promise." He was silent, waiting.

"Carter, it's embarrassing," she finally whispered.

"So? We're married now. We have an entire lifetime of embarrassment ahead of us." He grinned. "How did you imagine your wedding? A big ceremony?"

She sighed. "Yes, but only because my parents wouldn't have let me have anything else."

"Did they have a lot of friends?"

"Tons," she said, and then hastened to add, "while I was growing up, anyway. The numbers dwindled later, and of course, as you know, my parents passed on." Hilary Steele and Marly Alcott had that much in common—no family or close friends.

"I'm sorry."

"Thanks. It's funny, when I was little my life was filled with dreams. I always imagined a big church wedding, pews filled with people who'd come from all over just to see me walk down the aisle. Some of them I'd met before. Others I hadn't."

Carter closed his eyes. "Okay, I can see it. So what did you wear?"

Marly embraced the distant memory. "An ivory dress. Nothing fancy, not by today's standards. Kind of traditional, old-fashioned. Lots of silk and lace."

"Silk and lace," Carter echoed with an appreciative grin.

"Umm-hmm, underneath, too."

The grin faltered. "Underneath?"

"You know, bra and panties."

Carter didn't say anything.

"Well, I did do that much," she said, averting her gaze.

"That much when?"

"Today. At our wedding."

"You're wearing silk and lace under there?"

She shivered. Why should it matter what she wore underneath her clothing? Carter hadn't seemed interested in the kitchen. He was just being kind by asking now. "I'd better change if we're going to dinner."

He swallowed audibly. "You didn't answer the question."

"It's getting late." She felt herself flush and tried to turn before she gave herself away.

"Oh, no." He caught her shoulders. "You can't do this to me. You're the one who brought it up. Now it's going to bug me all night. Just tell me and get it over with."

She shook her head.

"Come on, Marly. Take pity. Put me out of my misery." His protests reminded her of the children at nap time.

"Carter King." She poked her index finger into his ribs. "I am not going to tell you what kind of underwear I'm wearing. That's the kind of thing you have to find out when you find out." With that, she crossed her arms and turned toward the windows, hoping he would go away so she could change.

He didn't. "When am I going to find out?"

She heaved a sigh. "Whenever you're ready, I suppose."

"Whenever I'm ready? Marly, I was born ready. I thought you wanted to wait."

"Because of the nightmares. Because I didn't want you to see me like that. Not because I didn't want to…didn't want you to…us to…" She pointed toward the kitchen. "I just told you I couldn't wait any—" A tug at her waist brought her backside flush against Carter's hardened length, and she stopped short, her eyes widening in surprise.

"Neither can I," he said in a growl.

Chapter 13

Marly gasped at the erotic brush of Carter's body against hers. Her head lolled back as his open mouth trailed hot kisses along the side of her neck, the scrape of a day's stubble wreaking havoc with her senses.

His nimble fingers worked the buttons of her linen suit free, and he slipped the jacket from her shoulders. Seconds later, the skirt pooled to the floor alongside it, and she stood wearing only the matching silk-and-lace bra and panties.

"Marly," he breathed against her neck. His voice sounded like gravel spread with honey, and it sent a ripple of waves crashing through her body. "You did wear silk and lace after all."

She should have felt more nervous, more hesitant, but her need for him surpassed all else. She wanted only to touch and to be touched, wanted only to feel and to be felt. She wanted her husband. Against her, inside her, in ways she couldn't even begin to name, only feel. And whatever she felt spiraled through her with a deep and growing hunger.

"Yes," she whispered, leaning against him. The contours

of his body, rugged and sturdy behind her, were infused with the most gentle strength she'd ever known.

After the fire, she never thought she could trust anyone again. Not even a little. But Carter proved her wrong day by day and minute by slow aching minute.

Marly felt suddenly weak in the knees and clutched his arm for balance. She wanted to absorb his strength, this man she had grown to admire and desire, and…

"Carter." She shook her head to stop her mind from racing into uncharted territory.

"Hmm?" He circled her waist, anchoring her body to his. His other hand moved to her breast, first one and then the other, grazing the tips until they pebbled and ached for release from their lacy confines.

She sighed at the sensations racing hot and fast through every nerve ending. "Eight years is a very long time to spend alone," she whispered.

"I'll make it worth the wait."

"You already have."

"Not quite." His hand dipped lower, spanning her flat stomach, and lower still, slipping inside her panties.

Marly cried out when he touched her.

"Too much?"

She shook her head. "Don't stop."

He didn't, but gently pulled her back with him, until he was sitting on the edge of the bed, her bottom pressed against him.

Carter squeezed a dusky nipple, rubbing it between his thumb and forefinger. The sound of her labored breathing made his own pulse race. The air stilled in his lungs as he parted her thighs.

Her panties were already moist, and she writhed against him, her head thrown back to expose the creamy expanse of her neck. He couldn't resist the invitation.

He couldn't resist her.

He bent to taste her neck, his fingers plunging deeper and deeper inside her. He'd never wanted a woman as desperately as he wanted Marly. Never.

She was so real, so genuine. She made him believe in things he'd stopped believing in long ago, made him hope for things he had no business hoping for. She inspired him to dream.

"Carter," she cried, grasping his thighs.

She tumbled over the edge quickly, splintering apart in his arms. It was the most incredible turn-on of his life. He wanted to take her like this, her soft breasts nestled in one hand, her womanhood in the other. But he held himself perfectly still, allowing her the time she needed to regroup.

After a minute, she rose from the bed and turned into his arms. Her eyes appeared slumberous, like a kitten awakening from a nap, and he grinned at the sight.

She smiled back with the expression of a satisfied woman and trailed her fingers along his jawline and over his lips. Then her expression slowly changed, and her hands lowered to his already loosened tie. She pulled it from his collar and discarded it along with her other clothing, then unbuttoned his shirt and added it to the growing pile.

"Take this off, please." She tugged at his undershirt, and he complied. "Thank you."

Her hands splayed over his shoulders, then drifted along his chest, blazing a fiery trail of need in their wake. Her knuckles grazed his belly. His heart skipped a beat when she moved to his belt buckle.

Carter stilled her fingers. "What are you doing?"

"Trying to undress you."

He swallowed. "Just checking."

Her gaze met his, wavered a bit, then steadied. "I want to make love with my husband now, if that's okay."

He nodded, figuring that was him, and this was inevitable, but his voice sounded strangely hoarse when he tried to speak, and the only intelligible words that came out were, "Uh, it's okay with me."

God almighty. He was the president of a regional bank. He served on numerous boards. He was quoted in the newspaper all the time. Could he possibly have said anything more lame?

Carter realized that for the first time in his entire life he felt like a complete idiot.

"Carter? I need you to show me how, okay?"

"How what?"

Marly unbuckled his belt and pulled it free, then lowered her hand to him.

The muscles of his lower body contracted in violent, involuntary response to the contact, and he sucked in a sharp breath.

Marly jerked her hand back. "Was that good or bad?"

"Good," he responded automatically. He almost replaced her hand, but didn't need to because she did it herself.

"Good." She rubbed against him, stroking him through the material of his suit pants. "I want you to show me how to do to you what you do to me."

Streaks of heat shot through his nervous system, until he was shaking like a man in the grip of a fever. "I don't think you need any help."

"But I do. I need you to show me how to make you feel like the entire world is spinning out of control and it's the best ride of your life." She kissed his shoulder, her petal-soft lips working up the side of his neck. When she got to his ear, she whispered, "Show me how to make you feel like you're the most desired man in the entire world, and that I lo— I want you beyond reason."

"Marly," he gasped, as her tongue touched his earlobe, her words threatening to ignite a wildfire that would damn near incinerate him. For a split second there, he'd almost imagined she had said *love*. But that wasn't possible, wasn't part of their agreement, and he told himself he didn't want or need to hear that word anyway.

"Show me."

Carter rose from the bed and drew her hard against him. She molded her body to his in equal measures of surrender and seduction, accepting his mouth with a throaty sigh. He deepened the kiss, savoring the hot, honeyed taste of her and the sweet smell of flowers after a rainfall.

He was acutely aware of the press of her nipples against his chest and the wisp of fabric that still served as a barrier. In one deft move, he remedied the situation.

Had a woman been created expressly for him, she could not have fit his palms any better. He cupped the weight of her breasts and bent to take a nipple into his mouth in slow, sensual possession. Marly moaned and threaded her hands into his hair.

Soon, the remainder of their clothing joined the pile on the floor, her silk-and-lace panties atop his white cotton briefs. He slid his arms around her back, arching her against him, and trailed his mouth down the side of her neck. He felt her pulse beneath his lips, and the furious beat both satisfied and excited him.

He picked her up in his arms, holding her tight against him, then set her down on the bed, covering her body with his. His fingers trailed down her body, grazing the curve of her breast, the dip of her waist, the swell of her hip.

"I need to be inside you, Marly," he whispered, his mouth brushing the sensitive skin beneath her ear. "I need to know you're mine."

Marly thought she would suffocate from the longing he evoked in her, that she would never get enough oxygen into her lungs to satisfy her hammering heart. Never in her life had she been drawn to a man the way she was to Carter. Never had she wanted another man as she wanted him.

"I need you, too," she said, her voice not much more than a strangled plea.

He shifted her beneath him, parting her legs so that he rested against her, the heat and hardness and need of him. She reached down and stroked his length, hesitant when he shuddered.

"That's good, right?"

"Too good." He reached for her hand and moved it to his shoulder. He pulled her legs up around his hips and eased inside her, just a little bit at first.

She winced, and he paused to allow her time to adjust to him. She forced herself to relax.

"Okay?" he whispered. At her nod, he inched a little more. The flexed muscles in his arms looked like bands of steel supporting the weight of his body, and his jaw was taut with strain. "Tell me if it hurts too much."

She bit her lip, not wanting to tell him, not wanting to lie to him. She pressed her head back into the pillows, rationalizing "too much" was a relative term.

Her fingers tightened on his arms as she clung to him. He seemed to know exactly how far to thrust before he retreated, and instinctively, her own body joined in the rhythm. Back and forth, they moved ever so slowly until the last trace of discomfort vanished, and their bodies became as one.

"I'm yours," she murmured in a voice full of wonder and awe.

Carter took a deep breath and then went still, burying his face against her neck, threading his fingers into her silky hair. "I've waited a long time to hear those words."

They savored the moment together before they started to move again, first gently and then not so gently.

The sensations that surged through Carter's body were as foreign to him as another language. Tenderness, need and a raging excitement battled in his veins. He never wanted the feeling to end, knew, even as he grew mindless, that he'd found something he hadn't even known he'd been looking for all his life.

In giving him her body, Marly was giving him so much more. This incredible act was so much more than the slaking of physical desire. He wanted to tell her that, but the words wouldn't come. So he kissed her and touched her and made love to her, telling her without words, telling her in the only way he knew how. Until she cried out, and he joined her. Then together they lay in mindless oblivion.

Afterward, he rolled over, taking Marly with him. She collapsed on his chest, their ragged breaths mingling for a second or an eternity, Carter didn't know which. His fingers skimmed over her back, memorizing the curves and hollows that made up his wife.

His wife. Would the wonder of those words never fail to overwhelm his senses?

"Carter?"

"Hmm?"

"There's something you should know."

"I know." His hand traced lazy circles over her back. "I haven't done this in a while, either."

"I haven't done this...ever."

Carter froze, his eyes boring into hers. "You weren't a virgin, Marly," he said, but he couldn't keep a note of suspicion from creeping into his voice.

She looked away.

"Marly?"

"Hmm?" She trailed her hand down his chest.

He covered it with his to prevent further descent. "Marly, come on. Don't distract me. I have to know."

"I'm glad you couldn't tell."

"Couldn't tell what?"

"You're my first, Carter."

"But what about John?"

Marly's mouth went dry. "John who?"

"Your college boyfriend of two years."

She stiffened, her entire body suddenly rigid. She almost stopped breathing altogether, though her heart clamored a turbulent rhythm she was sure Carter could hear if not feel.

"Hey..." He crooked his head to the side. "Don't look so worried. I'm not going to be jealous of a guy you haven't seen in ten years." When she didn't say anything, he added, "Okay, not too jealous." Silence. "Well, maybe just a little jealous, but it's only natural. I mean, you're my wife now, and I... Marly?"

She exhaled and gave a poor attempt at a halfhearted smile. "I—I wanted to wait for my wedding night. I guess I had a lot of stupid ideals back then, about how it was supposed to be between a man and a woman."

"No." Carter brushed his lips over hers. "They weren't

stupid ideals. They weren't stupid at all." He shifted and nuzzled her neck. "Don't worry. I'll take care of you. I promise."

"I know you will. You're my husband now."

He closed his eyes, but even then, he saw her. Her image burned behind his eyelids every second of every day. She was so beautiful. So very beautiful.

He didn't deserve her. But she was his. And God help him, he would cherish her until the day he died.

"Carter?"

He opened his eyes. While he watched, she kissed her fingertips and brushed them over his lips.

"From this point forward, we forget about the past. We're going to make our own past. Together, beginning now. Deal?"

"Deal."

"You're my first. And you'll be my only."

Something tightened deep in his gut. He didn't want to give it a name, let alone acknowledge that it existed, so he kissed her, instead, then kissed her again. It wasn't long before he wanted her again, just as he knew he would.

Marly gave a throaty chuckle. "Again?" she whispered, trailing her hand down his chest, this time reaching her target.

Yes, he wanted to answer. *Yes, please. Again and again.*

"You're insatiable, Carter. It's uncouth." Eva Ann's quips played like a broken record through his mind. He wanted to tune it out, but the voice spoke the truth.

Only, he wouldn't give in to it.

He had to be strong. His future with Marly depended on his willpower. Their pasts were dead and buried, but he had to make sure he didn't resurrect his own.

He caught Marly's hand and kissed her one last time. "Not tonight, sweetheart. You're still tender. I don't want to hurt you."

She acquiesced with a sigh, and he drew her closer, tucking her head under his chin. She fell asleep within minutes, stirring a few times in the night, while he lay as rigid as a board, afraid that at any moment, he would cross the line between desire and something more.

He couldn't let that happen, couldn't open himself up to that kind of pain again. Not with Marly. Certainly not with Marly.

From the window seat in the kitchen, Marly watched the sunrise in the meadow announce the arrival of a new day. Her first day as Marly King. Last night, Carter had helped create her—another name, another identity, but oh, so different this time, like a brand-new pair of shoes made just for her, instead of someone else's she'd had to borrow.

Maybe it wouldn't hurt so badly to break into these shoes. And maybe, in time, they would fit so well that no one would remember the loaners.

No one, except for her.

She *had* to remember. She could never again forget, as she'd done last night. Serendipity had a nasty habit of running out when least expected.

"Marly, have you seen my briefcase?" Carter called from down the hall.

She frowned, then rose from the window seat. "I think you left it in the car. Want me to check?"

"Could you?"

"Just a second." Dressed in a cotton nightshirt, she slipped outside and scurried across the driveway in bare feet. "Yes, it's there," she confirmed, closing the door behind her.

Two seconds later he yelled, "Do you know where I left my shoes from yesterday?"

"Don't you have at least fifty other pairs?" she teased, reaching for the phone to call Tyler.

"Yeah, but these are my favorite."

"Try the floor on my side of the bed."

"Found them," he bellowed. "What about—"

"Your wallet's probably still in your jacket. I hung it up in your closet."

"Thank you."

After she'd finished talking to Tyler, she placed the receiver in Carter's outstretched hand.

"Hey, ace. How's it going? Well, of course we're coming to see you this weekend. Is there anything you want us to bring?"

Marly shot Carter a warning look.

He straightened his tie and turned his back on her, twisting the cord around his finger. "What kind of books?"

"Carter…"

He glanced her way. "Storybooks for Miss Marly to read? Sure, I think we can manage that. Anything else? No? Okay, well, we'll see you soon." Carter hung up the phone and placed a finger over Marly's lips before she could say anything. "He wants you to read him some stories this weekend."

She swatted at his hand but grinned despite herself. "I heard. Carter, I swear. I'm going to have to keep a close eye on you, or you'll end up spoiling our kids rotten. I can just hear it. 'So, Janie, what do you want for your birthday this year? A horse? But Daddy already got you a horse last year. How about a new car?'"

"Wrong." Carter tugged at her waist, bringing her flush against his chest.

She stiffened, then relaxed. He had a way of doing that to her, making her forget all the reasons she needed to keep her distance, making her feel safe with him, making her wonder if maybe one day, she could tell him the truth…

"Daddy—" he repeated the word with masculine pride "—is going to foster a strong work ethic, don't you worry."

"Well, I'm glad to hear that."

"But you'd better believe little Janie's getting ice cream any time she falls off her horse." He raised his eyebrows with a devilish grin that made Marly go weak in the knees.

She laid a palm against his cheek. "You're going to make a wonderful father, Carter. I just know it."

His eyes darkened, and he gripped her closer. "That means a lot coming from you."

She trembled against him. "I mean it."

"Thank you." He dipped his head then, and his lips lingered over hers. "Have I ever told you how good you taste in the morning?"

"No…"

"Do you want me to stop?"

"No, but you're going to miss your board meeting if you don't get out of here soon."

"I know. I'm going." But he only took another step forward and nuzzled her neck.

"I suppose I should tell you, before you go…oh, hey…umm, that's nice…." She tilted her head to the side to allow him better access.

"Tell me what?" He nibbled a path to her ear.

"I, um, don't really like the name Janie."

"You don't say." He pulled back and stroked her hair, his eyes meaningful with his intent.

"Nope." She swallowed, her gaze on his descending lips.

"Thanks for telling me," he mumbled before he tipped her head back and closed his mouth over hers.

She opened eagerly for him, holding on to his shoulders with both hands, surrendering to senses only he could evoke.

Every time he touched her, an ache struck her belly and quivered through her nerves. Every time he kissed her she couldn't think for the rippling in her limbs or the heat pooling between her legs. When they made love, she forgot about their arrangement, about the forces that had brought them together, about the shared goal that would keep them together. How easy it would have been to let go.

So easy.

Carter moved more intimately against her, his mouth caressing the side of her neck. She hadn't imagined his desire for her last night—she could feel it even now, when he kissed her. But beneath her hands, the hard muscles of his back bunched as though he were restraining himself, as though he knew exactly how far he could go and when he had to pull back.

Maybe it was his restraint that urged her to try to blur his boundaries, to shift against him in greater invitation and brush her breasts against his chest. Maybe it was his answering moan that made her rub her hips against him, shivering when he clutched at her bottom through the thin nightshirt.

Or maybe it was the overwhelming desire to break through his barriers before he could penetrate hers.

She knew the instant Carter realized she wasn't wearing underwear. He let out a guttural sound as his hands slid under her nightshirt, wandering everywhere, dancing over her skin. Shards of heat lanced through her as his mouth slipped over her jaw, along the column of her neck and over her throat.

"Marly." He uttered her name in a ragged voice. "Where did you learn to do this?" And then, "Forget it. I don't want to know."

She remembered so well the feel his body wrapped around hers. She remembered losing herself in the depths of his hazel eyes, reveling in his need for her before her own needs stole the last of her reserve.

"I learned from you." She lifted her leg as he stroked her thigh and hooked it around his waist. "From wanting you."

All at once, Carter grabbed her tight and pressed her to him, burying his face in the curve of her neck.

He was losing it, but so was she. What made her think that she could crack the walls of his control without shattering her own? She wanted him. Again. Badly.

She reached for his belt, but he covered her hands.

"No, Marly," he told her. "No time."

She pushed his hands aside and continued her task. "Forget time. You started this."

He chuckled. "Why, Mrs. King. I never would have taken you for a delinquent. Tell me, what else are you keeping from me?"

Marly's hands froze in the act of tugging down his pants, and her leg slid down his thigh. His words hit home, to the hidden darkness in her soul, and she turned her head, unable to meet his gaze. Would he see the lies and deception in her eyes?

"Hey, why the long face?" Carter brushed his hand over

her hair. "This ain't no high-society boy you married. I like it when you talk dirty to me."

"It's not that…it's…"

"What?" He lifted her face and kissed her slowly, leisurely, sliding his tongue inside her mouth, tasting her, soothing her, once again arousing her to a fevered pitch as his hands roamed her body.

His touch filled her with liquid heat, made her feel whole, like a real woman, instead of the mere shell of one. He made her ache to believe again…in miracles and second chances…in the healing power of love. Maybe, just maybe…

If Carter could want her this much, if he could make love to her with such fierce tenderness, maybe one day he *could* learn to love her. And maybe someday, if he grew to love her enough, she could confide in him. And then, just maybe, he might find it in his heart to forgive her.

Then again, maybe the earth could just open up now and spare them both the eventual disillusionment.

Marly lifted her shoulder and said the only words she could, the words of a woman used to living on borrowed time: "I want you, Carter. Stay and make love with me?"

Carter thought about her question for a full nanosecond before answering with all the wit and charm and seduction he could muster, "You bet."

But Marly didn't seem put off in the least as she freed the button on his suit pants and pushed them down, along with his briefs. His breath caught in the back of his throat as she restlessly stroked his bottom and the backs of his thighs, groping beneath his shirttails to the hollow of his spine and around to his belly before dipping lower.

When she wrapped her hands around him, he closed his eyes and swore softly. For the first time in his married life, he felt his wife needed him almost as much as he needed her.

"The bedroom?" he managed to choke out.

"No time."

It pleased him to know Marly's desire stretched beyond the confines of propriety, that unlike Eva Ann, she didn't require a bed in a darkened room. She pleased him in so many ways—too many, but he couldn't dwell on that now.

Carter bent down and gathered her in his arms until she straddled him. Positioning himself, he lowered her hips until she eased around him, wrapping him in her tight warmth, her back to the wall. He closed his eyes and savored the moment.

Later, he would kick himself. Later, he would call himself every name in the book. Later, he would devise Plan B. But right now, he would have her. Right now, he would feast on her. Right now, he would love her.

When she started to move, he bit back a groan and drove into the heat of her. Together they joined with urgent hunger and lost control. They weren't sleek or sophisticated. They weren't charming or refined. They were artless, raw and primitive.

And yet as he guided her hips, Carter was every bit aware of the woman in his arms. *His Marly.* He was attuned to her needs, alert to the patterns of her body. He knew when to reach between their bodies, knew exactly how to stoke her fire, knew when she could take no more.

"Carter?" She started to tremble, her thighs squeezing his hips.

"I've got you, Marly. Just let go. Trust me," he whispered. "Let go."

With a cry, she clutched his back and arched against him. He held her as her body convulsed around him, and then with one violent thrust he joined her, gripping her hips with an anguished moan.

The room swam around him. Colors danced like sunlight filtering through cut crystal. Carter pivoted on his heel, trading places with Marly to sink against the wall. All energy sapped, he slid down his back, easing their bodies to the floor.

For long moments, he couldn't move, couldn't think, couldn't speak. He'd gone over the edge, into oblivion, the vast unknown. And yet with Marly, it felt strangely like coming home.

"That was incredible," Marly mumbled against his shoulder sometime later. "I suppose you want me to get off you now, huh?"

"No, don't move." He didn't want to open his eyes; didn't want to let go of her, to leave the warmth of her body for even a minute.

"Don't think I want to, but it's time for you to shake a leg, Mr. President."

"Damn. The board meeting." Carter raked a hand through his hair.

"Yeah, the board meeting." Marly pulled away to straighten his tie. She wore a content, satisfied smile, with a mischievous sparkle in her eyes. "How soon we forget."

He hadn't forgotten. That was the problem. He remembered all too well, where he'd gone wrong, and what factors had contributed to the demise of his first marriage.

Carter stared at the agenda in front of him, twisting his Cross pen open and closed as he half listened to the ongoing debate before the board.

"Carter, what do you think?" the CEO asked.

He shrugged and voiced the thought that had been eating at him all morning. "I think we've been going about it all wrong."

A flurry of murmurs erupted before one of the board members piped up, "Would you care to clarify your point, Mr. King?"

"Gladly. Our strategy's off." Carter went down the agenda, ticking off each point as he challenged its validity. "In summary," he said when he had finished, "I see this proposed acquisition as a quick fix. We've got a wad of cash burning a hole in our pocket, so we feel like buying something pretty and showing it off, something that will make us look good to our shareholders, at least in the short run.

"But if we expect to build shareholder value, we need to position ourselves to be competitive not just into the next fiscal year, but into the next century. We have to look long term, and that means merging—not acquiring."

Silence filled the boardroom. Twelve pairs of eyes stared at him, all the way down the length of the mahogany table. Finally, the CEO cleared his throat. "You've obviously given this a great deal of thought."

"I have," he realized. It had all begun the moment Marly agreed to marry him.

An acquisition, a quick fix—that's what Eva Ann had been. A dazzling trinket for a young man climbing up the corporate ladder. He'd been too young back then to see how high the ladder was, too concerned in his youth with reaching the next rung to worry about life at the top, too shallow to realize his expensive diamond was really cubic zirconia.

By the time he'd reached the top, he had the insight to know what he needed to survive in the long run. But even then, he'd gone about it all wrong in the beginning. He'd viewed his marriage to Marly as another acquisition, albeit a smarter one, but it wasn't an acquisition at all, in any form. He realized that now. It was a merger. And Marly was his true diamond in the rough.

The board meeting continued for another two hours, during which the members voted unanimously to postpone the acquisition until they could further explore other options.

For the rest of the day, Carter considered his own options while he sifted through heaps of never-ending work as if on autopilot. He tried not to think about Marly, not to remember how she looked when she slept in his arms, not to replay the events of last night and this morning over and over in his mind. It didn't work.

At six-thirty, he got up from his desk, went into the private bathroom and splashed cold water onto his face for two minutes straight. When he'd finished, he stared at his reflection in the mirror and shook his head in disgust.

"It wasn't supposed to be like this, buddy," he said to himself. "You weren't supposed to want her every second of every day."

He didn't know how it had happened, how he'd arrived at this sorry state, but here he was.

"You people are all the same. All you know how to do is breed."

Maybe Eva Ann was right. Maybe his libido was some sort of genetic defect, common among the lower classes. Marly didn't seem to mind.

No, Carter King had done his research this time, found himself the perfect woman, and in doing so, landed himself in the sorriest catch-22 of his life.

He wanted like hell to believe in forever, but experience had taught him forever took two, not just one willing party. If Marly ever stopped trying, if she ever gave up, if she left him…he didn't know what he would do.

Eva Ann had ripped his heart out, but Marly…if things progressed in the direction they were headed, Marly would have the power to shred his soul.

Gee, no big deal there. *Just his soul.* Carter gulped and loosened his tie.

So about Plan B… What he needed was some distance—and fast. Just enough to regain his equilibrium, so he could start thinking with his head again.

A few minutes before seven, his private line rang, and he answered, fully expecting to hear Marly's voice. But it was the private investigator, instead.

"Does the name Billy Ray Cameron ring any bells?" the P.I. asked.

"Unfortunately so."

"He's the one—been asking questions about your wife."

Carter frowned. "What kind of questions?"

"Where she's from and if she's got any kin."

He gripped the receiver even tighter. That lowdown scumbag, that two-bit hood, that bastard Billy Ray Cameron was looking to threaten Marly's family. *His wife's family.* Carter knew her parents were dead, but he didn't know about any distant relatives.

"Stay two steps ahead of him if you can," he ordered.

''Whatever he finds out, I want to know before him. And Mike, retrace everything we've got. Just as a precaution.'' He hung up the phone, and for a split second, he could have sworn he saw red.

Chapter 14

Marly spent the morning getting the center back up to speed and planning for the future. When the *Federal Register* arrived, she circled three grants and began writing preliminary proposals. The nutritionist stopped by, and they planned menus for the upcoming months.

In the afternoon, Marly phoned in an order for some new art supplies and arranged transportation for some local field trips. Her new name rolled off her tongue with such ease it brought a smile to her face.

Betsy Jean came running into her office, purple hair ribbons flying behind her. "Miss Marly. Is it true? Robbie says you got married."

"Yes, it's true. See my rings." She displayed the bands on her finger.

"Wow. Pretty." Betsy Jean beamed. "You gonna have a baby now?"

Marly laughed and hugged the little girl. "Maybe, honey. Maybe."

That evening, Marly found herself sneaking glances at Carter when he wasn't looking. She liked to watch him unawares, when his guard lowered and the man beneath the calm, professional exterior surfaced. She would catch certain expressions on his face—thoughtful, sometimes even melancholy—and wonder what went on in his mind.

But she couldn't access his inner world without risking his access to hers, and with each passing day, Marly grew more certain Carter would never forgive her dishonesty if he ever found out the truth.

"Marly?"

"Hmm?"

"I asked how your day was."

"Oh." Marly lifted her gaze from the salad she was tossing. "Sorry. I was daydreaming. Fine—my day was fine. And yours?"

"Okay. Marly, there's something I have to ask you."

"What?" She carried two wooden bowls of salad to the kitchen table and turned, trying to read Carter's expression.

"It's about your family."

"What about them?"

"I know your parents are dead, but do you have any distant relatives?"

"None that I'm aware of."

Was it mere curiosity that brought on the question, or was he suspicious for some reason? He had been oddly quiet since she got home, insisting he didn't need any help preparing their dinner, and she'd been content just to watch him. But now, she started to wonder if his pensive expression didn't indicate something out of the ordinary.

"Why do you ask?"

Carter pulled off his already loosened tie. "We have to talk about something."

"Something serious?"

He scooped two helpings of shepherd's pie onto their plates, along with two corn-bread muffins from the cooling rack, before answering, "Yeah."

She dropped her fork, and it clanked against a plate. She

went to retrieve it and realized her hand was shaking. "What is it?" she asked, folding her arms.

"I think you're going to want to sit down for this." He put their plates on the table and pulled out her chair.

Did he know something, something she didn't know? Something she had contradicted? Maybe Marly Alcott had estranged relatives?

"Carter, you're scaring me. Please, tell me what's wrong."

"Nothing to be scared about, not yet." He waited until she sat down, then took his own seat beside her. "Remember the P.I. I hired for your background check?"

She nodded and felt the color drain from her face.

"Well, he found out Billy Ray Cameron's checking up on your family."

She pushed her chair back from the table. Once on her feet, she started pacing. "Wh-what exactly did he find out?"

Carter stood, too, and placed a hand on her arm. "Nothing, so far. Nothing that isn't public record. Where you're from, where you went to school, your employment history. But when I heard he was looking for relatives—"

"My parents are both dead. I have no other relatives."

"That's why I asked."

"Carter, why?" Marly tipped her head back and stared at the ceiling. "Why is he doing this?" Her voice wavered, and Carter gathered her into his arms. She sagged against him, more tired than she had felt in a long, long time.

"Because he's a thug. And that's what thugs do. They find your weak spot, and they exploit it."

"Oh, God." She pulled back and stared into Carter's eyes. "Don't you see what this means? My kids, my center, you.... You're all in danger because of me."

"Now, wait just a minute. Let's not forget that you have the upper hand here."

She shook her head, burying her face against his shirt. "If I have the upper hand, why do I feel like some sort of puppet?"

Carter cleared his throat. "Mrs. King, if you would look up

for just a moment." When she complied, he continued, "You are the strongest woman I have ever known, and I mean that. I seriously doubt you could ever be anyone's puppet. Don't let Billy Ray Cameron get away with this." He said the words slowly, with deliberate enunciation. "Please, sweetheart. Just say the word. If you go to the police, you can crush him with your pinkie."

"Oh, Carter. I wish it were that simple."

"It may not be simple, but it's reality. That bastard isn't going to touch one precious hair on your head, Marly. I won't let him. I swear it."

"I believe you," she whispered, lifting her face to stare up into Carter's. He was a strong, powerful man, but he was also compassionate, honest and fiercely loyal. He expected the truth from his wife, and he deserved nothing less.

How she wanted to tell him. It was ripping her apart to look into his eyes day after day and to have to lie to him. She trusted him on so many levels, yet she couldn't trust him with the truth of her identity. To do so would have proved the ultimate test of faith, but Marly's faith had been tested enough for one lifetime. She wasn't a cat with eight more lives to spare.

She watched a myriad of emotions flicker across Carter's face before he chased them all away. She could sense him abandoning some resolve and knew he was going kiss her. She rose on her tiptoes to meet his lips, threading her hands through his hair as she held him to her, savoring his touch, his taste and everything that was Carter.

She sensed tension in his muscles, taut beneath her fingertips, but he started to loosen up gradually as she kissed him long and deep. And then his hands were moving, first meandering and then with purpose, rubbing her arms, her back, her bottom.

Every place he touched fueled a pulsating need inside her. It grew and grew, until she literally ached inside, as if her body were crying out for him, pleading for him, yearning for him to fill her and make her whole again.

What had Carter awakened in her? What switch had he flipped that made her want him so desperately? Whenever she kissed him, she forgot herself. She lost herself in him.

"Marly," Carter groaned, and she could not mistake the agony in his voice.

Did the same feelings rivet through his body, if not his heart? And could she get to one from another? When he held her in his arms and he touched her the way he was doing now, she almost believed she could do anything.

"Marly, we have to stop. Dinner—" He broke off with an expletive as she rubbed against him.

"What about dinner?"

Carter closed his eyes and swallowed, setting her away. "It's getting cold."

Marly took in the wonderful spread on the table before her. It was the kind of simple meal that completed the homey setting she'd craved as a young girl. The woman she'd become cherished it almost as much as she cherished the man who had created it. Almost. Because at that moment, all Marly could think about was clearing a spot on the table large enough for her to seduce him.

She pushed her plate to the side.

Carter's eyes darkened.

She moistened her lips and pushed aside her salad bowl.

He swore—again—then shoved a hand through his hair and turned from her. "I—uh, I think I'd better eat my dinner in the study."

"What?" His words penetrated her passion-filled haze.

"Work," Carter said without looking at her. "I have work to do. Lots. Big project. Potential merger. Preparation."

"Tonight?"

"Yeah." He swooped up his plate and salad bowl, balancing them on his arm as he reached for his glass. "I won't make this a routine. I promise. I just need to get away, just this once. I mean, I have a lot of work to do…to catch up on…before the night's over…for tomorrow, you know."

She didn't know what to say, and so she just nodded and

watched him gather everything. The plate and bowl clanked against each other, and she couldn't mistake the flash of regret in his eyes before he turned.

''Your dinner's getting cold, Mrs. King. You'd better eat soon.''

''I will.'' She slumped into her chair, staring at the table now set for one and telling herself that it was best, that she needed some distance to regain her perspective. But it didn't help. Nothing would. She was too far gone.

Carter pulled his spoon back and flung a wad of mashed potatoes into the fireplace. So much for willpower. For the third night in a row, he was eating his dinner in the study. He didn't like it, and he knew Marly didn't like it. But man, the way she looked at him….

Every time he thought he had things under control, one look. That was all it took before he was wanting her all over again—wanting, needing, craving. And when he kissed her, she was so damn responsive. So unlike Eva Ann. So unlike any woman he'd ever known.

Three nights' abstinence hadn't done a thing for his equilibrium, so until he could get a grip, there was no other way. No man with half a brain would allow a woman this much control over him.

Still, he hated for Marly to feel as if he were ignoring her. If only he could strike some sort of balance—and soon.

At lunch that day, he'd foregone his usual sandwich-at-his-desk and opted, instead, to walk down to the library. Didn't take long for him to find the information he wanted: the average married couple made love once a week.

Once. He could do that. Couldn't he?

He flipped open his Franklin Planner and circled last Monday. Today was Thursday. Damn. Four more days.

''Carter?'' Marly tapped the door before she came in.

''Hey.'' He shut the leather-bound planner and shoved it aside, feeling as though he'd been caught reading some nudey magazine.

"How's it coming?" she asked from the door.

"Fine, fine. You?"

"Okay, I guess. Can I get you anything?"

"No, thanks."

"I loved your raspberry cobbler."

"Did you? Great. Look, I've got a lot—"

"I know. I'm going."

"Marly, wait." He rubbed his jaw in an effort to keep from clenching it. "I'm really sorry about this. I promise, it won't be much longer."

She lifted her shoulder in a delicate shrug. "It's okay. I understand. I'd rather have you home, at least, instead of at the office."

Carter smiled as she left, and wondered if he looked as much the besotted fool as he felt.

Marly didn't look into the mirror as she brushed her teeth and washed her face. She didn't want to see what the rest of the world saw when they looked at her, didn't want to see what her husband saw when he evaded her touch, when he excused himself to his study each night, when he waited until he thought she was asleep before he came to bed.

She'd never thought herself a shallow woman—until now.

For the first time in eight years, she mourned for the face she'd lost, for the beauty that would never again be hers. She turned off the bathroom light and squeezed her eyes shut against silent tears of vanity.

It was past midnight, and Carter still hadn't come to bed, just like the past three nights. Of course, he'd said he had work to do, and it wasn't that she didn't believe him. She just wasn't entirely sure. And the guilt of that uncertainty ate at her.

Was she an awful and terrible, self-absorbed person for doubting him? Or was she intuitive in sensing that her husband was using any excuse to avoid her, to avoid intimacy with her? A man who had married her for the explicit purpose of having children, and now he couldn't bring himself to sleep with her? It didn't make sense.

She hadn't mistaken his desire. She hadn't!

Marly climbed onto the four-poster and pulled the covers over her. Her fingertips traced the dent in the pillow where Carter's head had been last night.

On impulse, she sat up and switched her pillow with his. Pulling it close, she inhaled his scent, seeking and finding the comfort she needed to contemplate her decision regarding Billy Ray.

Carter was right. She needed to go to the police. And she would. It was the right thing to do.

After the weekend. After she saw Tyler. After she reassured herself that she wasn't making the biggest mistake of her life.

She and Carter planned to leave for the mountains after work the following evening. She would tell Carter her decision on their drive. That way, she couldn't chicken out come Monday.

She'd tossed and turned most of the night, unable to stop thinking about what unknown facts Billy Ray had discovered about Marly Alcott. For that matter, she wondered again what Carter knew that she didn't.

Unanswered questions had nagged at her subconscious from the time Carter had brought up the subject of John, the college boyfriend, on their wedding night. She'd felt uneasy ever since, as if waiting for the next inevitable blunder, the one that would force her hand.

What would happen then? Would her treachery snowball the longer time passed, as Carter's deception had with Eva Ann? Would Carter never forgive her?

She must have fallen asleep eventually, because she didn't realize when Carter came to bed, nor when he woke up, but there was a dent in the pillow next to hers to suggest he'd been there and a note on the bedside table confirming their plans to visit Tyler.

That evening, Marly arrived home before Carter. She'd taken the Caravan to work that day and already had it fueled for their trip. She made a few sandwiches, cut up some raw veggies and tossed the plastic bags of food into an ice-filled cooler, along with some sodas. After grabbing her overnight bag, she went to load the Caravan. But when she slid open the side door of the vehicle, a cold, peculiar sensation crawled up her spine.

Marly's eyes widened, and she spun around.

Nothing. Just the stillness of the garage. She took a deep breath.

That made twice today. Twice that she'd felt that odd sense of foreboding. The first time was at her center, just before she'd left. She'd forgotten an important computer disk and run back to her office. Upon returning, she'd climbed into the driver's side and immediately frozen with a sick sense of apprehension. Only, she didn't know why. The parking lot was deserted.

In the stillness of the garage, she gave a nervous laugh. "You're being melodramatic, Hilary." With lightning speed, she clamped a hand over her mouth. Her heart racing ninety-miles an hour, she slammed the side door of the Caravan shut and ran into the house.

That background check was wreaking havoc with her mind. She wanted to know what information it contained, and she wanted to know right now. She cursed herself for not asking Carter before. Suddenly, it seemed imperative that she find out right away. Besides an obvious blunder on her part, she had to know if there was anything—anything at all—that could link her true identity with Marly's.

With shaking fingers, she dialed Carter's office.

"Carter King."

"Carter, it's Marly."

"Hey, just wrapping things up. Should be out of here in the next five minutes. You need anything from the store?"

"No. I packed some sandwiches. I—everything's ready. It's just—"

"Marly, are you okay?"

"No—I mean, yes." She slid down the wall until she was

sitting on the floor. She gripped the receiver in both hands. "Carter, that background check. The one you had done on me. Do you still have it?"

"Well, yes…"

"Where is it?"

"My desk in the study. The file drawer. You sure you're okay?"

"Yeah, fine. Come home now, okay? I want to hit the road before dark."

"I'm on my way."

In the study, Marly pulled open Carter's file drawer and thumbed through the file tabs.

Auto, Banking, Horses, Investments, Leisure, Medical, Mortgages, Newspaper, Personal Correspondence, Travel, Utilities. The man had a file tab for everything. Everything but *Background Checks.* Of course, it couldn't be that easy. Why hadn't she thought to ask him exactly where he'd filed it?

Marly rifled through *Leisure* and then through *Society,* where she found a newspaper clipping of a wedding announcement. "Eva Ann Putnam weds Roger Thornton IV." She stared at the picture of Carter's ex-wife. She had wide-set eyes and a coy smile. She was beautiful, the kind of woman who made men stop and take notice.

Carter had obviously stopped and taken notice. But he hadn't fallen in love with her. Just what kind of woman did it take to steal Carter King's heart?

Marly frowned and replaced the clipping, turning back to the hanging folders.

Cinderella Candidates. The file tab caught her eye. Curious, she reached for it.

Carter reached for the phone and answered his inside line. "Carter King."

"Mr. King," came his secretary's voice on the other end. "There's a Mike Rodgers here to see you. I can ask him to come back—"

"No, send him in. Please." He shot to his feet.

When the P.I. entered, he carried a large, yellow envelope.

The men exchanged greetings and shook hands before Carter closed the door. He indicated two chairs in the sitting area. "Something new?" he asked, eyeing the thin envelope.

"Yeah." The usually nonchalant P.I. appeared nervous for the first time, which made Carter nervous in turn.

"What is it?"

"As you instructed, I retraced all prior steps to make sure we didn't miss anything. If you remember, my initial report indicated Miss Alcott had undergone reconstructive surgery approximately eight years ago."

"Right. After the fire. She sustained numerous injuries."

The P.I. nodded. "Like you, I assumed the reconstructive surgery was in conjunction with her other injuries from the fire. That's why I didn't probe any deeper at the time."

"But now you have?"

"Yes, I have."

"And what have you found?"

"This." The P.I. opened the envelope and extracted a piece of cardboard. Lying flat on the cardboard were two black-and-white photographs. He handed the first to Carter. The woman who stared back could have been a model for a cosmetics ad in a fashion magazine. She had high cheekbones, a pert nose, pale eyes fringed with long lashes and well-shaped lips that didn't smile. Her mouth...there was something familiar about her mouth....

Carter didn't know what to make of it. "Who is this?"

"That's the 'before' photograph of the woman who came in for reconstructive surgery under the name of Marly Alcott."

He frowned. She didn't look anything like Marly. Maybe there was a slight resemblance to the photos taken before the fire. But this woman's face didn't have any cuts or abrasions, no burn scars like the ones on Marly's hands. Nothing that would indicate surgery was required.

"This isn't Marly," he said, shaking his head. "There's a resemblance, but it isn't her."

The P.I. handed him a second photograph. "Here's the 'after.'"

"That's her." Carter recognized his wife right away, then scowled, his gaze shifting from the 'before' to the 'after,' and back again. "The pictures must have gotten mixed up. This one's probably from someone else's file." He held up the 'before' shot.

The P.I. took a deep breath, then shook his head slowly. "I thought the same thing myself…at first. But there's no mix-up, at least not with the photographs."

"I'm not sure I understand what you're saying, Mike."

"I'm not exactly sure I understand, either, sir. But what these photos suggest is that whoever you've married, she isn't Marly Alcott."

Chapter 15

Carter came home to find his wife climbing into the Caravan. He stopped and stared at her. A pounding rhythm reverberated through his eardrums, sounding as though gigantic thunderclouds were colliding inside his head.

The blue of her jeans, the green of the Caravan and the strawberry blonde of her hair swirled together before his eyes. He could almost smell the sweet scent of her on the wind and feel the future narrowing before him like a tunnel.

Stop. It's not what you think. Nothing has changed.

The P.I. had obviously screwed up, mixed up the photographs and spewed some half-baked conclusions. In a matter of seconds, Marly would clear up the whole thing.

All Carter had to do was show her the photographs and tell her the P.I.'s crazy innuendo. Then they'd both have a good laugh and take off for Asheville. And soon, he would forget all about the uneasiness in the pit of his stomach.

"Hey, Marly," he called, surprised by the sudden lump in his throat. Why did his mind have to keep zeroing in on trivial details like her aversion to cameras, her nerves at the charity ball, her refusal to publicize their wedding or her self-proclaimed low profile? None of that had mattered before. Why did it matter now, just because some stupid P.I. had mixed up some ancient photographs?

Never mind that the P.I. was one of the best in the country, that he'd come highly recommended. Even the best made mistakes, and this was obviously one of them.

Marly turned then, and he noticed her eyes were red. "I left a note for you," she said, a funny catch in her voice.

He told himself he had no justifiable reason to doubt his wife's integrity. It wasn't as though she didn't know how he felt about secrets in a marriage, didn't know why he felt the way he did. She did. And if there was something to tell him—something this huge—surely she would have done it by now. She'd had plenty of opportunities, especially after he'd gone and spilled his guts to her.

So what kind of husband did that make him?

The kind who had the entire drive to Asheville to grovel. The kind who needed closure before that, for his own peace of mind.

"There's something I want to show you," he said, removing the photographs from the envelope. "Before we leave."

She closed the door, turned on the ignition and lowered the window. He handed her the photos, convinced he would soon have a rational explanation for everything.

Hadn't she trusted him with the truth about Billy Ray, as if that wasn't the granddaddy of all secrets?

The color drained from Marly's face, and tears sprang to her eyes. "Where?" Her voice held a note of hysteria. "Where did you get these?"

"From the P.I.," he answered, the rising bile in his throat threatening to choke him.

Her hands trembled as she tore the photographs to shreds with quick, jerky motions. "The negatives?"

"I don't have them."

"Get them. Please, Carter. Get them for me."

He took a step toward her. "Tell me what's going on, Marly."

She shook her head, and a cascade of tears spilled down her cheeks. "What did the P.I. tell you?"

Carter swallowed, each word slicing through his insides like a razor. "That you aren't Marly Alcott."

Her wide blue eyes turned to him. "And you believe him?"

"I don't know what to believe. That's why I'm asking you."

She opened her mouth as if to respond, then closed it again. Lifting a hand in appeal, she whispered, "I wanted to tell you, Carter. So many times, but I...I couldn't."

"Tell me now, Marly. Tell me it's just a mix-up."

"I can't." She bowed her head. "I can't lie to you anymore."

He felt ill. He'd wanted the P.I. to be wrong, wanted Marly to prove him wrong. Instead, he'd found his own wife was...what? Another person? That she'd married him, slept beside him, made love with him, all under false pretenses?

He took a deep breath, hoping for calm, for restraint, but finding it impossible. "Who the hell are you?" he demanded.

"Not like this, Carter. I can't tell you like this."

"How, then? With candles and soft music to break it to me gently?" He turned his gaze to the house, squinting into the distance as he tried to process the past hour of his life, to make sense of the chaos. His jaw felt stiff, and his temples throbbed in undeniable agony. "Are you going to tell me you're someone else's wife?"

She gasped and had the decency to look shocked.

"What do you expect me to think?" he shouted, bracing his hands on the door.

She didn't even flinch at his harsh words. Instead, she yelled back, "I expect you to think I had a good reason to do this—" Her voice broke, pitiful with accusation. "A damn good reason to give up my entire life and to live in someone else's. It's not exactly a commonplace occurrence."

"So explain it to me." He gripped the edge of the window. "Make me understand."

She shook her head, swiping at her tears. "When I get back. I have to go now."

"I'm going with you."

"No, please." She clutched the steering wheel with both hands, staring straight ahead. "I need some time alone, to think. Without distractions. I've decided to testify against Billy Ray."

"Great." Carter shoved a rough hand through his hair. "And when were you planning on telling me about this?"

"When you got home."

"I see," he said, but he didn't. He didn't see at all. He had no idea what in the hell was going on. Worse, he had no idea how to go about finding out. "My God, what happened between our last phone call and now?"

She shrugged as silent tears checkered down her face. "Reality bit us in the butt." Then she added in a soft voice, full of such sadness it tore at his gut, "You said you liked it when I talked dirty."

They both turned then. Their gazes met and held. If misery could have been painted, he imagined they would have made twin portraits.

He wanted to reach through the window and grab her, to throttle some answers out of her, to demand an explanation, to hold her close and never let go. He'd coerced this woman into his life, never intending to let her slip past his defenses. But she had, and now his need for her was crippling, like a cruel blow at the back of his knees.

In her eyes, he saw anguish, not fear. And for some reason, a cold, dismal knot coiled in his belly. Whatever inner battle waged behind those eyes, it evidently surpassed the likes of Billy Ray. That realization did nothing for his confusion, served only to heighten his uneasiness, thereby taking some of the edge off his anger.

He had no idea what lurked beneath the murky waters, only an innate suspicion that he'd need a big stick to test the depths.

"I'll be back Sunday night," she said softly.

He wanted to believe her, but like a photo negative, she'd reversed his entire world. He no longer knew if her leaving was a bad thing or a good thing.

"Drive carefully," he said, his voice sounding as tight as his throat felt.

He watched her leave, and for a long time stood rooted to the same spot in the garage. A strange, aching heaviness weighed in his chest, and he couldn't bring himself to go inside the house. When he finally did, his gaze searched the kitchen for her note.

As his mama had said, Carter always had been one to sniff the milk just to make sure it was really sour.

The note took the form of a yellow sticky paper, affixed to a hanging folder. A very familiar hanging folder.

Cinderella Candidates.

The message, printed in small, neat script read: "Dear Carter, your plain-Jane wife has gone to Asheville. Be back Sunday." She hadn't bothered to sign it.

Carter crumpled the note in his fist and flung the wad across the room with a vicious oath.

He would never forgive her. If ever there had been a glimmer of hope, it was gone now. Maybe if he'd loved her, she would have stood a chance, but he didn't, and he never would. His file had proved that. There, she'd seen the reasons Carter had married her methodically enumerated—on a spreadsheet, no less—right up to his specification of a plain-Jane wife.

Carter King, always the man with the plan.

No wonder he'd avoided her recently. He'd never been attracted to her, only faked it. Twice, in case he hadn't impregnated her on the first try, no doubt.

So why the hurt, why the outrage, when she'd gone into their arrangement knowing full well what to expect? Hadn't she agreed to serve as his incubator? A plain-Jane incubator who understood poverty because of her own humble upbringing.

"Well, hallelujah! Give the boy a bright, shiny gold star for finding such a perfect fit for his model. Too bad Hilary Steele had to surface and rip it off your forehead." She bit her lip, gasping as she drew blood.

Grabbing a tissue, she turned on the overhead light and used the rearview mirror to blot the dots of red. She'd turned off the light and refocused on the road, when a sudden chill crawled up the back of her neck.

Her gaze flew again to the rearview mirror. Nothing. Just inky darkness.

Since she'd left the interstate, she hadn't seen the headlights of another vehicle for miles. Yet, for some unknown reason, she couldn't shake the disquieting feeling that someone was watching her.

Nerves.

After all, it wasn't every day that a woman found out that the man who had made love to her with such aching intensity had feigned every touch, every kiss, every word of passion.

Remorse and humiliation flooded Marly's cheeks. Damn but she'd bought his act for a while there. He'd been so blasted convincing in his role as the good husband. The perfect husband.

Almost as convincing as she in her role as Marly Alcott. She bit her lip again, wincing anew.

Ahead, a crooked sign advertising a local diner indicated her turnoff for the school. Soon two roads diverged in the woods, and she picked the unpaved one, steering the Caravan up the long, winding mountain road.

At the gates, the guard asked for identification, which she produced from her purse.

"One moment," he said, verifying her name in his computer's databank. "Hope you didn't have any trouble finding the place."

"No, the directions were quite sound," she said, using the password. The guard admitted her. The beam of her headlights slashed through the night, and she drove through the grounds.

It was nearly midnight, but she didn't want to wait until

morning to see Tyler, even if it was just to hug him in his sleep.

She pulled into a parking spot and cut the engine. Dropping her head back against the headrest, she stretched her arms in front of her.

Something moved inside in the Caravan, and she craned her neck to peer into the back, expecting to find her overnight bag had fallen off the seat. Instead, she saw the silhouette of a long, thin ponytail.

A scream died in her throat. With lightning speed, Marly wrenched her seat belt free and jabbed the button that unlocked the doors. She hit the ground running.

Quick, but not quick enough.

An arm shot out, like a steel band across her chest, hurling her to the ground. And then he was on top of her, straddling her, pinning her with his weight. She lunged, trying to escape, when the ice-cold barrel of a gun bit into the flesh of her temple.

"Don't even think about it," Billy Ray admonished, his voice sounding cautiously vigilant, like a man who'd finally caught an errant mouse in his trap but hadn't yet discovered whether or not the rodent was dead.

"What do you want with me, Mr. Cameron?"

"Well now, ain't that an interesting question?" He snorted. "Seeing as *you're* the one who's planning on testifying against *me*. That's right. I heard you. But never mind that right now. Where is he?"

"Who?"

"Either you're denser than a box of rocks, or else you're messing with me. And I done already warned you *twice* now not to mess with me." The barrel of the gun dug deeper. "Ain't that so, pretty lady?" His gaze locked with hers. When she didn't reply, his hand rose to her neck. "Yeah, I believe it is," he said, answering his own question. "Now, where's our little witness? You ain't gonna be able to testify without him."

"I—I don't know what you're talking about."

"My son," he said through clenched teeth, his fingers tightening around the column of her neck. "I know you're hiding him."

"I'm not hiding anyone," Marly choked out, sputtering as Billy Ray increased his grip.

"You're lying."

"I'm not," she challenged with the belligerence of a woman who had nothing to lose.

"Then why are you here?"

"Because I'm a teacher," she whispered, her eyes watering at the bite of metal against her skull. "And this is a school."

"You're a natural-born liar, ain't you?" He gripped her head. "And you've had yourself a lot of practice, too, fooling all the good people of Durham. Your entire life's just one stinking lie, *Hilary*."

Her eyes widened in horror.

"That's right," he added with smug satisfaction. "I saw right through your righteous little act. Ain't nothing so pure as Miss Marly playing Miss Priss. I knew something was fishy from the start. Just didn't know what. But it all makes sense now, don't it?"

She didn't respond.

"Yeah, I think it does. Now I am done playing nice with you, so I'm gonna ask you one more time, and you'd better think real hard about the answer. Where the hell is my son?"

She closed her eyes. "You can go ahead and snap my neck, Billy Ray. It isn't going to change what I do and do not know. I told you before—I don't know where Tyler is."

"You lying whore," he swore. "I ought to kill you right now and get it over with."

"Why don't you, then? Why don't you just do it?"

He stared at her. "Uh-uh. You're just a little too anxious. I think we're going to have to draw this out. And don't be thinking it's gonna to be quick and easy after that stunt you just pulled."

He leaned over her, so close she could feel every revolting inch of his body. His mouth hovered inches from hers, and she could smell the stench of stale cigarettes on his breath. His gaze lowered to her breasts, then back up again.

In a flood of guilt and shame, she remembered that no other man had touched her before Carter, and remembered her avowal that no other man ever would. Dear God, it had been real for her, no matter what their arrangement. She had fallen in love with him, and she would take the memory of that one-sided love to her grave before she let Billy Ray touch her.

With the vestiges of her strength, she raised her knee, aiming for his groin. It connected with a solid thump, and Billy Ray cried out, doubling over in pain.

Marly shoved him away, scrambling to her feet. She managed to run thirty yards before he caught up with her and flung her to the ground again. She struggled, clawed at him, trying to get away, but he overpowered her, threw her on her back and pinned her beneath him. She shoved at him, bucking, trying to throw him off her. She swung her knee up, missed and tried again.

Billy Ray swore viciously, slamming the barrel of the gun against her thigh. She cried out in pain, and he gripped her throat, picking up her head and slamming it against the ground.

"Try that one more time and it's gonna be your kneecaps," he snarled, tightening his fingers until spots danced before her eyes. Until finally, she didn't see anything at all, except unbearable darkness.

When she started to come around, she realized someone was hitting her, slapping her arm. And then she felt a prickling sensation, like a pinch.

Like a needle.

"No!" she cried. But it was too late.

It was too late for Tyler to be up, but when he hadn't seen the Caravan at the motel, Carter knew where Marly had gone.

He'd paced the house for a good hour, and contemplated drowning himself in a bottle of bourbon. But none of those things had helped his situation. Nothing would, except answers. Answers only Marly could provide. And damn if he'd wait around until Her Highness showed up before he got them.

The yellow beam of the smog lights penetrated through the night, as he pulled past the guard shack and headed up the long, winding drive. He'd almost passed the first parking lot when the sight of the Caravan caught his eye. He saw it clearly through the fog because the interior lights were on.

Maneuvering into the adjacent spot, Carter realized both the driver's door and the side door were open. Strange. Why would Marly be unloading the car? Unless she planned to spend the night at the school, instead of the motel. But there were rules against that, and Marly knew them.

Carter shook his head. Something was wrong. He got out of the car and approached the Caravan, noting the keys dangling from the ignition, Marly's purse still in the passenger seat.

A peculiar sensation stole through him. His head jerked upright, his narrowed gaze combing the grounds.

He was here. Billy Ray Cameron, that sonofa—

He had Marly!

Marly's bleary gaze tried to focus on her surroundings. She was lying on a bed in a dimly lit room. There were three other twin beds arranged in the room, and painted murals on the cinder block walls, like at her center.

She must have been in the vacant dormitory by the parking lot. Vacant, save her and the man at the foot of the bed, the man tying each of her ankles to the bedposts.

No! She wanted to scream, but something obstructed her voice. A gag.

Gagged and bound. Oh, God. Of all the ways to die. Why like this?

Billy Ray finished his handiwork and came to stand beside her, a vile grin on his face. His hands went to his belt. "Still feeling feisty?" he jeered.

Tears rolled down Marly's cheeks as he slid the leather strap from around his waist and cracked it once.

"One last time," he said through clenched teeth, his beady eyes bulging from their hollowed sockets. "Where's Tyler?"

She closed her eyes, willing the nightmare to end, opening them again at the sound of a zipper being ripped down.

"Guess we'll have to play it your way." He lifted her skirt and ran his hand along the inside of her thigh.

Bile rose in the back of her throat, and a sound of agony tore from the depths of her being, low and dejected like a wounded animal. It echoed in the room, was bouncing back and forth between the cinder block walls, when, out of nowhere, came a thin streak of light, followed by a flash that nearly blinded her.

The door, she realized, had been flung open, but Billy Ray blocked her vision.

He whirled just as someone screamed "No" like a warrior's battle cry. She glimpsed surprise in his eyes as he lunged for the revolver on the bedside table.

In that split second, Marly saw Carter.

With the speed of a striking snake, he coiled his fist around Billy Ray's ponytail. The gun in Billy Ray's hand exploded as his body flew against the wall. His head smashed into the cinder block, and he slid to the floor, where he lay in a motionless heap.

Carter kicked the gun from his hand, then scooped it off the floor before running to Marly's bedside. He dropped to his knees, his hands shaking as he worked the knotted handkerchief.

"Marly." He chanted her name over and over. "I took a chance and started with the closest building. I almost walked past…if I hadn't heard you moan…damn this knot."

"Carter," she gasped like a diver escaping from a watery grave, when he'd removed her gag. Her mouth was so dry no more words would come out. And there was a strange pressure in her side.

"Two more seconds and we'll get you out of here." He started on the ropes that bound her hands, untying the first and moving to the other.

"Carter." She tugged at him with her free hand.

"I know. I could kill the bastard for this." He couldn't keep the venom from his voice.

"Carter!"

He'd heard the unmistakable sound of the switchblade an instant before Marly screamed his name. His hands—already in motion—grabbed the arm that held the knife dangerously close to slitting his throat.

It had been a long time, but some things, once learned, could never be forgotten. Like basic survival instincts.

Billy Ray hadn't anticipated the reaction, and Carter capitalized on the element of surprise, forcing the knife from his hand. It clattered to the ground, and they both scrambled for it. Carter stepped on Billy Ray's hand, kicking the knife away with his other foot. Billy Ray hurled at Carter's knees full force, knocking him off balance.

It was a street fight. Down and dirty. One Billy Ray could never have expected—not from Carter—but he caught on quickly. The streets had a way of recognizing their own.

Billy Ray went after him in blind frenzy, while Carter returned his own wrath with calculated precision.

They struggled, blow after blow, angry fists connecting with bone, their hands wrapping around each other's necks, each trying to choke the life out of the other. Finally, Carter maneuvered on top of Billy Ray. Pressing his advantage, he bashed the drug lord's head against the floor.

His vision blurred with raw fury, he barely noticed Billy Ray's face turn from scarlet to violet. Even when the slime was wheezing for air, his body jerking in violent spasms, Carter didn't let up. He dug his fingers into Billy Ray's throat, sorely tempted to rip out his larynx.

He could choke the damn life out of Billy Ray, but it still wouldn't be enough. Nothing would ever eradicate from his mind the image of Marly tied to the bed; nothing would make him forget the atrocities she'd suffered at Billy Ray's hand. As long as he lived, he would never forget—

Carter glanced up at that moment, to Marly, on the bed, and

his eyes widened in horror at the crimson spot staining her blouse.

The gunshot!

"Marly!" he cried.

She'd managed to free her other hand, and she was struggling to sit up.

"Don't move!" he barked, springing off Billy Ray and dashing for the hallway, where he grabbed a red emergency phone. "A woman's been shot. Call the nearest hospital. We need paramedics, a helicopter." He gave their location and hung up the phone with a last, urgent request. "Please hurry."

He rushed back to Marly's side and began tearing the sheets from the adjacent bed. "Help's on the way. You just hold on, okay?"

"Oh, God, he's—"

Carter spun around, his ears registering the sound of the revolver clicking into place, at the same moment his eyes took in the sight of Billy Ray coming at them with the knife. A second gunshot sounded, and Billy Ray jerked back, clutching his heart before he dropped to the floor.

"This is worse than Hitchcock," Marly whispered, lowering the gun. "Please…make sure he's dead."

Carter checked his pulse. "Nothing."

She closed her eyes. "Forgive me for feeling relieved. He drugged me, so it's not like I can feel too much, anyway."

Carter swore and dropped Billy Ray's wrist. "What did he give you?" He knelt at her bedside, applying pressure to her wound.

"Not quite sure. In a needle. Think I'll die this time?"

"You're *not* going to die."

"Don't be so sure. I'm not a cat, you know."

"You're not going to die," he repeated. "I won't let you."

"Not part of the plan, huh?" She tried to sit up.

"Stay still."

"Okay, but you know, it's not what I imagined."

"What?" He pressed the wads of cloth against her, trying to stop the bleeding.

"Getting shot."

Carter gave a derisive laugh.

"Fire hurts more."

He winced. "No one should have to go through what you have."

"I suppose I should tell you—"

"How you got such good aim?"

"No, the truth. About me...."

"Shh...not now. You need to save your energy."

"But you need to know. How else will you put things into those little compartments in your brain?"

"First of all, they're big compartments, and second, this conversation can wait."

"That's what you think." She wagged her finger with all the precision of the truly doped up.

"Come on, Marly." He covered her lips with one finger, hoping to silence her. "You need to stay still."

She bit his finger. "I'll stay still if you listen to me. Please, Carter," she implored. "You have to know I'm not that person in your file."

"I already know that," he said quietly.

"You don't," she repeated. "Remember that bomb I told you about, the one that exploded in the village and set that terrible fire?"

"Do we have to talk about this right now?"

"I'm not going anywhere. Are you?"

Carter's eyes stung. He was rapidly coming to the end of nerves already stretched to the limit. "How can you joke with me at a time like this?"

"No joke. I'm serious. They killed the wrong person. Do you understand what I'm saying? That bomb was meant for me. Your Marly, the woman you thought you married, died in that explosion. I'm Hilary Steele."

"Hilary," he breathed her name. "Of course. The one who witnessed the murder."

She nodded. "I was fifteen at the time. We lived in Boston. Old money, upper crust and all that."

"No more. No more talking." He pressed his lips to hers in an effort to silence the very words that had driven him to come after her, the ones he'd felt she owed him, the answers he'd been determined to force from her tonight.

He'd been angry—so angry. He'd felt used and betrayed and angrier than he'd ever remembered being. But he wouldn't have hurt her. God knows, he never would have laid a finger on her.

"Carter, I want you to know...."

"Not now. Marly, please." His throat felt raw, and guilt threatened to overwhelm him. "Not here. Not like this," he repeated her earlier request.

But she went on, as if she hadn't heard him. "My father was an investment banker, far as I knew. He used to have his business associates over to the house a lot. One night I couldn't sleep, so I went downstairs. They were...in the study. Three men and my father. I could hear...voices, but I couldn't really hear what they were saying.

"I went into the kitchen...poured myself some milk. All of sudden, the voices stopped. I didn't really think about it. I took my milk into the dining room...to a chair in the corner. I sat alone in the dark, staring into space. Then the door to the study opened. My father came out and looked around. He didn't see me...I didn't call out. Then two of the men started dragging out a body. It was the third man. They'd killed him."

"And you witnessed it."

"I saw everything. I still remember my father saying to watch the rugs...he didn't want any blood on them. I told my mother what I had seen, and she forced me to testify. I was just a kid...I couldn't have known. But my mother... I can't believe she never suspected. For years, she didn't care where the money was coming from, as long as it continued to flow." She gave a bitter laugh that turned into a coughing spasm.

"Sweetheart, enough." Damn. Where were those paramedics? "You need to rest."

"After they...killed my father, and my mother, they came after me...only, they killed my best friend, instead."

"So you took her identity." Yes, it all made sense now. But it didn't matter. None of that mattered. Only her. Only his wife, the woman he'd married. At that moment, he didn't care who she'd been before. He just wanted *her*. Safe, healthy, alive.

"It's okay," he whispered, kissing her temple, trying to reassure himself as much as her. "Everything's going to be okay. Please. Just rest now."

"It was the only way, Carter."

"I know…I know," he crooned to her.

"They would have kept trying…they wouldn't have given up." Her voice was growing more and more labored. "If they knew I didn't die…"

"It's not going to happen. I won't let it."

"Carter, I know you try…you put on a good act. But I can't fake it anymore.… I can't pretend to be the wife you want.… I can't help the way I feel.… I'm tired of fighting it…so tired of trying.…" Her eyes closed just as the paramedics arrived.

"We removed the bullet, but she isn't out of the woods yet," the doctor told Carter. "She lost an awful lot of blood. It's still touch-and-go."

"Can I see her?" he asked.

The doctor nodded.

Carter spent that night and the next in the intensive care unit.

"Fight, Marly," he whispered, his words rough and challenging. "Come out of this." He squeezed her hand. It was so cold, like ice, and he held it in his, rubbing it, willing the woman lying on the hospital bed to live.

He never left her side, until they kicked him out, made him wait outside, where he stayed through the night, pacing the hallways. Finally, at some point in the wee hours of morning, he collapsed into a chair and did the only thing he was truly good at doing: bartering.

Carter bowed his head and said a silent prayer.

Please, God. Let her live. It can't be her time. Not yet.

People need her—the children need her. Tyler needs her. I need her.

It wasn't enough. He knew that. He had to offer something in return, something that would make his request less selfish. There was only one thing, and his gut clenched in anticipation of the inevitable. But he didn't have a choice, just as Marly hadn't had a choice in marrying him. Because he hadn't given her one. He would right that mistake, if it wasn't too late.

He would give her what she wanted—he would let her go.

If she came out of this, Carter swore he would set her free.

Chapter 16

"Are you free?" Marly entered the study and closed the door behind her without waiting for Carter's response.

A small desk lamp illuminated the surface of his desk, leaving the rest of the room cast in darkness. Carter stood in the shadows by the Palladian windows, hands in the pockets of his faded blue jeans.

"How are you feeling?" he asked without looking at her.

"Pretty good, actually. It's nice to be able to move around again." The doctors had released her that afternoon, and she'd been delighted to find Tyler and Annie Lou waiting for her in Carter's car. "Everyone's gone to sleep, so I thought maybe you and I could talk now. We haven't had much chance since I got…back."

The word *home* felt presumptuous. From the moment she'd awakened in the hospital, she had sensed a change in Carter. Though he never left her bed side, his manner was markedly reserved, like a man caring for a distant relative instead of his wife.

"You must be tired. Why don't we wait until morning?"

A mere week ago, she would have done as he'd suggested. She would have maintained the distance between them, convinced herself that it was for the best and crawled into an empty bed to contemplate her solitary existence. Now that their secrets were in the open—her identity and his true feelings about her—any efforts at evasion would only prove futile.

She walked toward the windows, staring out into the night, where darkness had fallen like a black curtain. "I've waited long enough, for the outcome of this day. I can't wait any longer. I have to know. Where do we go from here, Carter?"

He turned toward her slowly, and when she glanced up, the expression in his eyes confirmed her fears.

"There's no easy way to say this."

She took a breath and steeled herself for the worst. "Just go ahead and say it."

"All right. I want a divorce."

Numbly, she grasped for the wall to steady herself. No foresight could have prepared her for the aching desolation that ripped through her.

Though she had foreseen their inevitable conclusion, she'd grown to dread the day it became reality. She had hoped for a twist of fate, appealed to the heavens and prayed for the impossible. But with Carter's words, the final sands of borrowed time slipped through the hourglass.

She felt strange inside, hollow and empty, like someone had taken her soul, leaving her with the mere trappings of a body. A woman without substance.

She cleared her throat and tried to speak, when all she wanted to do was sob. "You've already thought this through, then?"

"I have," his voice was low and monotonous, like a man who had never expressed any human emotion.

"I—I don't suppose this is negotiable?"

"No negotiating necessary. You can keep the donation."

"Just like that?"

"That's the only reason you married me, isn't it? Money for your center."

A dull ache throbbed in the area she used to call her heart. "Not the only reason...."

"Tyler doesn't need protection anymore."

"No." The art of stringing intelligible words together suddenly seemed an arduous task. She peered at the rings on her finger and willed them not to blur before her eyes. "Carter, I'm sorry, so sorry. I never meant to lie to you. I wanted to tell you. I just couldn't... I knew you wouldn't..." She swallowed. "I guess it doesn't matter anymore."

Carter shrugged. "Not really. The way I figure it, why not cut our losses and move on?"

Her head snapped up at his matter-of-fact tone, and she stared in amazement at his dispassionate profile. "Just write things off, like bad debt expense on the bank's books?"

"Exactly." His gaze reverted to the windows, and he raised his hand to massage his right temple.

Marly glanced again at her rings, then back up at Carter. She remembered the first time she'd seen him at her center, the way he'd scared her showing up in the bank's limo and then entranced her with his hazel eyes. It seemed a lifetime ago that they had gone to the charity function as two strangers and ended the night practically engaged.

Would they part in the same businesslike manner they had agreed to marry, as if nothing of significance had passed in the interim? As if they had shared nothing, meant nothing to each other?

How she wanted to believe she'd meant more to Carter than a bad investment in cattle futures, that some things, if not all, had been genuine and not faked. But she had seen his file. She knew the truth. They both did. And Carter had made his decision.

She wouldn't try to change his mind. She wouldn't cry. She wouldn't beg. She would handle their parting with the grace of a woman—not the grief of a child.

And then she would quietly fall apart in the privacy of Annie Lou's converted garage.

"Okay," she conceded, turning from the window. She slid

her rings from her finger onto the smooth surface of the desk, leaving her hand bare, the zigzagged pattern of her scars accentuated by the loss.

She deserved this. She had no one to blame but herself. It was all her fault.

"I thought you'd agree if I suggested it," Carter said, the monotone replaced by a clipped edge. "I've got a lot of work to do, so if you don't mind..."

"Yes, I know the drill." Gingerly, she folded her arms over her cardigan sweater, careful of the bandage beneath, and started for the door.

The short distance felt like an interminable journey, aging her with every step. She recalled each moment of her life with Carter—every look, every touch, every promise they'd made.

Though she felt his gaze on her back, she didn't turn around, knowing if she did, she would lose the last scraps of her tattered pride. She would cry. She would beg. She would plead. And in the end, she would gain nothing.

If she knew little else, she knew the man who, for a very short time, had been her husband, who in that time, had made her feel safe, revered, even desired. And she knew it was over between them. Real or not, she would mourn that loss, no differently than would a widow grieving for her beloved husband.

She raised her palm to her forehead, feeling suddenly lightheaded. "If it's okay with you, I'm going to let Tyler sleep through the night. I'll sleep in a guest room." Her throat felt swollen shut, and with great effort, she squeezed out her parting words. "We'll be gone in the morning."

"Marly, wait."

She stopped with one hand on the doorknob.

"Maybe...maybe we can have lunch sometime?"

Her hand fell to her side, and her shoulders slumped, but instead of crumpling like a paper flower, she shook her head in disgust.

Had he truly banished every memory they had ever made?

Was she the only one who felt any remorse over what could have been? Had he felt *nothing* for her?

Slowly, anger mounted, overriding all other emotions. She turned around and glared at him, flinging her widow's weeds to the ground.

"No, we cannot have lunch sometime." She gritted out each word, punctuated each with deliberate steps farther into the room. "This was never about having lunch, Carter. It was about a commitment for a lifetime, about working things out and not giving up. Or have you forgotten your own rules, too?"

He didn't say anything, merely stared out the window. His jaw, taut with tension, was the only indication he'd even heard her, and his complete and utter lack of emotion infuriated her further.

"Oh, I'm sorry," she said, her voice dripping with sarcasm. "I seem to have forgotten my impeccable breeding. I don't suppose it's very nice to be petty to a man who saved your life, donated a quarter million to your center and destroyed the negatives that could expose your secret identity.

"I *should* just walk out this door and get on with my life, since you're certainly prepared to do the same. But at the very least, I think I ought to try to return the favor in some small way, maybe give you some *advice* for the next time you go playing White Knight."

"There isn't going to be a next time." His voice sounded harsh, each word strained.

"Right, I'm sure that's what you said the last time."

That one put a dent in his armor. His face fell, and for the first time in too long, she glimpsed the emotions he kept hidden behind the impassive-businessman's veneer.

Good. Let him hurt. Let him feel a fraction of her pain. Let him know that he was equally to blame for the demise of their marriage, that it wasn't just her.

"First of all," she started, "don't be so damn nice all the time. Don't welcome your next wife into your home and make her feel it's her own. Don't ask her about her day and sound like you mean it. Don't cook—ever—especially not desserts. Don't be kind to children, so that even the most wary trust you in a matter of minutes. Don't try to make her feel better after a nightmare. Don't be late to board meetings, for any reason.''

His eyes closed. ''Marly—''

''I'm not finished.'' If she had to chisel away at that veneer chip by chip to make him remember her, she would. ''Don't stare at her across the room as if you can see your unborn children in her eyes. Don't make her believe in her dreams again. Don't give her a quarter million, no strings attached. Don't save her life. Don't preserve her identity. And if you remember nothing else, remember this, Carter King. Do *not* make her love you when she doesn't have a prayer.''

His face contorted in an expression of excruciating pain.

''Don't.'' She raised a hand before he could speak. ''I've said my piece.'' She spun and ran for the door.

He found her outside in the meadow on her hands and knees. Under the starless sky, he wouldn't have seen her if not for the hurricane lamp she'd taken.

''What are you doing?'' he asked.

''What does it look like?'' she snapped, letting him know in no uncertain terms what she thought of his presence.

''Marly, I—''

''I'm planting tulip bulbs for the spring, if you must know. I plant them every fall in Annie Lou's garden, but either the weeds choke them, or the mice eat them, or they just don't grow in her soil. I thought they'd have a better chance here. Maybe not, but at least I'll know I tried.''

Unlike you. He heard her unspoken words.

He crouched beside her, every muscle in his body taut with tension. The night air felt soft and balmy, still warm for an autumn night, even in the Carolinas.

He didn't want to ask the question, didn't want to give her the chance to take back her words, but he had to know. ''Marly, what you said earlier…did you mean it?''

She nudged him out of her way and pulled the box of bulbs between them. "Contrary to what you might think, Carter," she said, stabbing into the dirt with a spade, "I've only lied to you about things that involved my identity."

He stared at her hands, watching her scoop out the earth and drop a bulb inside. A cold sweat trickled down his spine. The words were going to hurt like hell, but he had to say them, had to make sure they were talking about the same thing.

He swallowed hard and tried to keep his voice steady. "You love me?"

"Well, if you really want me to tell the truth, it was a toss-up between you and Mel Gibson." She shrugged and covered the bulb with dirt, patting the mound with the back of the spade. "But with Mel already married, you kind of won by default."

He wanted to laugh. He wanted to cry. He felt like a convict released after ten years of false imprisonment. "I wasn't expecting this," he whispered.

"No, of course you weren't." She waved the shovel in the air before spiking it into the ground again. "One high-society, narrow-minded witch did a number on you, and now the rest of womankind has to suffer for it."

"I...I don't know what to say...."

"Say good-night, Carter. I'm about out of scintillating wit. It's going to get ugly really soon." She turned her face to wipe it on her sleeve, and the hurricane lamp revealed the tears she'd been trying to hide.

Guilt pierced at his gut. He'd done this to her, the last woman in the world he'd ever intended to hurt. His eyes stung with remorse, and he dropped to his knees. "I don't want you to leave, Marly."

"Save your pity."

"No, not pity. Never that. Try respect, admiration, awe—"

"Stop," she cried. "I read your file. You don't have to pretend any longer. I know why you married me."

"And I know why you married me. Because you had no other choice. And neither did I. But things didn't go as planned for either of us. I didn't want to want you,'' he admitted. ''I couldn't stand the thought of falling in love with you and risking you walking out on me. I couldn't risk anyone ever having that much control over me again.''

''Thank you, Eva Ann.'' Marly mock-saluted with the shovel. ''You turned an otherwise-brilliant man into a ding-dong in the relationship department.''

''I forced you to marry me, Marly.''

''Yes, you did,'' she said, jabbing at the earth. ''But you bought the wrong model, and fraud certainly entitles you a refund.''

Carter reached out and took the spade from her. ''I didn't buy the wrong model.''

Imitating her earlier actions, he proceeded to dig a hole, gesturing for her to plant the bulb before he went on to dig the next one. She must have surmised he wasn't going to leave any time soon. With obvious reluctance, she dropped a bulb into the ground and covered it with dirt.

''When Eva Ann found out about my past, she wanted a divorce the very next day. She said I wasn't the person she thought I was. You know what really got me?'' He stopped digging and waited for Marly to look at him. When she finally did, he met her gaze evenly and said, ''I hadn't changed. I was still me. Only her perception had changed.

''I was shocked to find out you were another person. Shocked, angry, hurt, confused. But I'm no hypocrite. Your birth, your upbringing, your true identity…they don't change who you are, the person you've become, the person you are inside. *You* told me that, and now I'm telling you. Your past can't nullify all the good you've done with the children and the center. Your past can't change the things that happened between us. You *are* my Marly.''

In the pale candlelight, he saw her lower lip tremble. ''I lied to you, Carter,'' she said in a broken whisper.

''You didn't trust me.''

She shook head. ''I didn't think you would forgive me. I was afraid of losing you.''

"And I was afraid of losing you."

She sniffled. "We were both ding-dongs."

"I forgive you. Please, forgive me. I don't want a divorce. I never did."

"Oh, God." She clutched her stomach, her breathing rough and uneven.

He threw down the spade and crawled to her on his hands and knees. "Say you'll stay. With me. Because you want to, not because you have to."

"But you don't want me—"

He tipped her chin up, his gaze roving over every precious inch of her face. "I want you, Marly."

"A plain-Jane?"

"You aren't the least bit plain, not in my eyes. You're…" He lifted a hand, then let it drop to his side. "You're everything to me."

"You can't honestly expect me to believe—"

"That I don't want you every second of every damn day? That I can't work? I can't think? Go ahead. Take your pick."

"You think about me at work?"

"I think about you all the time. I can't get you off my mind." He raked his fingers through his hair. "You have no idea, you couldn't possibly know, what it's like to want something so desperately it's almost inhuman. To lie awake all night, aching inside because you know you'll never have it. Do you have any idea what happens then, Marly?

"You start to die from the wanting, and the only way you know to survive is to convince yourself you no longer want it. But it's a lie. I never thought you would love me. I never thought I could be worthy—"

"Don't say that," she cried in anguish. "Don't *ever* say that again, Carter. Any woman would be damn lucky to be married to you."

"I don't want any woman. I want you. You have to know that. It's just you, Marly." He tucked a lock of her hair behind her ear. "Only you." He rubbed the pad of his thumb over her lips. "Always you." He reached into his pocket and withdrew his fist, opening it to reveal her rings. "Stay with me, Mrs. King."

A sob tore from her chest, like carbonation from a can of soda someone had shaken. She dropped the tulip bulb and covered her mouth with both hands.

Carter eased her left hand free and slid the rings over her third finger. He raised her fingers to his lips. "I want you right now, Marly," he whispered. "You can either take my word, or check for yourself. A guy can't exactly fake these things." He lowered her hand and placed it firmly on the evidence of his attraction, smiling when her eyes widened. "No more lies," he said just before his mouth came down on hers, hungry and insistent.

She didn't resist, not even for an instant, but leaned into him, one hand pressed to the back of his neck, the other boldly stroking him, returning his fervor with an urgency all her own.

Marly noticed how he held her in place, careful not to brush against her bandage. His tongue parted the seam of her lips, thrusting deep inside before tangling with hers in a swirl of mounting passion.

"Sweetheart, stop me now," he whispered, his voice ragged with desire as he pressed damp, moist kisses to the hollow of her throat. "You're in no condition to make love in the dirt."

"I'm fine."

"God help me, I can't resist you."

"Then don't stop." She threaded her fingers into his hair, unmindful of his protests as she rocked her hips against him. "Don't ever stop." She wanted so desperately for it to be true, to believe a woman like her really could evoke such longing in a man like Carter.

His hands went to her cardigan, and she noticed his fingers shook as he undid the buttons one by one. She held his hands on the last button.

"It's ugly, Carter. I just want to give you fair warning."

"Nothing about you is ugly." He opened the garment and pushed up her cotton T-shirt, gazing at her long and hard as pain and desire mingled in his eyes. "I want to see it."

She nodded, and he lifted the bandage. His fingers lightly traced the puckered purple tissue, all that remained from the staples and stitches.

"You are the most beautiful woman in the world to me. Don't ever doubt that."

"Carter." She whispered his name like a caress, her flesh quivering beneath his gentle touch.

"When you were lying in that hospital bed, I thought I would die if you didn't make it. I thought if only you made it through, I would let you go. I wouldn't force you to stay with me."

He lowered the bandage and raised her T-shirt higher. The night breeze rushed over her exposed flesh as he took a dusky nipple between his thumb and forefinger. Already pebbled, it puckered even more at his touch, straining against the lacy confines of her bra.

He bent his head and let his mouth follow suit, gently raining kisses along the trail. Then he lifted his head and gazed deep into her eyes. "Tell me what you want, Marly."

Her heart responded tenfold. "I want it all." She reached for the buttons of his shirt. Baring him to his waist in a matter of seconds, she pulled his shirttails from his jeans. "I want you." Her hands spanned the expanse of his chest, exploring the textures before dipping to his belt buckle. She touched her tongue to the hollow of his throat. I want you to need me the way I need you, she thought.

I want you to love me.

She unbuckled his belt, her nimble fingers working loose the button-fly of his jeans. The zipper made a sensual ripping sound as she inched it lower, exposing the white material of his briefs, which were stretched taut over his hardened length. She slipped her hand inside the denim and rubbed her palm against him.

Carter opened his mouth as if to protest, emitting only a strangled moan. She leaned forward and kissed his cheek, nibbling a path along his jaw. She brushed his mouth—once, twice. He pulled her into his lap and captured her face between two hands.

"I want you, Marly," he said, his voice rough with emotion. "I want you more than I've ever wanted anyone or anything, and that scares the hell of out me."

"A wise man once told me that we're all scared. Every one of us. We wouldn't be human if we weren't. So don't think for one second that you've got some kind of monopoly going here, Carter."

"A wise man said that, huh?"

"The wisest man I know. I'm just hoping he's smart enough to make love to me soon, before I die from the wanting."

With his palms on either side of her face holding her still, Carter covered her mouth with his, kissing her hard. His hands tilted and tipped her head, his lips moving against hers as if he would never get enough, as if the dam of his reserve had broken and splintered into a million tiny pieces, never to be repaired.

"I love your mouth," he whispered between ragged kisses. "Your lips, your smile, the way you taste. I love kissing you, but it always makes me want more."

Her arms twined around his neck, tightening until they ached. When his tongue thrust into her mouth, she suckled it with a reckless hunger, then dipped her own into his mouth, urging him forward as she slowly leaned back on the ground. His body covered hers, limbs tangled together, kneading, groping in a primitive dance of unabashed desire.

"I love the way you feel against me, the way you move, those incredible curves." Carter unclasped her bra. The scrape of his late-night whiskers electrified her senses as he trailed his tongue along the valley between her breasts. His mouth closed over one aching nipple, teasing it with his teeth, then blowing softly until she thought she would explode.

His face had changed before her eyes, the mask he'd worn for so long slipping, baring to her gaze the hunger he'd hidden for so long.

"You don't know how long I've waited to see you look at

me…like this,'' Marly whispered, her hands trailing over his body.

Carter groaned deep in his throat as her touch sent a sheet of white-hot fire through him, a fire fueled by furious need and long-suppressed passion, a fire unlike any he'd ever expected to battle. ''I waited a lifetime for you. I can't believe I nearly lost you, nearly threw you away. How could I have been so stupid?''

And then his head was dipping lower, his mouth exploring the contours of her belly, then lower still, he shoved her jeans down, his fingers tugging at the elastic of her panties. She wiggled out of them, then gasped as Carter parted her thighs.

''Don't leave me, Marly.''

''I won't. I can't. I love you.''

A conflagration of desperate, almost violent need burst within him, her declaration singeing his control to ashes. Flames licked through him, blazing a trail of hot, wanton desire, leaving the charred cinders of reservations and doubts in their wake.

He wanted to take her right here, right now, in the meadow, in the dirt. Again and again. He wanted to slide his rigid flesh into her, to watch her passion mount with every thrust. He wanted to kiss her with every fiber of his being, to drink the soul of her existence and absorb it into his. He wanted to explore every inch of her, to uncover every mystery, to lose himself in her. For the moment, he didn't even care if he had anything left afterward, if only he could assuage this primal, burning need.

His need for her.

Only her.

Suddenly, the need felt as vital as his next breath, if not more critical. He stripped out of his jeans and lifted her hips, positioning himself. She was so wet, so incredibly ready for him, that he slid into her in one quick thrust, careful not to hurt her wound.

They both cried out at the same time, the thrill of their joining almost too much to bear. Carter started to pull back.

It was too much, too soon. Too soon for her. He was ready to explode.

"Don't you dare hold back on me, Carter King. Don't you dare." She reached between their bodies, taking him in her hands.

"Marly, what are you…?"

"Trust me," she whispered.

But then he could only cry her name, over and over as his aching flesh convulsed inside her.

"You weren't ready," he said afterward, as they lay in the meadow bathed in the dim light of the hurricane lamp, Carter on his back, Marly draped across his chest. "I could have waited."

She drew lazy circles on his stomach. "I didn't want you to wait. I wanted *you* to lose control for once."

He felt the muscles in his belly contract as her hand drifted lower, closing around him.

"Again?" she whispered, moving her thigh restlessly against his.

"Yes," he answered. "Yes, please. Again and again."

"You are insatiable, you know."

He froze, then slowly pulled back, surprised to see her smiling up at him. And if he wasn't mistaken, she wore a decidedly smug expression on her face.

"Don't ever change," she told him, drawing her body over his.

He grinned then, and held her close to him.

"Carter, can I try something?"

"Sure. Whatever you want." When he realized her intent, he took her hips and helped guide her down.

She smiled, her eyes heavy lidded with passion, and flung her head back. Her hips rocked against his, slowly at first, then gaining momentum.

Carter levered himself up on his elbows to kiss her, while his hand slipped between their bodies. She cried his name as she splintered apart, her back arching like a bow. Just the sound of his name on her lips was enough to throw him over the edge. He gripped her hips and thrust into her with his own shattering climax.

"Do I have to move?" she asked afterward.

"No, please don't." He pressed his lips to her temple. All the while, his hand stroked her back.

"Can we stay here until spring?"

"And watch the tulips come up?"

"Umm-hmm. They will this time. I just know it."

"Marly." He breathed her name, gathering her closer. "I love you, you know," he said, his voice raw with emotion.

She froze, her playful smile wobbling before falling entirely. "You…you don't have to say that just because…"

"What if I *want* to say it just because? What if I *need* to say it just because? What if *you* need to hear it as much as I do? For no reason other than the fact that it's true. I do love you, Marly. I've loved you for a long time."

A cry escaped her lips, just before his mouth descended on hers. She threw her arms around his neck and hugged him with all her heart. Tears spouted from her eyes, dampening their cheeks.

"You're not supposed to cry," he murmured, kissing the tears away. "Just love me back."

"I do." Marly choked back a sob. "I love you so much, Carter. I just never thought that you…that you would… Oh, God, I can't even say it."

"I can. I love you, Marly. I love you more than life. Do you want to know when I fell in love with you?"

"When?"

"The night of the fund-raiser, when I saw you all dressed up like Cinderella going to the ball. The night you dumped your drink in the plant."

"No, that was your drink. I told you—I drank mine."

"That was the night I knew. I tried to deny it because I never thought you would—"

She pressed a finger to his lips. "Say it again, Carter."

"I love you, sweetheart." He kissed the tip of her finger.

She shivered, deep inside. "Carter, about those two kids…"

"One down, one to go." At her perplexed expression, he clarified, "Tyler needs a little brother or sister, don't you think?"

"Oh, Carter." She bit her lip. "Yes. Oh, yes. I don't think I've ever been this happy."

"Me, either." He brushed his mouth against hers.

"We're going to have such a great life. I love you so much."

"More than Mel Gibson?" he asked, rolling over and taking her with him.

"More than anyone or anything. You're my very own Prince Charming." Gently, she reached her hands up to cup his face. "Carter, can we make love again? Just one more time. I want to make your baby tonight. Nothing would make me prouder."

He shuddered and gathered her close. "Say it again, then."

"Which? I love you, I want you or I need you?"

"Yes."

Marly laughed, then grew serious. "Please don't ever tire of hearing me say that."

"Never." Carter smiled, trailing his fingertip along her collarbone. "Never in a million years." He kissed the hollow of her throat. "You'll always be my Cinderella."

* * * * *